AN AJ DOCKER

SIN CITY TREACHERY

GARY GERLACHER

Black Rose Writing | Texas

ISBN: 978-1-68513-431-0
PUBLISHED BY BLACK ROSE WRITING
www.blackrosewriting.com

Printed in the United States of America
Suggested Retail Price (SRP) $21.95

Sin City Treachery is printed in Minion Pro

*As a planet-friendly publisher, Black Rose Writing does its best to eliminate unnecessary waste to reduce paper usage and energy costs, while never compromising the reading experience. As a result, the final word count vs. page count may not meet common expectations.

PRAISE FOR
THE AJ DOCKER & BANSHEE THRILLER SERIES

"*Last Patient of the Night* is M*A*S*H* meets Detective Harry Bosch.
It's a thriller that won't disappoint."
–Gregory D. Lee, author of *Stinger: An International Thriller*

For Rick, whose light burned brighter than most,
but was extinguished too soon.
The world is a better place because of you.

SIN CITY
TREACHERY

CHAPTER 1

Monday, October 16
2:11 p.m.

"911, what's your location?"

The caller responded in a harsh southern drawl, the voice modulated by an electronic device. "Is this call being recorded?"

"Yes, sir. What is your location?"

"For too long, our country has allowed the shadows to spread unchecked. The Aryan Federation of Las Vegas is bringing light in these times of darkness. Look to the start of the day at the beginning of night, when our light will explode forth and eliminate a bringer of shadows. White power now rules in Las Vegas."

The caller hung up as a stunned 911 operator turned to her supervisor. "What do we do with this?"

"Play it back again." The operator and supervisor listened to the call.

"Try calling the number," the supervisor suggested.

The operator called the number, but hung up when she heard the number was no longer in service. "Probably a burner, and probably in a trash can already. What do you want to do?"

The Supervisor had been on the job for fourteen years and had heard innumerable crazy calls. Most people called 911 with good intentions, but some were inspired by alcohol and drugs, by a desperate need for attention, or by other mental illness. The hard part was to determine which calls were genuine threats. This caller bothered to use a voice modulator, and the message was cryptic enough to be useless in the moment.

"Not much we can do. Flag it and wait and see if anything happens, or if it's another crank call."

"What's your gut tell you?"

"Something bad is about to happen in Las Vegas."

. . .

"For the last time, Jen, Charlie Daniels lost the fiddle battle." The speaker was a towering figure dressed in Spider-Man scrubs, looming over his adversary. Most people would be intimidated by his bulk, but not Dr. Jen Schumer.

"Rick, I'll cut you some slack since you were raised by a pack of wolves on a diet of raw meat, and God only knows how many head injuries you've suffered over the years, but let me assure you of one thing. Charlie Daniels out-fiddled the devil in Georgia. It says so in the song."

Rick was not finished arguing, not by a long shot. "Everyone assumes Charlie won, because it's his song, and he said so, but the devil was better. Ask any professional fiddle player who was better, and they'll tell you the devil."

"Are you aware of any actual professional fiddle players?"

"That's beside the point. Doc, what do you say?"

I mulled over my answer. "Rick, the only thing I know is you don't know shit about fiddling; Jen doesn't know shit about fiddling; and I for sure have no knowledge of fiddling. In the absence of any intelligent insight, I will vote with Jen, and say Charlie Daniels won."

Rick stared at me in disbelief. "Why do you always side with her?"

Jen grabbed her stethoscope from the table and stood to leave. "Because everyone enjoys that silly look on your face when you lose an argument."

Rick turned to me. "Do I have a silly look on my face?"

"Probably best you get back to work. Patients are waiting to be seen."

I looked out over the emergency department, appreciating the energy as people moved about in controlled chaos. Sunrise Hospital, located less than ten minutes from the strip, was the main trauma hospital serving Las Vegas. I had been working there as an emergency medicine physician for five months and really enjoyed the staff. Jen Schumer was the medical director for the ED, and one of the most competent ER doctors I had ever met. She was incredibly empathic with patients and staff, brutally sarcastic with friends, and just barely politically correct enough to deal with administration. She fought hard to assure that every patient received the best possible care and that every staff member thrived in a friendly work environment.

Dr. Rick Merden was a force of nature. His six-foot-two athletic frame helped him achieve All American status as a college decathlete and as a nationally ranked triathlete. In his early forties, Rick could still run, jump, swim and bike at a competitive level. He wore only superhero scrubs, and in his free time he dressed up as a superhero to visit kids in the hospital with gifts. He had roamed the halls as Superman, Batman, Spider-Man, and his personal favorite, Thor.

I leaned over to scratch Banshee behind his ears. "C'mon good boy. We got patients to see." Banshee thumped his tail in anticipation. Banshee is a former police dog who came to live with me after being injured on the job. He knows hundreds of commands and can operate on a spectrum between a compassionate service dog and a war machine. Most of his time in the ER, he functioned as a service dog, but occasionally, he helped with security. A low, throaty growl and bared teeth convinced even the toughest of patients to lower their voices.

Banshee and I were intercepted by a friendly face as we walked to our next patient. "Hey, Banshee, how are you today?" The speaker was already sitting on the ground to get snuggles from him.

"Hello there, Little Mac. Is your shift just starting?"

"Yes, sir, Doc. I have the evening shift this week. Do you think Banshee needs to go outside for a walk?"

"I think you have to walk him now that you said the word 'walk.' Look at how his ears are all perked up."

Little Mac scratched those ears vigorously. "Yeah, I think he has to go now. It seems like a good time, since it's quiet in here right now."

I winced as he used the Q word. "Little Mac, remember what we said about using that word in the ER? It's bad luck."

"Sorry, I forgot. I won't say quiet, again."

I visibly flinched at the second use of the word in a short time frame. "Thanks. You know where his leash is. Have a nice walk."

Banshee and Little Mac scampered away with Little Mac chatting incessantly to the dog, putting a smile on everyone's face. Mac Kennedy, now an important persona in the ER, had been a patient in the hospital as a child when his Down's Syndrome required multiple heart operations. In his teens, he had volunteered in the ER, and now in his twenties, he worked full time as a medical assistant. His childhood nickname was given to him early due to his love of Big Macs and his short stature. He carried it with pride and reminded everyone that the best things come in small packages. Little Mac proudly proclaimed that he wasn't short; he was fun-sized. His smile, infectious laughter, and positive attitude were always welcome in a workplace often overrun by stress, and he had some extraordinary talents as well.

He loved Banshee and often took him for hours at a time on shifts, always happy to take him for a walk. Little Mac's only flaw seemed to be his frequent use of the word "quiet" in the ER. The ER staff is superstitious, convinced something bad would happen after the word's utterance to disrupt the current calmness. Who knew what a double quiet might bring?

. . .

Dr. Kelly Williams gazed on her staff with pride. "Great job by everyone today, especially that last delivery. No better way to end the day than a successful stat C-section. Anything else before I speak to the family and call it a day?" Her Jamaican accent gave her speech a musical quality.

"No, ma'am. Get some rest. We'll finish up here."

Dr. Williams hurried to the recovery room, where she found the happy family together. The exhausted mom beamed with pride, as she stared into the eyes of her newborn son curled on her chest. A relieved dad fidgeted at the bedside, trying to help and stay out of the way at the same time.

"Congratulations, everyone. Was that enough excitement for the day?" Her patient had suffered a mild uterine rupture requiring a stat C-section.

"More than enough. I'm just happy he's out and doing well," the mother replied.

"I'm just happy I didn't faint in there," the father added.

"It was close. I saw you turning pale, but that's normal. Emergency surgeries are a bit overwhelming for most people. Everything should be fine. You had some bleeding, but we controlled it quickly. We'll be watching you closely, but I don't think you'll need a transfusion. The epidural will stay in place tonight, so pain should not be a problem. Get some rest and make sure to eat well. You're going to need your energy with that little one."

"Thank you so much, Dr. Williams. You've been great this whole pregnancy. When is it your turn to deliver?"

Dr. Williams cradled her expanding stomach with a smile on her face. "I have another ten weeks to go. Fortunately, the hospital provides scrubs in all sizes. Get some rest, and let the nurses know if you need anything. They can reach me at any time."

Dr. Williams thanked the staff again and headed to her office. She hung her white coat on a hook on the back of the door and collapsed into her desk chair. Despair threatened to overwhelm her as she looked at the stack of paperwork on her desk. She loved her patients, but hated the paperwork that took more of her time from her patients with each passing year.

Movement in her abdomen interrupted her thoughts. She cradled her belly and forgot about the paperwork to savor the moment. It had been a long journey for her to get pregnant. She had married in her mid-twenties, but her OB/Gyn residency had been too busy for her to contemplate a pregnancy and a newborn. By the time she finished residency in her thirties, she needed to start her practice. More years had passed, and finally she was ready for a baby of her own.

The irony of her having a difficult time getting pregnant was not lost on her. She had counseled hundreds of couples in similar situations, but it was easier for most doctors to give advice than to listen to it. A work up revealed she had endometriosis, a common cause of infertility. After years of treatment from specialists and two miscarriages, she finally sustained a healthy pregnancy. She rubbed her abdomen as she imagined her son coming home to his new nursery.

She pushed the paperwork to the back of her desk and struggled to stand to leave the office. She greeted colleagues as she wove through the halls of Sunrise Hospital toward the employee parking garage. She imagined a long, hot bath as she left the hospital. The mere thought of the warm water eased the ache in her swollen feet.

As she approached her 2020 silver Lexus sedan parked on the lower level, her world exploded. A too bright light blinded her, as her optic nerves were overwhelmed. The roar of an explosion followed, rupturing both ear drums, leaving her temporarily deaf and blind, a mercy considering what came next.

A wave of shrapnel exploded from the epicenter of the bomb at over 25,000 feet per second, ten times faster than a bullet. Small pieces of plastic and metal from the exploding car became lethal projectiles as they easily passed through tissue and broke bone on impact. The projectiles lost velocity as they spread out from the explosion, but were still potentially lethal when they struck her.

The final arrival was the pressure wave from the explosion. A compressed wave of air traveled outward from the explosion and struck her like a brick wall, throwing her backward fifteen feet. The blast wave was like getting hit everywhere at once, but damaged her lungs the most. The fast moving, dense air caused rapid expansion of the lungs, resulting in damage to the small airways that handled oxygen exchange.

One moment Dr. Williams had her car in sight, and the next, she lie flat on her back fifteen feet away, partially blind and deaf, confused, and struggling to breathe. She slowly became aware of a dull roar and the acrid smell of smoke from a nearby fire, and then came incredible searing pain screaming from her legs. Her hands ran over the curve of her pregnant belly and were soon covered in bright red blood. All thoughts went immediately to her unborn child as she held her belly and sobbed.

CHAPTER 2

Monday, 5:10 p.m.

An ICU nurse arriving to start her shift had parked far enough from the blast to avoid shrapnel, but she felt the concussive force deep within her chest. She turned toward the blast to see Dr. Williams writhing on the ground, surrounded by smoke from a burning car, and ran to her side.

"Stay still. We're gonna get you some help." The nurse gently pushed her head back onto the pavement and began her assessment. Airway appeared open, although she clearly struggled to breathe. For the moment, she could move enough air to talk. Her strong pulse beat at over 150 times a minute, likely due to adrenaline in her system. The nurse noted no trauma to the chest, but small wounds peppered her pregnant abdomen. Both legs, shattered, bled profusely.

A surgical resident arrived and focused on the bright red blood pulsating from the left leg. She recognized arterial bleeding that could kill a patient in minutes. "This is gonna hurt like hell, but I need to put some pressure on this to slow the bleeding." The resident pressed down on the thigh as Dr. Williams screamed in agony. The outwardly unfazed ICU nurse scanned the growing group of onlookers. "You, call 911. You, run over to the ambulance dock and get a unit over here. You, run to the ER and tell them we have a major trauma coming, and it's one of our doctors." The three bystanders leapt to their assigned duties.

The nurse looked into the resident's determined eyes. "Don't let up on that pressure no matter what." She held Dr. Williams' hand and tried to comfort her as they waited for the ambulance.

•   •   •

A frantic nurse's aide burst through the open door, as I sat at my desk completing charts. "There's been an explosion in the garage, and one of the doctors is badly injured and headed this way!" Everyone momentarily organized their thoughts before jumping to play their parts to set up for a trauma victim. I rushed to her side with the charge nurse to get more information.

"There was some sort of bomb or explosion, and one of the doctors is hurt really bad. Her legs are blown up. People are helping her, but they said to get ready for major trauma. She's a doctor here, and she's pregnant."

The charge nurse, on hearing the words bomb and explosion, activated his portable radio and called security. "We have a possible bomb or explosion in the garage. Lock down the ER, and let me know when we have some information."

I entered the trauma room to find the team calmly preparing for the patient's arrival. "The patient may be pregnant, so let's get the ultrasound set up, and be prepared for an emergency C-section if needed. Get the neonatal warmer ready in case we have a delivery down here. Inform the NICU we don't need them yet, but to be prepared for a possible patient from us."

Nervous energy dominated the room as all tasks were completed, and we could only wait. All nine team members mentally rehearsed their priorities in silence before the patient arrived. Adrenaline surged and collective focus narrowed when the ambulance bay doors opened, and the stretcher approached.

The paramedic gave a report as they entered the trauma bay. "Patient is a 37-year-old female, thirty weeks pregnant, caught in a bomb blast of unknown origin in the parking garage. Patient is awake and alert, but with significant trauma to both lower extremities. The left leg has a tourniquet and compression due to arterial bleeding."

Rick assumed responsibility for the airway and breathing. He listened to her lungs while watching the monitor. Diffuse crackles were present in both lungs, and the patient struggled to catch her breath. Despite the nonrebreather mask delivering 100% oxygen, her oxygen saturation hovered at 87%, well below normal.

Jen focused on the leg wounds, calling for orthopedics and vascular to be notified. Both legs had massive injuries, and a surgery resident held pressure on the left thigh in addition to the tourniquet. She felt a pulse in the right foot, but could find none in the left one.

Nurses and medical assistants attached leads to monitor vitals and started a second IV to transfuse blood when it was ready. The patient's oxygen saturation decreased to 85%, and Rick prepared for intubation.

I recognized Dr. Williams as they transferred her from the stretcher to the bed. Her terrified eyes met mine, and she gasped, "The baby…"

I motioned for the ultrasound to be brought over, as I leaned over to reassure her. "We're going to take care of you and the baby. Can you still feel movement?" She nodded affirmatively. "Any problem with the pregnancy so far?" She shook her head. "We're going to need to intubate you for pain control and prep for the OR."

"Let me see the ultrasound before you intubate," she pleaded.

I turned the screen toward her as I placed the transducer on her abdomen. The active baby moved on screen. Dr. Williams reached her hand down to the transducer I was holding and guided it as she scanned the screen through tearful eyes. She held it in place and pointed at the screen with her other hand. "Placental abruption. Need to get the baby out." She fell back on the bed from the effort.

Little Mac was at her side and squeezed her hand. "Don't worry. You have the best doctors in the world here. Everything's going to be okay." His kindness and relentless compassion reassured her.

Dr. Rivers, one of Dr. Williams' partners, arrived at the bedside, alerted of her injuries. He examined her with the ultrasound transducer and confirmed that the baby needed to be delivered immediately. He leaned over to reassure Dr. Williams, as I addressed the room.

"Listen up, everyone. We have a partial placental abruption. We're going to intubate down here, then transfer to the OR. OB is doing a stat C-section, and trauma surgery will do a quick exploration for any other abdominal injuries. Then vascular and orthopedics will work on the leg injuries. We're saving her baby and her leg. Let's move."

Rick intubated her with a 7.0 endotracheal tube, and oxygen saturations increased to 96%. Jen supervised management of the leg injuries, bandaging the worst injuries after X-rays were obtained. Fifteen minutes after her arrival in the trauma room, x-rays had been completed; blood hung; labs sent; and pain meds administered. Dr. Williams was intubated, sedated, and on her way to the operating room.

A wave of calmness overcame the trauma room, as the patient departed. Everyone looked around at the pools of blood, bandages, and debris that littered the room after every trauma resuscitation. Rick summed it up best. "What the fuck just happened?"

CHAPTER 3

Monday, 5:42 p.m.

As the acrid smoke in the garage dissipated, order returned. Two other victims had received minor lacerations from shrapnel and had walked to the ER for repair. Fortunately, that was the extent of the other injuries.

The fire department had doused the last of the flames, revealing the extent of the blast. Dr. Williams' Lexus was completely destroyed, along with three adjacent cars. Every car within fifty feet of the blast suffered damage, and the debris field extended to a radius of about a hundred feet.

Detective Roger Stillman surveyed the scene, as the firemen cleaned up their gear. "What a fucking mess. Who's in charge here?"

An officer stepped forward. "I am, sir. Lieutenant Powell." The overweight Lieutenant in his rumpled, sooty uniform contrasted with the fit Detective standing tall in his pressed designer suit and without a hair out of place. His shoes, polished to a shine, reflected the sickly fluorescent lights that dimly lit the ashen garage.

"Get your notebook out, Lieutenant. First, I want all firemen and their gear out of this garage in the next ten minutes. Next, I want a solid perimeter locking down the entire garage until I say it can reopen. No one goes in or out without my permission. And if I see a single media member in here you'll be writing parking tickets for the next twenty years."

"Sir, a lot of doctors are going to want to get to their cars in a few hours."

"Tell them to Uber. Next, I want someone to secure all security camera footage for the entire hospital for the last two weeks. Work with our IT team to get those images transferred to us. I need officers to start collecting a witness list. I want the names and contact information of everyone who even thought they might have heard the explosion. Anyone within ear shot of the explosion needs to be on that list. Finally, set up a site for folks to submit videos and pictures of the explosion. Half of Las Vegas had their phones out videoing this thing, and I want every single one. Questions?"

"No, sir."

Detective Stillman watched the firemen load their equipment and leave the garage, following them to the garage exit. A senior detective on the Las Vegas force, he had worked his way up from street patrol, to robbery, and finally to major crimes. Stern, but fair, his ability to piece together evidence into a coherent story was envied by many of his fellow officers. He occasionally bent the rules, but only for a just cause. He generally worked by the book, and his integrity was not for sale.

A group of officers kept onlookers at bay. "I want the crowds back another hundred feet to give us room to work. No one enters the garage except the bomb squad and the evidence team, and everyone better be signed in and wearing full protective gear." The officers scattered to enforce the orders.

"Looks like you fucked up another pair of shoes."

Stillman glanced at his shoes. "Nah, it'll buff out easily. Nice of you to join us, Mary."

"I was up north working on something when the call came in. Traffic's a bitch all the way down here since they started setting up for the race. What we got?"

Mary Roland had been on the force for seventeen years and had built a solid reputation from her work on sex trafficking cases. Her team had taken down three large rings and had saved countless girls from horrific conditions. Three years ago, Stillman had requested her as a partner over more senior candidates. They may have had more experience than she, but he recognized that she was a better cop. The Chief approved it, and the last three years had validated the decision. Roland and Stillman were a formidable force and took the most complicated cases Las Vegas produced. She had a unique ability to read people and to get them to talk to her. When she turned on the charm, everyone opened up to her, and she was equally able to play the bad cop.

"Looks like a car bomb in there with one car exploded. Fire's out; scene is secure. Waiting for bomb squad and evidence teams to arrive."

"Car bomb, huh? That's a first for me. I thought that only happened in old Las Vegas movies. Who got the call?"

"Tim fucking Roberts"

"Fantastic. A narcissistic jackoff insecure about his height is just what I need in my life."

"He's as tall as you."

Roland turned to her partner with a raised eyebrow. "He wears two inch lifts in his shoes. He's maybe 5'6" without the lifts."

"No shit. I never knew."

"Stand tall around him. Drives him nuts. How about injuries?"

"Could have been worse. One doctor with severely injured legs, though, is in surgery now, and she's pregnant."

"That poor lady. Hope her baby is okay."

· · ·

In the OR, anesthesia gave the thumbs up to proceed, and Dr. Rivers, scalpel in hand, wasted no time making the abdominal incision. In under thirty seconds, his incision extended through the skin, fascia, muscle wall, and peritoneum to expose the abdominal cavity. A small amount of free blood oozed, but his attention focused on the uterus, where he made a four inch cut and spread the sides open to reveal the fetus. The baby boy squirmed, and he gently lifted the three-pound infant through the incision. A nurse clamped and cut the umbilical cord and handed the baby to the neonatal intensivist.

A warmer set up in the corner of the room held the baby, as the neonatal team went to work. The infant was dried and monitors were attached to the body. The airway was clear, but the infant struggled to breathe due to prematurity. A breathing tube was placed in the trachea and hooked up to a ventilator, which took over breathing for the infant. Immediately, oxygen saturations rose, and the dark, mottled skin turned a vibrant, rich color. The team started IV's, stabilized the baby, and moved him to the NICU.

On the table, Dr. Rivers sewed up the uterus before handing the case to the trauma surgeon. A quick scan of the abdomen revealed two puncture wounds from the blast, one of which had hit the liver, the apparent source of the free blood in the abdomen. The surgeon repaired the damage before inserting drains and closing the abdomen.

A separate team of vascular surgeons and orthopedists already worked on the legs. The right leg had broken bones and torn muscles, but the vasculature was intact. The toes were well perfused with good blood flow.

The left leg was in much worse condition. A tourniquet remained in place to control the bleeding, and the surgeon ordered for the slow decrease in pressure on the tourniquet to identify the source of bleeding. As the tourniquet pressure decreased, bright red blood pumped from the thigh.

"Here it is. The lateral circumflex artery is torn. Hand me a clamp." The clamp was placed gently above the tear. "Slowly decrease pressure in the tourniquet." The tourniquet was fully deflated to show no evidence of further arterial bleeding. "All right, team. Let's get this artery patched and restore some blood flow to that leg, and then make a decision if we can save it or not."

· · ·

I was finishing my notes in a chart when Little Mac tapped me on the shoulder. "Hey Doc, this is Mr. Williams, Dr. Williams' husband."

I stood up and introduced myself to the distraught man. "I'm AJ Docker, but everyone calls me Doc. I helped take care of your wife."

"How is she? How's the baby? What happened?"

"Let's go in here where it's a little quieter." I led him to a consultation room designed for family conferences. "We don't have all the information yet, but there was some sort of explosion in the garage, and your wife was injured. She was brought over here awake, but with significant injuries to her legs."

"And the baby?"

"Ultrasound showed good movement and heartbeat, but a small placental abruption. Her partner, Dr. Rivers, was at the bedside and took her straight to the OR for a C-section. At the same time, orthopedics and vascular surgery are going to work on her leg injuries."

Mr. Williams collapsed back in his chair, crying. "I can't lose her, and we can't lose the baby. She spent ten years trying to get pregnant."

I reached over and squeezed his hand. "Mr. Williams, we're not losing anyone today. We have a top trauma team and NICU team. Your wife and your child are gonna get the best care that can be provided anywhere in the world."

"Any idea what caused the explosion?"

"We haven't heard anything yet, but half the police in Las Vegas are in the garage. Don't worry about them, let's focus on your wife and child. Are you expecting a boy or a girl?"

He smiled for the first time. "I don't know. She wouldn't tell me. Wanted it to be a surprise."

"Let's go upstairs and find out."

Mr. Williams dried the tears on his face, and we walked together to the elevator with Banshee silently appearing beside us.

"Is this your dog?"

"Yes, sir. This is Banshee. He provides comfort and security around here."

Mr. Williams reached over to scratch Banshee's ears. "I hope they send you after the asshole that did this."

"Banshee would like that. If we find the guy, I'll make sure Banshee introduces himself."

After a brief discussion with the charge nurse, Mr. Williams was gowned up and allowed into the NICU where his child was getting settled in by a team of nurses. Dad reached his gloved finger out and gently touched his son's tiny hand.

"Congratulations. Looks like you have a son. What's his name?"

Dad teared up as he replied. "We'll have to wait for his mom to get better and weigh in on it."

I quietly slipped away to the nurses' station, as dad gazed at his new son. I called the House Supervisor, explained the situation, and requested that Mr. Williams have VIP treatment while his family stayed in our hospital. A staff member would ensure that he had access to his wife and son, their doctors, and a place to sleep.

Banshee and I stepped back into the elevator. "We need to find that asshole, don't we, Banshee?" He tilted his head, trying to understand. "And when we do, you're gonna show him your teeth."

Banshee recognized the command and instantly bared his teeth, as a low growl rumbled from within. "Good boy. Save it for the asshole." Banshee was smiling by the time we returned to the ER.

.   .   .

Tim Roberts, head of the Las Vegas Bomb Squad, was suited up in protective gear from head to toe in a Tyvek suit, booties, gloves, glasses, and a hair net. Detectives Roland and Stillman adjusted their own protective gear as they listened, Stillman subtlety nudging Roland as he stood up on his tip toes.

"We're going in for a quick overview. Don't touch anything or go anywhere I don't go. We'll get a quick look at what we have and then make a plan. Let's move out."

Roberts, Stillman, and Roland, along with four other members of the bomb disposal team, entered the garage. The immediate site of the blast was darker with the lights blown out, and even their powerful flashlights failed to penetrate the layers of ash and soot. Residual water from the fire department trickled away. The team swung their lights back and forth as they moved forward.

Roberts commented as they advanced. "You can see the debris all the way out here, and even these cars have some minor damage. This is much more than a simple fuel tank explosion. Definitely a bomb of some type."

The car, now an unrecognizable twisted pile of metal, announced the obvious origin of the blast. Roberts stopped everyone twenty feet from the car and pointed. "This looks like where the doctor was injured. You can still see the blood stains and bandages on the floor." He turned his light on the car, and then slowly moved it back and forth over the area. He moved it to the ceiling above and stopped, turning to his team. "You seeing what I'm seeing?"

The team agreed, as Stillman and Roland looked on in confusion. Roberts explained. "You can see the main force of the blast is up towards the ceiling based on the amount of damage to the concrete and embedded debris. The cars on the side did not receive nearly the damage as the ceiling."

"What's that mean?"

"That means it was a shaped charge designed to blow up a person sitting in the car. It was not designed to blow up people around the car. This just got way more interesting."

"So what's the plan?" Roland asked.

"We'll get some samples and should know what explosive was used within an hour. We'll set up a grid and start sifting debris to find the bomb parts. Once we have the detonator and design we'll know a lot more."

"You're gonna find the detonator and parts of the bomb in this mess?" Stillman asked.

"When the bomb explodes, the device is blown apart, but the parts don't magically disappear. They're in there, and we'll find over 90% of the bomb, reconstruct it, and go from there. Get out of here, and go do some Detective shit while we get this done."

Stillman and Roland retreated to the exit and disrobed from the protective gear. "All right, partner. What sort of Detective shit do you want to do first?" Roland asked.

Stillman took out his notebook and started reviewing his entries from earlier, when his phone rang. Caller ID showed central dispatch.

"This is Stillman, what you got?" His expression revealed incredulity as he listened. "Send it to us. Thanks."

"Are you gonna make me guess what that was all about?"

"Our bomber called in a threat to 911 earlier today before the explosion, and they're emailing a link to the recording."

"Looks like we know what Detective shit to do next."

CHAPTER FOUR

Monday, 5:50 p.m.

Lana Hearns hurried to the scene of the explosion, along with a growing number of journalists and reporters. At thirty-eight, Lana had been a freelance reporter in Las Vegas for fifteen years, selling her stories to the networks. She had grown up in a small town in Ohio and had earned a journalism degree from Ohio State. Six months of working for the Columbus Dispatch convinced her she wanted something more. She looked for an exact opposite of Columbus and settled on Vegas.

Over the last decade and a half, she had established a robust network of informants among the criminal, legal and police communities in town, groups with more overlap than one might expect. She traded information, but never sources, and collected favors from people for times like this. Intensely focused, she wouldn't stop until she had the whole story. Las Vegas had produced some incredible stories, but an explosion targeting a pregnant doctor made national news, and she was determined to take the lead on this story.

A quick call to a cell phone at police headquarters uncovered a 911 call prior to the blast. Calling in a favor, she had a copy of the recording texted to her before the detectives heard it. It was public information that would be released eventually, but having it early gave her a leg up on the competition. She found a quiet spot away from the growing crowds and played the recording. Her pulse spiked as she listened again to the entire call, then replayed it to take notes. She had no idea who the hell the Aryan Federation of Las Vegas was, but determined to find out, she knew who to call first.

When Lana met Mad Dog Maclin, a small time drug dealer, an avowed white nationalist, and a certified sociopath, he had been falsely arrested for assaulting a cop. He had been pulled over on his Harley, and the cops claimed he had aggressively attacked them. Lana scoured the area and found a video from an Uber driver who had been pumping gas into his car pointed directly at the traffic stop. Although distant, the video clearly showed Mad Dog's cooperation prior to his arrest. Lana interviewed Mad Dog as part of her story after the video led to dropped charges and his quick release. Mad Dog told her that he owed her big time and not to hesitate to reach out if she needed something. While she never expected to need a favor from a sociopathic white supremacist, Lana didn't hesitate to call him.

"Who the fuck is this?" Mad Dog answered.

"This is Lana Hearns, and I need a favor."

"Happy to help after what you did for me, but not sure what a respectable lady like you needs from me."

"I need some information on a white supremacist group."

After a prolonged pause, he spoke. "Just to be clear, I'm not a part of any of those groups."

Lana thought about the swastika tattoo on his neck and "88" on his knuckles and doubted his denials. "I'm not saying you're a part of any group, I'm just looking for information about one specific group."

"Is this off the record?"

"Absolutely off the record. You're a protected anonymous source."

"Okay. Let me hear the question, and I'll decide if I can answer or not."

"Great. What do you know about the Aryan Federation of Las Vegas?"

"Who the fuck is that? There ain't no Aryan Federation of Las Vegas."

"Are you sure? I have it on good authority they exist."

"Your good authority sucks ass. Those groups are independent, but everyone knows everyone in that world, and there ain't no Aryan Federation in Las Vegas. Besides, that's a stupid fucking name."

Mad Dog continued to mutter about the name's stupidity, as Lana contemplated options. She had hoped for a name she could track down before everyone else was on the story. Despite his denial, Mad Dog was well connected with white supremacist groups in the area, and if this group existed, she would expect him to know about it. "No chance they're a new group you haven't run into yet?"

"Could be one guy masturbating to a nazi flag in his parent's basement, but it ain't a group. New groups are not exactly welcomed with people lining up to join, either."

"I understand. Can you please ask around, and let me know if anyone has heard of these guys?"

"No problem. You did me a solid with that video, and I owe you. I'll ask around, but make sure to keep my name out of your stories."

"Thanks, Mad Dog. You got my number if you hear anything." She hung up and wondered who the hell the Aryan Federation could be, and how she could track them down.

CHAPTER FIVE

Monday, 7:42 p.m.

"Jen, the ship is yours. I'm outta here," I announced, as I gathered my belongings.

"Enjoy the walk home. Your car is still locked down in the garage."

"Thanks for the reminder. I'm gonna run upstairs and check on Kelly and her baby."

"Hold up. I'll join you," Rick said, as he grabbed his bag. "Make sure Banshee doesn't bite me. I don't think that dog likes me."

Jen laughed. "That's because that dog has good sense. He probably doesn't want to catch anything from you." She punctuated the statement with a one finger salute.

Rick tried to look dejected. "That hurts, and I was just about to wish you a quiet shift. Really quiet. The quietest ever." Rick headed for the elevators chanting "quiet" all the way.

Banshee and I followed as Jen shouted down the hall, "Make sure to feed and water Rick before he comes back here."

The elevator pinged at the third floor, and we stepped aside for a pediatric patient who was walking in the hallway with a physical therapist. The patient pointed at Rick and exclaimed, "Superman!"

Rick puffed up his chest and held out his hand. "Superman at your service. What is your name, young man?"

"I'm Joe, and I wish I could fly like you."

Rick leaned over to whisper to the physical therapist and received a nod in return. "Good news, Joe. You're cleared for flight today."

Rick gently lifted the child and held him at head height, parallel to the ground. "Get those arms stretched out, Joe. We got some flying to do."

With the therapist carefully following with his IV pole, Rick strolled up and down the hallway raising and lowering Joe as he walked. Joe laughed and told everyone he passed he was Superman. Banshee and I watched until Rick brought Joe in for a soft landing.

"Okay, Joe. You work on getting those legs stronger. And let me know if you need anything."

"Thanks, Superman." With a high five, Joe returned to his exercise.

"Another memory created," I said.

Rick shrugged. "The world needs more laughter. Let's go."

That was classic Rick. He made a lifetime memory for that child and thought nothing of it.

We approached the ICU main desk to be confronted by a stern-faced charge nurse. "I hope you aren't expecting that dog to enter my unit."

"Are you talking about Banshee or Rick?"

"Both are unsanitary, and both distract the nurses' attention."

"But only one of us came up here to thank our colleagues in the ICU for their tireless efforts to care for our ER patients," Rick said with his most flirtatious smile.

"Your appreciation is noted and will sustain us through another day. She's in room six. Keep the visit short, please."

"How's she doing?" I asked.

"About as well as can be expected for delivering a baby and losing her left leg."

"Seriously? I was hoping they could save the leg," an angrily disappointed Rick said.

"They tried, but there was too much damage. Had to take the leg off below the knee."

"Can we stick our heads in for a minute?" I asked.

"Sure. Leave the dog here." She turned to Rick, waving a finger in his face. "No flirting with my nurses. We've got too much work to do."

Rick saluted, as I commanded Banshee to lie down. He curled up at her feet, as we aimed for the room. We both instinctively checked the monitor to evaluate her vitals as we entered.

"Numbers look good, but her color looks like shit," Rick quietly commented. I had to agree. She had fourteen separate pumps infusing blood and medicine into three IV's. She was intubated and the quiet beep of the machine kept time with her expirations. Her right leg was in a long leg splint, with only her toes showing. Her elevated left leg ended in a stump below her knee. Sedated and paralyzed, she looked like a skeleton of the vibrant person we knew.

"Who the fuck does something like this?" Rick asked.

I didn't have an answer, and I advanced to hold her hand. "Dr. Williams, it's Doc and Rick from the ER. You're doing great. Just keep fighting and get well. We'll make sure you and the baby get everything you need. Take care."

We left the room and sorrow ignited to anger. Rick was right on target. What kind of fuck up would do something like this? "C'mon Rick, let's go see the baby."

Banshee joined us as we left the ICU and walked down the hall to the neonatal ICU. Banshee had to wait outside with a volunteer as we gowned up to enter. Baby Boy Williams (no name yet) rested comfortably in a warmer. Hooked up to a ventilator, his tiny chest moved evenly twenty-four times a minute with the machine. His father slept peacefully in a chair at the bedside.

Rick whispered. "I didn't pay attention in neonatology. Is he doing well or not?"

The nurse overheard him and smiled at Rick. "He's actually doing fantastic and acting like a normal preemie, even though he was delivered by stat C-section after an explosion. He's doing great."

They thanked the nurse and stared impotently at the baby for a few more minutes before Mr. Williams stirred in his chair. He looked thirty years older than when I had seen him earlier in the day.

"Hey, Mr. Williams. Sorry to disturb you. It's Doc. We talked earlier in the ER, and this is Dr. Merden, he helped care for your wife in the ER as well."

Mr. Williams stood to shake hands, trying to shrug off his deep weariness. "Please, call me Isaac. Thanks to both of you for everything. I can't stand the thought of losing them."

"No worries. Glad we were there to help. Sounds like your son is doing well."

"That's what they tell me. Hard to believe with all these machines and monitors on his tiny body." Isaac teared up as he reached to touch his son's tiny hands.

Rick put his arm around Isaac. "Don't worry. We got the best baby doctors in the state looking after your boy, and a great team taking care of your wife, too. We'll take care of them, and you focus on taking care of yourself."

Isaac returned the hug and sat back down.

"Get some rest, sir. If you need anything let the charge nurse know. And if you want to speak to us just ask them to page us. They can reach us 24/7," I said.

Isaac nodded his thanks and closed his eyes, exhaustion once again overtaking him.

Rick and I silently exited. "Doc, we gotta do something about this."

"What did you have in mind? They are both sedated and intubated with twenty people caring for them. Not like we need to sign up to bring them a chicken casserole."

"No, I mean we need to get the assholes who did this."

"I'm pretty sure the police have a few people on the case already."

"Maybe, but we're smart. We're motivated. You got a bad ass dog, and I'm good at breaking things. We could do this."

"Rick, I'm gonna head home and get some sleep. Let's talk about it in the morning. These guys may already be caught by then."

We walked outside to see a mass of police cars, media, and yellow tape still surrounding the parking garage. A line of taxis were queued up to take advantage of the shift change. Banshee and I settled into a minivan for the ride home.

.   .   .

Tim Roberts exited the garage, doffed his protective gear, and took a long drink of water, while Detectives Stillman and Roland waited somewhat impatiently. "Sorry. It's a bit hot in these suits during the Las Vegas fall season." Fall was a relative term in Las Vegas, as the temperatures had dropped only to the low nineties.

Roberts led them to the evidence tent where hundreds of bags were already laid out and being catalogued. He pulled up his iPad as he explained. "A few things we know for certain. One, the car was definitely Dr. Williams' Lexus. We were able to locate a VIN number on the door and match it to her vehicle. Two, the blast was centered underneath the driver's seat. You can see here from the pictures the way the force of the blast is upwards, not outwards. Notice all of the debris embedded into the ceiling above the car, which is way more than the debris blown sideways. Which brings us to number three. The guy who did this is a pro."

"How do you know that?" Mary asked.

"Because I know professional work when I see it. This was a shaped charge. The blast was designed for the majority of the force to blow upwards, with minimal force blown outward. It takes real skill to design a bomb like this. If she had been sitting in her seat when the explosion occurred, we probably wouldn't have found any pieces of her more than a couple inches long. She was lucky it went off before she sat in the car."

"She might argue as to the relative level of her luck, but why did it go off before she was in the car?" Stillman asked.

"Come over here." He led them to another table, and after a brief search, held up a bag containing a burnt mass of plastic. "The bomb was triggered by this phone."

Roland looked dubiously at the bag. "That's a phone?"

"A very cheap phone that has been through a very powerful explosion. We won't get any more info from it, but it's a cheap burner phone, the kind usually used in bombs."

"How do you know it wasn't just a phone in the car?"

Roberts turned the package over. "You can just see the ends of a burnt wire attached to the battery. That, along with where it was found, makes us confident that this was the triggering device."

"That means someone had to make a call from another phone to trigger the device?" Roland asked.

"Correct. A better way to do it would be a pressure switch that would detonate when she sat in the seat, but that would require access to the inside of the car and takes a while to set up correctly. This device could be attached to the underside of the car in a second."

Stillman thought through the scenario. "That means our bomber had to be watching and manually call the number to detonate the bomb. Why didn't he wait until she was in the car?"

"Could be a number of reasons. He likely hadn't practiced the detonation, so he may have expected more of a delay between when he called and when the explosion occurred. He may not have had a direct view of the area and estimated her arrival time at the car, or he may have just been hyped up on adrenaline and fired too soon."

"Not an uncommon trait from men," Roland observed. "We keep referring to the bomber as a male, but how do we know it's not a woman?"

"The vast majority of bomb makers in the US are males. Statistically, it's a male behind this. Now, for the most interesting discovery of the day, chemical analysis of the residue showed that C4 was used, not unexpected, given the shaped nature of the charge. C4 is the best choice for this type of bomb."

"Do we have any information on the source of C4?" Roland asked.

"We know exactly where it came from. Every batch of C4 manufactured has chemical identifiers in it. We compared our results to the national database, and we know the date and location of manufacture. We know who it was sold to and where it has been. Want to know the crazy part? We have some from the exact same batch sitting in our evidence locker downtown."

"What the fuck did you just say?" Stillman asked.

"The chemical signature is a match for some C4 we seized about six months ago. Remember that asshole who stole seventy-eight blocks of C4 from the construction site, and then tried to sell it online? We monitor for that, and my guys answer those ads. Dumbass tied to sell us seventy blocks, about 87.5 pounds. He took a plea and is doing five to eight years right now."

"You said he stole seventy-eight blocks, but you recovered only seventy. Where are the other eight blocks?" Roland asked.

"The company records were thorough. He denies any other sales, but there are definitely eight blocks missing."

"So he either made a sale we don't know about, or someone stole eight blocks from him. So there are ten pounds of C4 on the streets?" Roland asked.

Stillman held up his hand. "There is one other possibility. Are we sure all of the C4 we seized six months ago is still in the evidence room?"

Roland and Roberts looked at each other as Roberts pulled out his phone.

CHAPTER SIX

Monday, 9:08 p.m.

Back at police headquarters, Roland and Stillman faced more questions than answers. "What do you mean they don't exist?" Roland asked.

"I mean four major white supremacist groups operate in Las Vegas, all pushing girls, guns and drugs. Fifteen minor groups dress up and play white supremacist on weekends, but no one takes them seriously. They make videos about how tough they are and then go back to their day jobs as accountants and bus drivers. No Aryan Federation has ever popped up on any radar." Detective Billy Bunger, or Billy Bong as he was known, headed the task force that tracked hate groups. His average size, scruffy beard, long hair, and tattoos allowed him to blend in unnoticed, as he mingled among the underworld of Las Vegas.

"Any of the known groups capable of pulling off this bombing?" Stillman asked.

"All of them would love to do shit like this, but I'm not sure any of them have the talent to pull this off. From what I hear, the blast was pretty sophisticated."

"We're still gathering evidence, but it appears the device was more than a weekend warrior could produce from YouTube videos."

"It also doesn't make sense. These guys hate minorities, and aren't against roughing up some folks if they get the chance, but mostly they stay under the radar and operate their groups for profit. The last thing they want is attention from the police, and they know we will be all over them after an event like this. Blowing up a pregnant doctor at the hospital is asking for a shit storm of trouble."

"That's what we need you to do. Go cause some trouble. Call in all your favors and rattle everyone on the streets. I want to know who the fuck the Aryan Federation is, and I want to know today."

"Already started. Everyone is out now rousting the usual suspects. We'll let you know as soon as we have something."

"Thanks. We gotta go update the Chief."

Billy Bong laughed. "Next time I see those asses there is gonna be a big bite missing out of them." Stillman and Roland held up single middle fingers as they walked away.

．　　．　　．

Tim Roberts lounged in the only available chair in front of the Chief's desk when the detectives arrived. Chief Olson had been on the force for thirty-one years and in the top position for two years. Stillman figured they must have been dog years based on how quickly the Chief had aged. His gray hair, the dark circles under his eyes, and his perpetually slumped shoulders depicted an image of a man heading to his retirement party soon. Despite his evident physical weariness, his sharp mind still deftly managed multiple crises at once.

"All right, give me the short version, and I'll let you know if I need more details." The Chief leaned back in his chair, as Roberts began his report.

"The bomb was a C4 shaped charge placed under Dr. Williams' car and detonated remotely by phone. The C4 is a chemical match for the explosive we confiscated six months ago from that mine heist. There were about ten pounds missing from what we collected, and this device used about a quarter of a pound."

The Chief's eyes narrowed. "There better not be any C4 missing from evidence."

"Already confirmed. Triple checked by my team after we got our initial results. All C4 in our possession is accounted for."

Roberts leaned back in his seat, and the Chief swiveled his attention to Detectives Stillman and Roland, who continued the report. "There was a 911 call before the blast with Aryan Federation of Las Vegas claiming responsibility. The call was from a cell phone and too short to trace. Voice was male, who likely used a modulator to disguise his voice. No one has heard of this Aryan Federation."

"And the victim?" The Chief asked.

"Dr. Williams is in the ICU and stable. Massive damage to her legs and lung. She lost the left leg below the knee, but she should make it, unless there are complications. The baby is in the NICU and doing really well. We have just started our background on her, and it's unclear why she was targeted. The phone call points to a racial hate crime, of course, but we don't know why they chose her."

"Analysis of the caller?"

"The call came in over three hours before the explosion. Out of context, it was assumed to be a prank until the explosion. The call was from a Las Vegas area code cell phone, which is now out of service and untraceable. In retrospect, the caller gave us some hints. The 'start of the day at the beginning of night' is consistent with Sunrise Hospital in the evening. The 'bringer of shadows,' in retrospect, is likely a crude reference to Dr. Williams. In her OB practice, the majority of her patients are African American."

The Chief pursed his lips as he leaned forward. "So to summarize, we don't know shit right now. We got a sociopath, who is a genius at building bombs, blowing up a black, pregnant doctor as part of a group we've never heard of. Did I get that right?"

"Yes, sir," Roland answered.

"And on top of everything, it's race week. Ten F1 teams with twenty of the best drivers in the world are going to be racing at 220 MPH on the Strip Saturday night. Almost a million people are descending on the city, including high dollar sponsors and VIP fans. Traffic will be a nightmare, and about half a billion people worldwide will be watching the race live on TV. And now we have a psycho racist bomber to deal with?"

The Chief's summary hung silently in the air, like a toxin. Everyone jumped as he slammed his hand down on the desk.

"Whatever it takes, you will catch this bomber before the race. Roberts, focus on that bomb, and figure out who built it. Can't be too many people in town able to build a shaped charge. You two focus on that call and on Dr. Williams. If we can figure out why she was targeted, maybe we can figure out who did this, and squeeze the shit out of that asshat who stole the C4 initially. I don't have to tell you that the Mayor, the ACLU, a senator, the head of the FIA, and a few billionaire casino owners are already all over my ass looking for answers. I don't care what resources you need, but find me this asshole. Dismissed."

.   .   .

I relaxed on my cushioned outdoor couch on the covered patio in the back yard, watching the sun set behind the Spring Mountains, while Banshee gnawed on a tree branch he had discovered two days ago. The branch was disappearing as quickly as the evening sun. I lived alone in a one story rental in the southern Las Vegas suburbs, but over the last three weeks, my girlfriend had moved in her share of supplies. I still controlled about a quarter of the bathroom sink space, but that area shrank by the day, as she added more essentials.

Banshee paused from chewing his stick to give a low growl, perk his ears, and tilt his head toward the house. "Are we under attack?" Banshee didn't understand the question, but remained alert. When he heard a key in the front door, Banshee happily leapt into the house. I didn't move from my comfortable position. It was likely my girlfriend, and Banshee would lead her to the back yard. If it was anyone else he would drag them outside kicking and screaming.

Banshee barked excitedly, as she came in the front door, knowing he would receive an undue amount of praise and maybe even a treat. Sure enough, a moment later he bounded out the back door with a piece of jerky in his mouth, followed shortly by Lana with a bottle of beer in her hand.

"Is there room on that couch for me?" she asked, as she slid out of her shoes.

I patted the cushion, and she plopped down beside me, swinging her legs into my lap. "Tough day?" I asked, as I massaged her calves and feet.

"Been chasing down the bombing story all day, and I'm not getting anywhere. I had the early lead on the story, but it just fizzled. I don't suppose you know anything useful?"

"Nothing that hasn't already been publicly reported. Dr. Williams had surgery on her legs and delivered a healthy preemie. What did you figure out?" I made it a point never to share confidential patient information.

"Not much after a lot of time and effort. Nobody has ever heard of this Aryan Federation that claimed responsibility. My sources tell me it was a shaped C4 charge that was remotely detonated and relatively sophisticated. There were some early rumors the C4 came from the evidence locker downtown, but that was quickly corrected. Background so far on the victim hasn't identified any leads. Other than her race, there is no obvious reason she was targeted. To summarize, I got nothing."

"Did you summarize that in your story?"

"Of course not. I'm an independent journalist and ahead of the pack. I filed my story first and all the major outlets have picked it up. Now everyone else is playing catch up, while I get my feet massaged and enjoy a beer."

I considered her words, as I continued to work on the knots in her feet. "Sounds like you learned a lot today. What's your next step?" I was always amazed at how quickly Lana could gather information. After fifteen years covering crime in Las Vegas, she had contacts everywhere, from billionaire casino owners to leaders of the crime syndicates that flourished in town.

"First thing, I am going to finish this beer while you finish massaging my feet. Then I am going to take a long, hot shower while you order some food. Then, I'm gonna call around until I can find something useful for my story."

"What do you think about me helping on this story?"

"I know we share a toothbrush sometimes, but not sure I want to share a story with you."

"Don't worry. You can have all the glory and the Pulitzer, but this one is personal. Dr. Williams is good people, and she may never walk again. Whoever thinks blowing up doctors is a good idea needs to face some justice. Besides, Banshee and I have some experience dealing with people like this."

Banshee perked his ears, as Lana considered the offer. She had admitted that she had run a background check on me after we started dating. Among my medical accomplishments, she had learned about my role in bringing down a Ukrainian crime ring in Houston as well as a corrupt rancher and Sheriff in Montana. She had also learned that I was wealthy, and that Banshee was a force multiplier in the field.

"Okay, I might regret this, but let's give it a try. You have to promise me you'll follow directions, and maintain absolute secrecy. We don't share our leads with anyone until the story is published, and no violence. Deal?"

"Deal. How do I get started?"

She stretched and rose from the seat. "Order some dinner while I take a shower, and then I'll make some calls, while you stay out of my way."

I looked at Banshee. "Being a reporter's assistant is a lot like working with surgeons. C'mon boy, let's go find some food."

Banshee thumped his tail enthusiastically, as if he sensed a new adventure.

CHAPTER SEVEN

Monday 11:52 p.m.

The bomber made it home late that night, relieved and confident that he wouldn't get caught. The sensationalistic news networks vied to outperform each other. They had very little factual information beyond a cryptic 911 call before the explosion and an injured doctor and her premature baby. In the absence of more material, they created their own narrative. Phrases like "domestic terrorism" and "hate groups" were repeated, as experts rambled about the meaning behind the attack. Their continuous drivel amounted to erroneous speculation at best. The only thing they got right was the suggestion that probable future attacks could escalate in scale.

The bomber smiled at the thought, as he prepared for his next performance.

CHAPTER EIGHT

Tuesday, October 17
7:13 a.m.

Stillman and Roland rolled up to the fence line with the already bright sun rising in their faces. "This place always depresses the hell out of me," Roland said.

"That's kind of the point of prison, I guess." High Desert State Prison, located about thirty miles northwest of Las Vegas, boasts a capacity of over 4,000 inmates, the largest prison in Nevada. The 160-acre facility is surrounded by an electrified fence with seven armed towers overlooking the entire prison. The fence probably wasn't necessary, as a hellish landscape surrounded it. A barren land of simmering dust, devoid of any meaningful vegetation, would encourage any escapee to beg to be let back inside. It's most famous guest, O.J. Simpson, called it home for a brief period in 2008. Stillman and Roland were responsible for many of the other guests who currently resided on site.

"At least they get lots of sunlight," Roland commented. Stillman winced, imagining living in that concrete hell hole through a Nevada summer. They pulled to the first gate for one of several ID checks. They locked their weapons in the car before entering the prison. The smell of four thousand desperate men overwhelmed them, as if even fresh air feared to enter. The gray, concrete walls, two-inch thick windows, and poor lighting subdued hope and optimism. Roland muttered, "Fucking depressing," as they signed in.

A guard led them to an interview room where the prisoner waited. Milton Meacham, or Milly as he had been known since childhood, wore the prison uniform of a light blue top and dark blue scrub pants. His hands were cuffed to an iron ringlet on the top of the table, and he raised his arms until the chain clinked. "What do you say? How about we lose the cuffs? I promise not to hurt anyone."

Roland smirked, as she motioned for the guard to uncuff Milly. He was maybe 160 pounds after a good meal and certainly not a physical threat to them. At forty-one, he had been a disappointment to everyone who had tried to care about him. Early involvement with gangs and drugs led to his dropping out of high school and to his first arrest at age sixteen for stealing a car. Since then, he had been in and out of prison for theft.

"How's it going, Milly?" Stillman asked.

"Fucking awesome. This place has everything. Free food, free clothes, an exercise program, the chance to shower with a bunch of psychos that may want to kill you or rape you. You guys should try it out. See if you like the place."

Milly was a well documented smart ass. "Thanks for that offer, but we're just visiting today."

"Let's start with who the fuck you guys are and what the fuck you want."

"I'm Detective Stillman, and this is Detective Roland. We want to ask you a few questions about that C4 you stole a few months back."

"Allegedly stole. I'm still on appeal."

Stillman conceded the point. "Fine. The C4 you allegedly stole from Diamond Head Mining a few months ago. Tell me about it."

"Why the fuck should I talk to you?"

Roland leaned forward. "Because I'm going to talk at your next parole hearing, asshole, and I'm either going to say nice things about you or talk enough shit to make sure you serve your full sentence."

Milly whistled. "I love it when the hot detective plays the bad cop. Okay, this is all theoretical, off the record, and you do me a solid to get me out of here early."

Stillman regained his attention. "If you provide us with useful information, we will put in a good word for you. Now, about the C4?"

"Theoretically, those dumbasses stored their explosives behind a shitty door with a shitty lock, covered by one camera which was not monitored in real time. A motivated individual could visit at night wearing a mask, avoid the drunken security guard sleeping in his office, spray some paint on the security camera, snap the lock off, grab some explosives, and be home in bed before anyone noticed."

Roland shook her head in disgust at how easy it was to steal explosives. "How much did you take?"

"Theoretically, if it was me, I would have taken everything they had, and they would have had almost one hundred pounds of the stuff. I would have hoped they had more, but that would have been all they had. Why the interest?"

"I just want to clarify. Theoretically, there were seventy-eight blocks of C4 in that office. Any chance that number might be wrong?"

"Nope. There were seventy-eight blocks of C4 weighing just under a hundred pounds in that theoretical office."

"Where did the missing ten pounds go?" Stillman asked.

Milly looked visibly confused. "What the fuck are you talking about?"

"When you went to sell the C4, allegedly sell the C4, you had only seventy blocks on you. Where did the other eight blocks go?"

Milly looked back and forth between the detectives. "Why don't you tell me why you're here. That job was months ago. Why the interest?"

"Yesterday, a bomb exploded in a hospital parking garage, seriously injuring a doctor. The C4 used in the bomb was a chemical match for the C4 you allegedly stole and tried to sell."

Milly sat back and crossed his arms. "I got nothing more to say."

"Milly, we aren't coming after you. We just want to know where the remaining C4 went."

"We're done here."

"You're gonna fuck up your parole."

"At least I'll be alive. Guard!"

Milly refused to say anything else and was cuffed for the return to his cell. Stillman and Roland gathered their belongings and passed through three solid doors to reach the already hot sunshine and fresh air. "He knows something," Roland said as she inhaled deeply.

"Fucker definitely knows who has the missing C4."

Roland looked around as they buckled into their car. "This place gets more depressing every time I visit." Stillman couldn't agree more, as he turned the car back to Vegas with a trail of dust obscuring the prison behind them.

CHAPTER NINE

Tuesday, 10:40 a.m.

Lana called me late in the morning. "What time are you done with your shift?"

"Three o'clock. Things aren't too crazy here, so I should get out on time, as long as some psycho doesn't blow up our parking garage again."

"Okay, I'll stop by around three with a change of clothes for you. I've got a hot date planned."

"Dinner?"

"Not quite. We're going to visit a thief in prison." She ended the call before I could respond.

· · ·

I pushed thoughts about the prison visit to the back of my mind to focus on a steady stream of patients. A young boy who broke his arm falling from his bicycle received a splint and a thank you for wearing his helmet. An older lady with chest pain warranted quick admission to cardiology. A steady supply of coughs and colds trickled through the system. Abdominal pain workups and breathing issues continued the routine patient flow for the day.

"Cheerleading injury? What the hell do you suppose that is?" I asked.

Rick leaned over my shoulder and glanced at the chart. "A twenty-three-year-old female with a cheerleading injury. Could be about anything. Five bucks I can do a better back flip than her," Rick called out.

I gave a thumbs up to Rick as I entered the exam room and did a double take. "Identical twins, I presume?"

The girls responded in perfect synchronicity. "Yeah."

Petite, athletic frames covered in athletic wear and topped with curly, red hair and light blue eyes stared back at him. "Not creepy at all. I feel like I'm in The Shining."

The girls responded in perfect unison, each holding out a hand. "Come play with us," before bursting out in laughter.

"As a survivor of Catholic schools, I can't begin to explain how creepy that is. Who is the patient?"

The girl on the left answered. "Me, I'm Jessica."

"I'm Hannah," the other sister offered without prompting.

"Nice to meet both of you. Okay, what happened?"

Jessica averted her eyes as Hannah took charge. "We were tumbling and stunting in the gym like normal. We threw our flyer in the air, right when our coach yelled that the ice cream was here. Jessie turned to look at the ice cream and our flyer landed with her knee on Jessie's sternum. Who knew ice cream was so dangerous, huh, Jess?"

I examined her as the sisters argued over how they could have caught her without getting hurt. "You may have cracked a rib. Not much to do about those except rest and ibuprofen, but we'll make sure it's nothing more serious. Wait here for an X-ray." The girls were still arguing as I left the room.

Not much had changed when I returned twenty minutes later, as the cause of the injury was still debated. I briefly waited for a break in the conversation before telling her the results. "You have a small crack in one rib. Nothing serious, but it's gonna hurt for awhile."

"How long?" Jessica asked.

"It usually takes three to five weeks."

"You can double that for Jess. She's a drama queen." Hannah added. A new debate ensued.

I finished my discharge instructions, answered their questions, and prepared to leave the room when I turned to Hannah. "Can you do a back flip?"

Hannah rolled her eyes. "Can you check a pulse?"

"I'll take that as a yes. How would you like to help me with something?" I explained my plan, and she readily agreed.

I exited the room with Hannah holding her side and called for Rick. "She's got a cracked rib, but I told her you were out here bragging about doing a better back flip than her, and she claims she is still better than you, even injured."

Rick looked dubiously at the small girl holding her ribs. "I don't think it's a good idea to try that injured."

Hannah stood up straighter. "Doc said you would be scared to lose." She then jumped straight up and performed a perfect back flip. She landed rock steady on her feet to applause from the staff.

Banshee watched with great interest, and I signaled a twirling motion with my hand. Instantly, he jumped up and performed his own back flip, landing steadily on his feet. Everyone clapped even louder as I challenged Rick. "Good luck. You're competing for third place."

Rick didn't waste a moment, emptying his pockets and clearing out space. He took a deep breath as he mentally rehearsed his moves, then jumped in the air and threw his head backwards. He rotated, but not quickly enough. He almost made the landing, but didn't quite have a full rotation, and tumbled forward onto his knees. The staff gave him a round of boos as he rose from the floor.

Jessica came out of the room, holding her ribs, and stood next to Hannah. "Not bad, but you have to elevate straight up, and then rotate.

You rotated too soon and lost elevation, and don't throw your head back."

Rick laughed. "At least I lost to the healthy one."

Hannah stepped forward. "She would have beat you, too, even injured. Here's what you need to do." Hannah and Jessica spent the next few minutes coaching Rick on his form. Several attempts later, Rick flew higher and landed solidly on his feet. Rick gave each girl a high five and asked what else he could try next.

"I've created a monster," I muttered as I went back to work.

· · ·

"Hey, Doc, some bomb squad guy wants to talk to you, because you were one of the doctors who took care of Dr. Williams right after the explosion. Just a heads up, he's kind of an asshole," the triage nurse informed me.

"Any particular kind of asshole?"

"The short kind who compensates by convincing himself that he's more important than everyone else."

"Bring him back, and let's get this done." I called over to Little Mac. "You got a free moment to take Banshee for a walk?"

"Sure thing, Doc. Let me get his leash."

Little Mac was adjusting the leash when the scowling nurse approached with a man in a shiny suit. He held out his hand. "Tim Roberts, head of the bomb squad. Nice to finally meet you," he said as he stared icily at the triage nurse who had delayed him.

I stood up to my full height, a good six inches taller than he, and wrapped my hand around his smaller one in a firm grip. "AJ Docker, but everyone calls me Doc. How can I help today?"

"Is there somewhere we can talk in private?"

"Yes, sir. Follow me."

Little Mac called out. "Adios, Doc. Me and Banshee are off on an adventure."

Roberts looked appreciatively at Banshee. "I assume that's a former police dog."

"Yeah, he was injured in the line of duty, and I adopted him. He took a bullet meant for me."

"Sounds like an interesting story."

"An interesting story for another day. How can I help you?" I asked again, as I led him to an empty conference room.

"How are the lady and her kid doing?"

I answered through gritted teeth. "The lady, Dr. Williams as she is known and respected around here, and her son, are doing okay. Both are very sick, but they should survive, unless there are major complications."

"That's a relief. It's a lot more paperwork when the victims die."

"I can see how that would be inconvenient for you."

"You got a problem with me, Doc?"

"I have a problem with a lead investigator who doesn't bother to learn the severely injured victim's name, and I have a real problem with people who find death inconvenient because it increases their paperwork."

Roberts held up his hands in defense. "Sorry, been a stressful couple of days with the explosion and the race coming up."

"Been a bit stressful around here as well."

"I imagine so. Can you call me if there are any changes in their condition?" He asked as he stood and handed me a card.

I stood to my full height. "Probably best if you communicate with our media team. Good luck catching the guy. He sounds pretty smart."

"He is, but I'm smarter. Good day, Doc."

I walked him out to triage and watched him exit. "Was I right?" the triage nurse asked.

"You were right, definitely an asshole." I dropped all further thoughts of Tim Roberts and went back to my patients.

CHAPTER TEN

Tuesday, 2:58 p.m.

Lana arrived as I finished my last chart. "Anything interesting today?"

Rick jumped up and performed his back flip, about his hundredth of the shift. "Rick learned a new skill and is very proud."

"As he should be. Ready to go?"

"Where you guys headed?" Rick asked.

"Doc takes me to the classiest places. Today, I'll be one of the only women there, the center of attention."

"Sounds like a fun date."

"Prison, Rick. We're going to a prison," I said.

"You're investigating the bomb? I wanna go, too."

"Unfortunately, Rick, your skills are needed here in the ER."

"Let me know what you find out. And I get to go on the next interview. Deal?"

"Sure thing, Rick. Try not to embarrass yourself while I'm gone."

"No chance of that." Rick punctuated the statement by doing yet another back flip, this time unaware of the chair behind him, which caused him to fall on his ass. Not discouraged in the least, Rick flipped onto his stomach and proceeded to do ten one handed pushups before returning to work.

Little Mac came over and saluted. "Don't worry, Doc. I'll take good care of Banshee while you're gone." He leaned down to give Banshee some ear scratches and a kiss on the head.

"Thanks a lot, Little Mac. We should be back in a couple hours."

. . .

Lana and I made the depressing drive to High Desert State Prison with little traffic in our way.

"Not a very popular destination, is it?" I observed.

"Have you ever been to a prison before?"

"I've spent a week in a small town jail, but never been to a prison."

"A small town jail is a luxury vacation compared to this place. Four thousand angry men live closely contained in a concrete box, and a hundred guards get by just above the poverty line."

"Hopefully, we can rely on the concrete to hold."

"Don't count on it. The whole structure was built by the lowest bidder. Just stay calm in there, and remember, you're my assistant."

"Why did he agree to a media interview?"

"Maybe he's bored. Maybe he's got something to say, but most likely, he's tired of looking at naked guys in the shower, and the prospect of some time with a female is intriguing."

I thought back to the week I was locked up and understood how overwhelming the boredom of prison life must be. "All right, let's do this."

We spent twenty minutes going through ID checks, a metal detector, and a pat down before we were led to an interview room. Lana carried a pencil and a notebook, and I had a small tape recorder. I fidgeted after the door clanged shut, locking us into our half of the room.

"You gonna be okay?" Lana asked.

"Yeah. Just bringing up some bad memories."

A few interminable minutes later, a guard opened the door on the other side of the room and escorted Milly to his seat. He raised his hands to the guard. "How about removing the cuffs."

The guard smirked, as he turned away. "How about you fuck off. You got fifteen minutes." The guard left the room, leaving Milly to stare at Lana.

"Holy shit, you're a looker."

Lana, ever the professional, ignored his hungry gaze. "Mr. Meachem, my name is Lana Hearns, and I am a reporter investigating the recent bombing at Sunrise Hospital. Is it okay if we record this?"

Milly nodded, and I turned on the recorder.

"I heard from my sources that the C4 used in the device was an exact match for some C4 that you had previously stolen."

"Allegedly stolen. I'm on appeal."

"Apologies. The C4 you allegedly stole. I'm trying to figure out how it ended up in the hands of the bomber."

"Seems like everyone is trying to figure that out."

"Do you have any thoughts on the subject?"

"I have plenty of thoughts about it. The question is why I should share anything with you."

"Mr. Meachem, I'm trying to get the truth out there on why a white supremacist group tried to kill a pregnant African-American doctor."

"Shit, that's easy. Those motherfuckers are crazy and hate black people."

"Okay, but I'm trying to understand how C4 was allegedly stolen from a mine, confiscated during an undercover sting, and ended up being used by this group. If I can understand that, I'll be one step closer to figuring out who did this."

Milly sat back in his chair and let the silence build. Eventually, he came to a decision and leaned forward. "I'll share some thoughts, but off the record."

Lana glanced at me, and I turned off the recorder and laid it on the table.

"You ever see those pictures on TV with the police standing behind a big pile of drugs, money or guns, stuff they confiscated during an arrest, looking all proud and tough with their spoils of war?"

"Of course."

"How big do you think those piles were at the time of seizure? Maybe 10% bigger? Maybe 30% bigger? I can guarantee you this. Not everything seized gets entered into evidence."

"Are you claiming an officer took the C4?"

"Here are the facts as I know them. Allegedly, I took seventy-eight blocks of C4 from the mine. Allegedly, I showed up with seventy-eight blocks of C4 to sell to an undercover officer. At my trial, there were seventy blocks of C4 admitted into evidence. I may not have finished high school, but seventy blocks is less than seventy-eight blocks. Somewhere along the way, some C4 went walking."

I leaned forward. "Are you saying a cop is behind this?"

An exasperated Milly directed his response to Lana. "Why does an intelligent and beautiful lady such as yourself hang out with this dumb fuck? No, I'm not saying the cops are responsible for the bomb. I'm saying one of those lying chuckle fucks stole the C4 and sold it on the street. That's what they do. They know who the buyers are and the street value of the stuff. It's easy, untraceable money, and the buyers know if they ever say a word they'll end up in a barrel in Lake Mead."

Lana tapped her pencil thoughtfully on her notepad. "Any idea which cop might have done it?"

"No idea. Never met any of them fuckers before, but all their names should be on the arrest report. One of those asswipes stole it and sold it. He's the one should be in here instead of me."

The guard came back and announced time was up. Milly stood and shook his finger at Lana. "The answer is in that report. If you're as smart as you are hot, you'll find him. Don't count on limp dick here being any help. Pretty boy wouldn't last five minutes in here."

Lana and I gathered our things and left the same way we entered. Upon escaping through the final door, we both instinctively stopped and took a deep breath of fresh air and admired the expansive landscape in the evening sunlight. I glanced at my phone. "Hard to believe we were in there for only forty-seven minutes. Felt like two days."

"Imagine what ten years would feel like."

"No, thanks. Do you believe him?"

"I believe some of what he said, certainly enough to chase down that arrest report and take a closer look at the cops. I've got to find a source for that."

"How do you find a source?"

"Keep following leads. Eventually, the story writes itself. Not so different from what you do in the ER. Avoid the Strip on the way back. They're starting race preparations, and it's a nightmare already."

"Gonna be a crazy weekend, even for this town. Do you really believe what Milly said? That a cop is involved?"

"Most of what he said, but he wasn't right about everything."

"What did he get wrong?"

She leaned in closer to kiss his ear. "You're not a limp dick."

I watched the prison recede in the background until it disappeared altogether. I hoped it was my last vision of any prison.

· · ·

A guard pulled out a burner phone and texted to a memorized number.

"Two reporters showed up after the cops."

"Names?"

"Lana Hearns and assistant."

"Thanks. Five hundred is on the way."

The guard turned off the phone and returned it to his pocket. He had no idea who was on the other end of the text and didn't care. He was paid for information and five hundred dollars of Bitcoin would be in his account by the end of his shift.

The bomber quelled some anxiety over the reporter's tracking down Milly so quickly. He guessed that it would happen eventually, but he needed more time. Milly had to go.

The bomber opened a Tor browser on his computer and entered the dark web. He went to a site with a twenty digit alphanumeric name. It had taken many hours perusing chat boards to find the site. He had hoped not to need it, but believed in preparation. Every possibility had been considered and every contingency planned for.

He opened a chat window on the site.

"I have an urgent problem at High State Prison."

"How urgent?"

"By morning at the latest"

"$5k. Bitcoin. Up front. No refunds. Target?"

"Milton Meachem."

"Send funds here," followed by a link.

The bomber, amazed at how easy it was to order a hit on the dark web, logged off, accessed his crypto account, and transferred the $5,000, then the $500 to the guard. The key was to find a secure site not set up by the Feds. The bomber had no idea who was on the other end, but they were known to be reliable. Reputation was everything in their business, and if word got out that they walked on a contract, they would be finished. The best part was that if they were caught, they had no idea who the client was, totally secure for him. The bomber quickly fell asleep, satisfied that he had solved another problem for only fifty-five hundred dollars.

·   ·   ·

I returned to the ER to pick up Banshee and found Little Mac blindfolded at the nursing station. Jen explained, "Rick is sure he can fool him this time. He brought a special guest and may actually have a shot."

Little Mac had the gift of absolute pitch, the ability to identify or recreate a given tone without the benefit of a reference note. A rare talent found in only about one in ten thousand people, Little Mac could recognize any voice he had ever heard, no matter how long ago he had heard it. His brain somehow catalogued the pitch and cadence of individualized speech, and he could identify that voice as soon as he heard it again. Rick was always trying to stump him and had always failed.

Rick asked for quiet, as he led an older lady into the nurses station. "Are you ready, Little Mac?"

"Yes, sir."

"What do you want her to say?"

"It doesn't matter. She can say anything she wants."

Rick opened the weather app on his phone, handed it to her, and whispered into her ear. The lady read, "The high temperature today will be eighty-seven degrees with plenty of sun and no chance of rain. The low temperature tonight will be…"

"That is Ms. Lisa, who used to work the middle cash register in the cafeteria a few years ago." Little Mac raised the blindfold and hugged Ms. Lisa, as everyone clapped.

Rick looked on in amazement. "How in the hell does he do that? She hasn't been in the hospital for over five years! I happened to run into her while she was visiting a family member upstairs. Wow, just wow!"

"We all have our special talents," I offered.

"Rick, it looks like your special talent is losing. Nice try, though. You had him stumped for about 0.3 seconds." Jen laughed, slapped him on the back, and headed back to her patients.

"How did the prison thing go? Did you join a gang? Get a tattoo? Start a riot?" Rick asked.

"No, but I did give your phone number out for anyone who has medical questions or an interest in muscular men. Milly seems to think the cops stole the explosive and sold it on the street, so Lana's following it up."

"What do you need me to do?"

I handed him an iPad. "Go see some patients. Banshee and I are headed home."

CHAPTER ELEVEN

Wednesday, October 18
7:35 a.m.

Breakfast at High Desert State Prison was consistently awful with oatmeal that tasted like it featured sawdust from the wood shop, watered down powdered eggs, and a piece of toast, either burnt or soggy. Today's toast was burnt, which he actually preferred. Milly carried his tray to his usual table, picked through the food, and wondered how the larger inmates stayed huge on the paltry diet.

Trouble began in the serving line when a black prisoner bumped into a Hispanic prisoner, who yelled at him in Spanish, resulting in the black prisoner throwing his tray at his adversary and tackling him to the floor. The exchange of punches caused instant chaos, as everyone stood to shout encouragement. Individuals pushed each other, leading groups to square off against each other. The prepared guards hit the alarms, locked down the cafeteria, and called in reinforcements, as they attempted to reach the original combatants.

Milly, standing on his bench and cheering on the chaos like everyone else, had managed to stay out of any gang and was not expected to join the violence. His only task was to stay out of it. Unfortunately, his attention focused on the fight and not on his surroundings. He never saw the fist that hit him, not that it would have made a difference. The massive punch from a colossal inmate landed squarely on his temple and caused catastrophic damage. A broken jaw and cheekbone were followed by a broken collarbone as he hit the floor, mercifully already unconscious with a small subdural bleed in his head. The inmate leaned over, jammed a sharpened spoon handle into Milly's neck, and worked it back and forth, as he held a tray with his other hand to deflect the shooting blood. The carotid artery, as well as the internal and external jugular veins, were completely severed in seconds. The inmate dropped the spoon and tray and calmly walked away.

Milly bled out in seconds amidst the chaos, alone on the cool cafeteria floor. The investigation lasted slightly longer than the fight with no witnesses to the murder. Milly's unremarkable death contributed only to one more statistic at High Desert State Prison.

.   .   .

Lana scrolled through her phone, as I made my famous waffles for breakfast, my mixing interrupted by her exclamation, "No fucking way!"

I laid down my black mixing spatula and stilled in anticipation, as her eyes moved rapidly through the story. "You gonna elaborate on that thought?"

She quickly finished the story, then turned to me. "That dude we met with yesterday, Milly, he's dead."

"Seemed healthy enough when we left him."

"A spoon jammed into the neck tends to have a deleterious effect on one's health."

"As a medical professional, I concur. Do you think it was related to our visit?"

Lana looked at me like I was an idiot. "Sometimes I can't figure out how you got through high school, let alone medical school. Of course it was related to our visit. Someone had him silenced."

"Pretty quick work, isn't it?"

"That just means it was important."

"What's your next step?"

Lana thought for a moment, tapping her pencil on her cheek, as she flipped through her notes, an adorable mannerism that I knew not to interrupt. Finally, she dropped her notes and picked up her phone.

"Who're you calling?"

She ignored me, found the contact she was looking for, and placed a call with her phone on speaker. "Detective Roland, this is Lana Hearns, and I'm working on a story related to the hospital bombing. Do you have any comment on the violent murder of prisoner Milton Meachem this morning?"

She paused, "I'm sorry, did you say Milly was murdered?"

"Yes, stabbed in the neck during breakfast. Apparently, a fight caused a distraction, and no one saw anything. Milly told me you met with him earlier in the day yesterday."

"Wait. You met with Milly yesterday?"

"Yes. We stopped by around four o'clock."

"We?"

"My assistant and I."

"Did Milly have anything interesting to say?"

"You know I can't reveal that information."

"Actually, you can. The question is whether you will."

Lana tapped her pencil on her notes as she thought. "How about we make a deal, help each other out?"

"I'm listening."

"I tell you all about my conversation with Milly, but I need you to get me a copy of Milly's arrest record in the next hour."

"Done."

"And if you need any information out to the press, you leak it to me first."

"No guarantees we'll share info, but if we do, you get the call, and if you come across anything useful, I want it. We have a killer out there."

With the agreement in place, Lana shared the details of her conversation with Milly, concluding that Milly felt a cop had stolen the explosive and sold it.

"That is one of the unfortunate scenarios we are evaluating," Detective Roland said. "I'll get you the report, and feel free to check out everyone in it. It'll be easier for you to do than for us. Blue on blue investigations are complicated, but if you find anything, let me know immediately. If it's a dirty cop who has already killed one person, a second murder will be no big deal to him. Be careful out there."

Lana hung up and turned to me with excitement gleaming in her eyes. "That's how you get information in my world."

I gave a slow applause. "Impressive. I think that effort deserves a reward."

"I'll take the waffle. Make it quick. There's work to be done."

. . .

Detective Roland tracked down her partner and updated him on Milly's death. "Someone's worried and cleaning up loose ends," she concluded.

"I agree. Let's notify the Chief. If a cop is involved, this could get real ugly, real fast."

"Set it up. I need to email a copy of the arrest report to Lana."

Twenty minutes later they were in front of the unhappy Chief. "You're telling me a cop may be involved? How confident are you?"

Stillman responded. "Nothing definite, but it's a real possibility that needs to be followed up."

They waited silently, as the Chief pondered his options. "We have media from every country in the world in town for the race, and now this. Who knows about this?"

"Only the three of us at the moment, sir."

"That's one good thing, at least. Bring in Chambers from internal affairs, and let him run background on the cops. You guys focus on suspects not wearing a uniform. No leaks. This stays between the four of us. If a cop is involved, we take him down, but control the narrative. If no cops are involved, this conversation never happened. Questions?"

"None, sir."

"Good. I want this asshole in cuffs before he strikes again. Dismissed."

"I'll get Chambers up to speed," Roland offered as they entered the elevator.

"And I'll go see if Roberts has any leads."

CHAPTER TWELVE

Wednesday, 10:27 a.m.

"Whatcha got there?" I asked

"Police report of Milly's arrest. Detective Roland sent it," Lana responded.

"Is it normal for cops to share info with reporters?"

"More common than you might think. As long as our interests are aligned, we can help each other. They have information, and we have sources."

"What's your next step?"

"The report clearly states that 87.5 pounds of explosive were seized, and Milly insisted he had 97.5 pounds. If ten pounds went missing, one or more of these guys had to have been involved."

She showed me a note card with four names handwritten on it.

Sergeant Jim Armond

Sergeant Ron Bertrand

Sergeant Kenny Krug

Detective Tim Roberts

"Now I need to find out everything I can about them. I'll start with finances, as anyone skimming off the top has likely done it before. Dirty money tends to leave a clear trail."

"You need help with that?"

A surprised Lana stared at me. "What do you know about getting financial info on cops?"

"I know a guy. Hacker. Can get anything on anybody in hours."

"Is he discreet?"

"Very."

"Give me his number."

I laughed as I batted away her outstretched hand. "He won't talk to you. He's a bit paranoid, but he likes Banshee, and he likes me, because I take care of Banshee."

"Sounds a little crazy."

"He's a lot crazy. Just be quiet and listen."

I put the phone on speaker and hit my contact for The BT. Before it could complete a ring on the other end, a harried voice answered. "How the fuck are you, Doc? And how's the dog? What do you need this time?"

"I'm good, Banshee's great, and I need financial profiles on four guys."

"What type of guys?"

"Possibly dirty cops."

The BT laughed. "You're being redundant, Doc."

"I'm looking for dirty money."

"Aren't we all. Give me the names."

I recited the four names.

"How long you need?"

"Cops are easy to track. Give me a couple hours, usual price of $500 per person sent to my account. Later."

The BT hung up as Lana asked, "Who the fuck is that guy?"

"He's a twenty-five-year-old who can hack any system and thrives on Adderall and energy drinks."

"And he can get all that info in only two hours?"

"Guaranteed."

"You need to introduce me. My guy would take a couple days."

"If you like the results, I'll introduce you, but right now I need to get ready for work. I'm covering for six hours today. Extra staffing for the race folks coming into town."

.   .   .

A 747 landing at Harry Reid International Airport in Las Vegas had originated in Macau, China, and the seven-thousand-mile flight had taken over sixteen hours. It pulled to a delicate stop at terminal 3 along with other international flights, but only this one had an immigration agent waiting, as the tunnel was attached and the door opened, to usher him inside to meet the VIP visitor. The agent stared in wonder at the interior opulence, which more closely resembled a five star resort than a plane.

The billionaire and his associates lounged on white leather couches, as an aide stepped forward to offer six diplomatic passports. The agent glanced at each passport before stamping them and handing them back to the aide. "Welcome to the United States. Please follow me. Your transportation is ready, as requested."

They deplaned, and instead of walking down the jetway, they exited down a set of stairs directly to the tarmac and ducked into the open doors of two dark SUVs that proudly displayed the Chinese flag on the antennas of each vehicle. Security men closed the doors to keep the guests cool and safe. The Kevlar lined doors and bulletproof glass would stop anything short of an RPG.

The two SUVs pulled forward and were joined by a lead and a chase SUV to sandwich the VIP guests. A Las Vegas police cruiser led the procession off airport grounds, his lights clearing a path for the small convoy. Twelve minutes later, they pulled into the underground parking lot at Mandalay Bay and took a private elevator to their suites to recover from the long journey.

Mr. Zhang, the billionaire from Macau, was only thirty-four years of age and enjoyed a net worth beyond the comprehension of most. Unlike many of his more modest family members, the billionaire enjoyed drinking, gambling, recreational drugs, the nightlife of Las Vegas, and especially race cars. In town for the F1 race, he had access to all of the teams on pit lane.

Mr. Zhang paid over a million dollars a night for an entire floor to accommodate the eighty staff, security, cooks, and personal assistants who traveled with him. The billionaire laid down to rest for a big night of adventure, while his staff moved his personal belongings into the hotel.

CHAPTER THIRTEEN

Wednesday, 11:54 a.m.

I walked into work to find a small crowd centered around the nursing station, taking sides as Rick and Jen prepared for their challenge.

"What's going on?" I asked a medical assistant.

"Rick claimed that he is more than twice as strong as Jen, who didn't take too kindly to that and challenged him. Jen has to hold two pounds with her arm extended, while Rick has to hold four pounds. First one to drop their arm loses."

I edged over for a better view. Rick, dressed in Black Panther scrubs, flexed his shoulders, as Jen calmly sipped her coffee. "Let me know when your male insecurity stretches are done, so I can get this over with."

Rick dramatically flexed a few more times, before he stretched his arm outward. "Let's do this." Jen stood next to him and held her hand outstretched with the palm up as well. A nurse approached with a two pound and a four pound weight borrowed from the sports medicine clinic. On the count of three, she placed the weights in each of their hands.

Rick raised his arm up and down a little. "Might as well get a little workout, since this competition won't last long." Jen ignored him. By sixty seconds, Rick stopped messing around and focused on his arm. By ninety seconds, Rick's arm trembled, and he gritted his teeth. Jen remained immobile.

At a hundred twenty seconds, Rick visibly shook and grunted, as he tried to steady his arm. Finally, at two minutes and twenty seconds, Rick gasped and dropped his arm with a small cheer from the assembled crowd. Jen turned to stare at him, reaching down with her left hand to take a sip of her coffee. Her right hand remaining rock steady with the weight.

She handed the weight to Rick, "Girl power." Rick looked at the weight in disbelief as Jen walked away.

"Tough morning," I observed.

"There is no way in hell I'm not twice as strong as she is."

"Probably not, but you're not five times stronger, which is what she just challenged you to."

"Huh?"

I picked up the weight. "This is two pounds, but if you extend the weight, the relative weight increases the further the weight gets. She held her shoulder in tight while you extended your much longer arm all the way out. Relatively, you were holding much more than twice the weight that she did."

Rick jumped up to seek a rematch, but I restrained him. "She already looks stronger than you are. Don't admit that she's smarter, too."

"You think she knew?"

"Definitely. She is smarter than you. Let's go see some patients."

• • •

A text from The BT two hours later told me to check my email. As usual, he gave a succinct summary of the attached report.

"Cops Armond, Bertrand, and Roberts are boring. Ignore them. Focus on Krug. He's bleeding money, likely to gambling. Best, The BT"

A forty page attachment detailed the finances of each of the four cops. I forwarded it to Lana and got back to work. My next patient was a drunken tourist with a broken arm from trying to climb a statue at Caesar's Palace. Another failed Instagram adventure ended in the ER. Viva Las Vegas.

. . .

Lana dug into the financial data as soon as she opened her email, amazed at the amount of detail The BT had collected in only a few hours. She quickly dismissed Armond and Bertrand as well. Both were family men living normal lives on cops' salaries with a little bit of debt and a little bit of savings. Roberts' finances were equally dull, with the exception of a $200,000 withdrawal six months before. Further notes revealed that he had used the money to pay off his parents' home. Lana gained a small amount of respect for the narcissistic bomb squad leader. At least he cared about his family.

Sergeant Krug's finances told another story altogether. He earned a base salary of $62,000, with another $20,000 or so in moonlighting. He was single, lived in a small three bedroom home, and drove a six-year-old Honda Accord. His salary and moonlighting should have been plenty to cover his modest lifestyle, but he was drowning in debt. A second mortgage had his house leveraged to the maximum, and all credit cards were maxed out and overdue.

Lana turned to the information from the Casinos, instantly clarifying that Krug gambled a lot. He had platinum status and open lines of credit at multiple casinos. The casinos were no longer lending him money, but they accepted his cash when he came to play. Sadly, Krug was a gambling addict and in serious financial trouble. Like any addict, he would do whatever was necessary to get money to make the next bet.

Lana reached out to Mad Dog, who answered on the first ring.

"If you're calling about the Aryan Federation of Las Vegas, they still don't exist."

"I have to agree with you on that one. No one has heard anything about them, but I called for another reason. If I had some stolen explosives, and I wanted to sell them, who would I contact to broker a deal?" It was a bold move by Lana, and she knew she was pushing her luck.

A wary Mad Dog hesitated before responding. "I don't know anyone like that, and even if I did, I wouldn't share that name on a call that could be recorded."

"I understand your concerns, but I can assure you I am not working with the police. In fact, my lead suspect right now is a cop."

"Are you really going after a cop?"

"I am going after the truth, and right now the truth leads me to a cop. I'm hoping to find someone who is familiar with moving explosives to see if I can confirm anything."

"Messing with cops and stolen explosives is a dangerous game for a young lady like yourself. I suggest you take the night off and relax a bit. Go out for a drink. I recommend you try the Iron Cross 14. There's a guy who works the bar named Tito who makes a good drink and knows a lot of people. Fair warning though, it's a little rough in there, so you may want to bring some company. And I don't need to mention that you don't know me."

"Never heard of you, Mad Dog. Thanks."

Lana disconnected and looked up the Iron Cross 14 bar on her laptop. Located northwest of the Strip in the heart of one of the most violent neighborhoods in America, it could clearly entertain a white supremacy stronghold. She planned to pick up Doc after his shift.

CHAPTER FOURTEEN

Wednesday, 7:53 p.m.

"Well look who showed up. Banshee, Guard."

Banshee lowered his head and growled as he stood between me and Lana, who was approaching down the hall. Lana laughed and bent down as she reached Banshee to give him a kiss on the top of his head.

"Calm down you sweet little puppy." Banshee rolled over on his back and kicked his back leg, as she scratched his belly. "Quite the guard dog you have here."

"He's scarier with strangers. What brings you here all decked out?" Lana wore black skinny jeans, a sleeveless black blouse, and black boots. Her short hair was flipped to the side, and dark eyeliner completed her sleek look.

"Tonight, I am a bad ass biker bitch, and you are coming with me to a bar."

"Seriously? A biker bar?"

"Yes. It's for the case."

"The case? Did somebody say the case? I'm in." Rick appeared with his iPad in hand.

Lana raised her eyebrows at me. I shrugged, "It's up to you. It's your idea."

She turned to Rick. "Okay, but you need to be on your best behavior, and it could be a little dangerous."

Rick puffed up his chest. "I am in a danger mood. Let me clear out the rest of these patients."

I turned back to Lana. "I hope we don't regret this. How dangerous are we talking about?"

"Nothing to worry about, sweetie, but bring Banshee in full gear, just in case."

I finished my charts and ran upstairs to check on Dr. Williams and her son. I found her husband at the bedside. "How's she doing today?"

"Better. The infection is under control, and her lungs are healing. Her legs are a mess, but the docs are confident she won't lose her right leg. Still a long road ahead, but she's out of the danger zone."

"Great news. How's your son doing?"

A smile lit up his face for the first time. "Really well. He no longer needs the ventilator, but is still on oxygen. No signs of infection and no signs of any bad effects from the blast."

"That's the best news I've heard all day. Anything I can do for you?"

"I'm good here. Everyone has been great. If you get bored and want to catch the bomber, that would be much appreciated."

"I'm sure the police have their best teams working on it. Glad to hear they're both improving. Get some rest and remember to eat."

I left with a little more bounce in my step. Seeing improvement in both of them and a spark of hope in her husband doubled my determination to get to the bottom of things.

· · ·

Twenty minutes later we slid into Lana's car and headed for the bar. I wore jeans and a black t-shirt with cowboy boots that Lana had brought for me. Rick had chosen jeans, Converse high tops, and an old Blink-182 t-shirt with the sleeves cut off. He happily flexed to show off his arms. Banshee sported his full tactical Kevlar vest. Lana pronounced the ground rules as she drove.

"I'll handle the interview. You guys are there to provide some security. I did some research on this place, and it is all about white supremacy. Lots of losers in there, needless to say, but some hard core dangerous types, too. I don't expect any trouble, and don't go looking for any."

Rick flexed and kissed his bicep. "No one's gonna mess with me in there."

Lana shook her head, as she turned off the Strip. "The bar is called Iron Cross 14, which refers to a German military medal given out by the Nazis during World War Two. The 14 references the 14 Words, which is a white nationalist slogan. 'We must secure the existence of our people and a future for white children'."

"That slogan sucks. They need better marketing people. 'Just Do It' is a slogan. That 14 words is just babble," Rick observed.

"Maybe keep that opinion to yourself for the next hour. The plan is to get in, find a guy named Tito, ask a few questions, and get out without a fight."

"That doesn't sound fun, but I'll behave."

We parked amidst a sea of motorcycles and pickup trucks. I put Banshee on a leash for appearance sake, but it was a breakaway leash that allowed him to move freely if needed. Small groups clustered around vehicles, sharing beer and pills openly, while others were already passed out on the cement. Leather outfits and tattoos were all the rage, and personal hygiene did not seem to be a priority.

"The fat ones are the drunks. The skinny ones are on meth or heroin." Rick commented.

Everyone did seem to be overweight or underweight. "I think they let their Pilates memberships expire."

Lana ignored us and led the way to the front door. A partially lit, crooked sign of "Iron Cross 14" struggled to defy gravity above the door.

Inside, neon lights filtered through smoke, as heavy metal music blared from old speakers. Cheap, wooden tables with mismatched chairs were scattered throughout the room, mostly occupied, with dozens of empty beer bottles littered across them. Chicken wings and nachos appeared to be the chef's specialty. Nazi paraphernalia hung on the walls alongside pictures of Hitler and his infamous salute.

Lana aimed for an opening at the bar, garnering a few appreciative stares along the way. Rick, Banshee and I attracted significantly more negative attention. Lana held up her hand and ordered three beers from the bartender.

I leaned over and talked directly in her ear. "You do remember I don't drink, right?"

"You don't need to drink anything. Just wanted you to have a weapon if necessary."

Not a bad idea, considering the increasing hostility thrown toward us. Banshee sat attentively at my feet, observing everything.

Lana called the bartender over and yelled over the music. "I'm looking for Tito."

The bartender looked her over. "You're not his type."

"I just want to talk. Can you let him know?"

The bartender turned away and went back to work, ignoring her.

"That didn't seem to go so well," I observed.

"Just wait, he'll talk to me. This is what I do."

I turned back to the crowd and noted three large men rise and head toward us. I tapped Rick to get his attention and signaled Banshee to be alert. The largest of the three stopped six inches away from my face. Although a few inches shorter, he outweighed me by a good sixty pounds. His clenched fists signaled his intentions, and his oft broken nose confirmed that this was not his first instigation. Two equally large men flanked him, and most concerning, the man at my left side slowly slid his right hand from his pocket to reveal a knife.

CHAPTER FIFTEEN

Wednesday, 9:15 p.m.

The center man spoke. "You're in the wrong bar. Why don't you and your dog and your faggot boyfriend get the fuck out of here. You can leave the girl."

Rick drew himself up to full height, took a deep breath that enlarged his chest, flexed his shoulders and arms, and actually did look gigantic suddenly. Rick's expansion resulted in their taking a step back, and Banshee's low growl pushed them back further, leaving Banshee with room to jump.

Lana tried to deescalate. "We're not looking for trouble. I just want to talk to someone, and then we're out of here."

The man's fake smile displayed dental decay and rot. "You can talk to me, and you leave when I'm done with you."

The building tension seemed to lead to an inevitable fight. Although Rick and I would get some punches in, and Banshee would take one of them out, a fight would be a losing battle, probably a deadly one.

Another man rose from his rickety chair and approached, staring at Rick. As he got closer he broke into a real smile, "Holy shit! Is that you, Dr. Rick?"

We all turned to Rick, who looked as dumbfounded as the rest of us. The man gave a confused Rick a bear hug.

"Do I know you?" Rick asked as he gently separated from the man.

He turned around and took off his shirt, revealing a tattooed hairy back with a recently repaired knife wound running from his right shoulder blade to his left lower back, bisecting several picturesque tattoos, like a reflection of a grotesque faded painting in a broken mirror. Rick leaned forward to examine the healing scar. "That's looking even better than I expected. I lined the edges up perfectly."

Lana and I looked on in wonderment, as their bromance blossomed. Rick turned to us. "He came in about three weeks ago with that knife wound to the back. Wasn't deep, but he worried about his tattoos. I promised him I could get everything lined up. Took about an hour, but it looks great."

The tension evaporated, as the man invited him to his table. I patted Banshee on the head, and he calmed down. The bar resumed its usual business, ignoring us.

"Glad we brought him along," I whispered to Lana.

"He has proven unexpectedly useful. I would not have bet on Rick's deescalating a bar fight."

We glanced back to see the bartender speaking to a young guy at the end of the bar, who approached us. "Follow me, but leave the dog if you want to talk with Tito."

I called to Rick and sent Banshee to him. Rick had Banshee perform tricks for his growing audience, as Lana and I followed the younger man up a back staircase to a dark hallway. A giant stood at the end of the hallway blocking access to the door with his arms crossed in front of him.

"Weapons?"

"None," Lana replied.

"Hands up." He frisked us, spending a little extra time on Lana. He stood aside and opened the door.

Lana paused and looked up into his face. "You ever touch me again, and I will come back and shoot your fucking balls off." I followed her into the office, opting not to threaten the giant.

Tito, seated behind a desk, could have been mistaken for an accountant, but for the tattooed scenes of nightmares creeping up his neck and down his forearms and hands. An average sized guy dressed in jeans and a flannel shirt, he sat behind a neatly organized desk topped with precisely stacked files. Bookshelves lined the wall behind him, displaying a mixture of classics, fiction, and business books. He took off his wire rim glasses and motioned to the seats in front of him. "Please be seated. My associates indicated you wish to speak. Can I offer you a drink?"

Lana took the seat, poised as if she expected to be greeted like a senior executive at a financial firm. "No, thank you. I appreciate your giving us a moment."

"Please, how can I help you?"

"My name is Lana Hearns, and I'm a reporter looking into the hospital bombing. This is my assitant. I have a few questions."

"Please continue."

"The explosives used have been traced to a robbery from six months ago. I met with the man who stole them at the prison yesterday, and he thought that some of what he stole may have been taken by the police and sold to the bomber."

"Interesting story. I would like to talk to him myself."

"He was stabbed in the neck at breakfast this morning during a riot."

Tito leaned forward, listening intently.

"Another source indicated that if a dirty cop was selling explosives to a white supremacist, you might have information regarding the sale."

Tito folded his fingers together, as he stared at Lana, who held his gaze. "I would very much like to speak with this source as well, but I'm sure your journalistic integrity prevents that." He leaned back and waved at the room around him. "As you can see, I am a humble businessman trying to earn a living and stay out of the limelight. Your question threatens my privacy."

"Sir, I am not looking to invade your privacy. I'm chasing a story. You're considered a confidential source, and anything you say in here is off the record. The same journalistic integrity that prevents me from sharing my source with you also prevents me from sharing your information with anyone. I'm only after the bomber."

"This bombing is bad for business and brings unwanted attention to this establishment and to some of its loyal patrons. Our interests appear aligned."

"Even if the bomber turns out to be one of your associates?" I asked.

Tito turned his attention to me. "I can state confidently that the bomber is not one of my associates. Although not always friendly, everyone knows everyone else in our world. If any of my associates did something this stupid, I would have handled it already."

Lana pulled out a photo of Sergeant Krug from her back pocket and pushed it across the desk. "Do you recognize this man?"

Tito studied the photo and shook his head. "Who is he?"

"He's a cop who had access to the stolen explosives, who also happens to have a significant gambling problem. It's possible he stole the explosives and sold them to cover some debt."

"May I keep this photo? If he was trying to sell explosives, some of my associates would likely have heard of him."

Lana stood and handed him a card. "Keep it, and please call me if you hear anything."

I stood and pointed to a diploma on the wall behind him. "USC Business School? Impressive."

Tito laughed. "I'm one of their more successful alumni, but they don't talk about me much for some reason."

I looked at the name on the diploma, which read Mike Hampton. "Where did Tito come from?"

Tito slipped off a shoe and pointed to his foot. "An unfortunate incident with a shotgun in my youth led to the loss of three of my toes. I was nicknamed Two Toes, which became Tito."

"Could have been worse," Lana remarked. "A little higher up and your nickname would have been No Nuts."

Tito genuinely laughed, "Ms. Lana, you have shown courage to come here, and you're welcome any time. If anyone recognizes this man, I will let you know. It has been a pleasure to meet you."

Lana and I walked past the giant, who deferentially stepped back from her. Lana shushed me before I could ask anything. "Wait until we're outside before you say anything. Let's get Rick and Banshee and get out of here."

Downstairs, we found Rick and Banshee in the center of a large group of men. Tables had been pushed back to clear a space for them. A countdown began, three…two…one. In perfect synchronicity, Rick and Banshee leapt into the air and performed backflips, landing on their feet. The crowd roared, and more drinks were ordered. We motioned for Rick to head outside, and he said his goodbyes through the protesting crowd.

A winded Rick joined us outside. "Took you guys long enough. I was running out of tricks to entertain the drunks in there. Did you learn anything?"

Lana replied. "Tito is missing three toes on his left foot and has a handsy giant for security."

"Anything useful?"

"Tito didn't recognize Krug, but he'll ask around. If Krug was shopping the explosives, Tito will find out."

"What if he doesn't find anything?"

"If he didn't sell it, then Krug may be the bomber himself."

"He agreed to help you? Just like that?"

"I happen to be charming, and he wants the bomber off the streets as much as we do. It's bad for his business."

"This investigating job kinda sucks. Next time I want to ask some questions, and one of you can entertain the drunk skinheads."

Lana patted him on the back. "You did good, rookie. You kept us out of a fight. Maybe next time you can ask a question. For now, you can sit in the back seat with Banshee."

. . .

A patron of the Iron Cross 14 walked out of the bar to his truck, where he pulled a cell phone from the locked center console and called a contact.

"This is Johnny at the Iron Cross 14. You said you wanted to hear if anyone asked about explosives. Some reporter named Lana just met with Tito."

"Was she alone?"

"Nope, brought two guys and a trained dog."

"Thanks. I'll send a payment your way."

The bomber disconnected. The reporter was becoming a problem, but first, he had to prepare for tomorrow. Act two was going to be spectacular.

CHAPTER SIXTEEN

Wednesday, 10:20 p.m.

Roberts stopped by the nearly deserted detectives' area that night and sat down at a worn table covered with paper across from Roland and Stillman. "I sure hope you guys are making some progress, because I ain't got shit."

Roland and Stillman communicated with a glance, like long term partners often do, and reached an agreement in silence. Stillman stood, "Let's continue this discussion in one of the conference rooms."

"Go ahead. I need to make a call real quick," Roland said.

Stillman led Roberts to an empty conference room and settled down at the far side of the table. Roberts sat across from him. "I'm on a bit of a time crunch. Can we get started?"

Roland glanced at his phone. "Mary should be quick. Give her a minute."

Awkward silence enveloped the room as both men looked at their phones to avoid small talk. The clock ticked slowly through the three-minute wait before the door finally opened. Roland walked in, followed by Chambers from Internal Affairs, who took a seat across from him.

Roberts sat up straight, his glance rotating among the three of them. "What the fuck is IA doing here? What the fuck is this?" He stood up ready to leave.

Chambers was used to that reaction when he entered rooms with other cops and responded in a calming voice, "This isn't about you. Please, sit down."

A still irritated Roberts fell back into his seat. "This better be good, and you two better have a good reason for springing IA on me unannounced." He punctuated his words with a death stare that Roland and Stillman ignored.

Chambers continued. "One branch of the investigation involves the possibility of police involvement, and I have a few questions about some members of your team. As you know, Milly stated there were ten pounds of explosive missing from the seizure at his arrest. IA is investigating to see if any of the officers involved in the arrest may have had sticky fingers."

"You don't really believe that piece of shit, Milly, do you?"

"Whether I believe him or not is irrelevant. As I said, this is just one aspect of the investigation that needs to be cleared. Four officers were involved in the arrest, Armond, Bertrand, Krug, and yourself."

"So now I'm a suspect? Do I need a lawyer?"

"You're not a suspect and don't need a lawyer, but we do have some questions about one member of the team."

"Who?" Roberts asked in a guarded voice.

"Of the three, who do you think is most likely to steal explosives and sell them on the street?"

"If I thought one of them would do that, they wouldn't be on my team. I'm not painting a bullseye on any of my guys."

Roland leaned forward. "Fair enough. Are you aware of any team members who might be under some financial strain? Keep in mind, we've already reviewed everyone's finances, including yours."

Roberts knew IA had broad authority to investigate other officers without the need for warrants.

"Everyone on the team is solid. Krug likes to gamble, and he goes on hot and cold streaks, but it's never been a problem."

Chambers lifted a paper from his folder and slid it across the table. "Are you aware that Sergeant Krug has over $360,000 in gambling debt with overdue payments?"

Roberts whistled as he looked over the paper. "I had no idea." He slid the paper back.

Stillman spoke up. "Krug is now a person of interest in this investigation. He had the means, motive and opportunity to acquire that explosive. We are now trying to determine if we can connect him to the sale of the explosive to a third party."

Stunned, Roberts sat back in his seat. "Un-fucking-believable. A member of my team? I'm gonna kill the son of a bitch myself."

Chambers took over. "You're going to do no such thing. You will continue to do your job and let us do ours. He is only a person of interest. I will continue to investigate him while Roland and Stillman look at other possibilities. You will continue to work your sources to see if we can trace the explosives or components. It's important that Krug is not aware we are watching him. If we need your help, we will let you know, but no one hears about this outside this room. Understood?"

"Yes, sir," a dejected Roberts agreed. He stood to leave. "If he's innocent, I don't want any mention of this in his record. If he's guilty, then he can face his consequences."

Roland waited for the door to close before speaking. "Is IA always this fun?"

"Sometimes it's much worse. Cops don't like hearing that they may have criminals on their teams. Roberts took it better than most. He's loyal to his man, but willing to let him face consequences, if he's guilty."

"What are the odds he's our man?" Stillman asked.

"I put it at 60% to 70% that he stole the explosives and sold them to our bomber. If so, he's probably freaking out. Let me take care of him, and you two work the rest of the case."

"As long as one of us clears it before the weekend. We don't need this problem hanging over our heads during race weekend."

"I want it solved, too. I have tickets, and I'll be damned if I'm missing the race for an idiot with a bomb."

.　　.　　.

At Mandalay Bay, Mr. Zhang prepared to go out. Plans for the evening included dinner, gambling at a private craps table reserved for him on the floor, followed by a visit to a Club with a VIP table reserved for him. Across the room, his three companions for the evening giggled as they tried on jewelry to match their outfits. The billionaire smiled as he encouraged them to choose more. He loved to enhance the beauty of already gorgeous women.

CHAPTER SEVENTEEN

Thursday, October 19
10:07 a.m.

The call was answered on the second ring.

"911, what's your location?"

The familiar southern mechanical drawl responded, "I hope you take this one more seriously."

"Sir, what is your location?"

"The shadows spread throughout the day but disappear when the day's half done. Their song is silenced in a burst of light, as they circle high to meet the sun. Better luck on this one." He abruptly disconnected.

The 911 operator called her supervisor. A protocol in place, the supervisor copied the recording and sent it to senior management. Within minutes, all of the top administrators at police headquarters and at City Hall received transcripts of the recording. Roland, Stillman and Roberts gathered to decipher it.

. . .

Lana was not on the initial distribution list, but still received the message only minutes later than the Mayor, due to a favor owed from yet another source on the police force. I was finishing my waffle when the message dinged on her phone.

"Shit. He called again. Looks like another bomb threat."

"Seriously, it's my day off."

"Not today. Let's listen."

She played the recording, and we listened to it three times. Lana had handwritten the bomber's words onto her notepad. "What do you think?"

I ate the last bite of my waffle before answering, "I think if they can't convict him on the bombings, the grammar police should throw him in jail anyway."

"Be serious for a moment."

"I am being serious. That's a really shitty clue. It's too obvious. He might as well say he's blowing something up at noon."

"Okay, Dr. smarty pants, where's it going to happen?"

I reread the cryptic words. "One of three places I can think of. 'Shadows circle high to meet the sun' suggests people circling high in the air, which means The Stratosphere, the High Roller, or the roller coaster at New York New York."

"Which one is it?"

"The coaster has some loops, but it's not very tall. I think it's the least likely. The High Roller is a Ferris wheel that goes over 500 feet in the air and overlooks the Strip. Not a bad option, but I think the most likely is the Stratosphere. It has the tallest observation deck in the country, and most importantly, a revolving restaurant at the top of the building. Stratosphere is the best place to circle high to meet the sun in Vegas."

"Not bad, rookie. What about this nonsense about silencing their song?"

"No idea. Need some smarter folks than I am for that part."

· · ·

At police headquarters, a group of smart detectives was coming to the same conclusions. "It's gotta be Stratosphere or High Roller, but my money is on the Strat," Roberts offered.

"I tend to agree, but I would like some confirmation before we throw everything at one site," Stillman pointed out.

"How about we split up and send half to each site?" Mary suggested.

"Bad idea. We have less than two hours, which is not enough time to search even one site, let alone two," Roberts added.

A sergeant entered the room and cleared his throat. "Excuse me. I just heard from the Stratosphere. The Florida A&M University band is in town for the race. They are the top band representing historically black colleges and universities, and they have a lunch scheduled for noon today in the revolving restaurant at the top of the Strat."

A second of silence burst into activity. Roberts spoke as he stood, "Let's lock down the Strat and evacuate the top floors first. We're gonna block all cell signals in or out of the area to prevent him from detonating, and search every square inch of the place."

Everyone rose from their seats with phones pressed to their ears, issuing orders. Time was of the essence.

.　　.　　.

Lana received one of those calls, with an update that the police were mobilizing toward the Strat. She gathered her things, "I'm headed down there to see what I can learn. Are you coming?"

"No, I think I'm gonna head down to the High Roller with Banshee."

"Why?"

"First of all, there's nothing I can do at the Stratosphere that the police aren't doing already, but it just seems too obvious. I'm not sure the bomber would make it that easy."

"You do realize we're talking about a psychopath here, don't you?"

"True, but he's an organized psychopath. So far he has been one step ahead of the police and hasn't made any mistakes. I think he has the whole thing planned out, and if he's like other psychopaths, his actions will escalate over time."

Lana gave me a quick kiss on the top of my head as she grabbed her purse. "Sweetie, you're an ER doctor, not a forensic psychologist."

"True, but a good ER doctor keeps an open mind to all possibilities."

"Good luck with that. Love ya," she said as she bolted out the door.

Banshee thumped his tail vigorously on the floor as he looked at me with big imploring eyes. I scratched behind his ears. "What the hell. Even if I'm wrong, it's still a nice day for a walk. Ready for an adventure?"

The tail thumping increased, and he leapt when I reached for his tactical vest. To be on the safe side, I packed my medical kit in a backpack and made sure Banshee's vest was fully loaded. Five minutes later, we were on our way to visit a Ferris wheel.

CHAPTER EIGHTEEN

Thursday, 11:03 a.m.

At the Stratosphere, security ushered the last few people from the top of the rotating tower, as Roberts arrived with his team. The evacuation had gone smoothly with four double deck elevators servicing the tower.

"Team one search the restaurant level, two the observation level, and three the exterior. We are blocking cell signals, so he won't be able to remote detonate again, but to be on the safe side, everyone is back on the ground by ten minutes 'til noon, if we haven't found the bomb. That's a hard deadline for everyone. I don't need any fallen heroes today."

The three teams dispersed. Each team included a bomb sniffing dog trained for this very scenario. Their noses were over 100,000 times more sensitive than a human nose, and with the correct training, these working dogs could detect the smell of common explosives with a high degree of accuracy. The Las Vegas bomb squad included a German shepherd, a Belgian Malinois, and a Labrador.

Lucy, the golden Labrador, was tasked with searching the restaurant level. Her handler left her off leash, and she playfully ran among the tables, searching for the scent that would earn a treat. She recognized hundreds of scents and detected a few new ones she would like to explore, but none of them would produce a treat. She determinedly searched and in less than ten minutes, she identified her prize. She sat and waited patiently for her treat.

.   .   .

I had difficulty finding a parking spot due to the race traffic, but I finally found one and trekked toward the giant Ferris wheel with Banshee. A crowd of race fans had already descended on Vegas. At the Ferris wheel, a large stage had been erected to host events throughout the week. I pushed forward to take a look at the schedule of events posted nearby.

At noon, a group of schoolchildren from England were scheduled to sing to honor Sir Lewis Hamilton, a British driver racing that weekend. One of the greatest drivers of all time, Hamilton had won seven world championships and was the only black driver in F1. A picture of the choir was posted behind Hamilton, and most of the members were black.

I called Lana to explain that these kids fit the bomber's clue about silencing black voices.

.   .   .

Standing ready to defuse any bombs discovered, the explosive disposal crew couldn't help smiling at Lucy, who happily crunched her treat as her handler led her to the exit and pointed to the bomb's table.

Doug Henne, the most experienced member of the team, approached in an explosive ordnance disposal suit. EOD suits combined layers of Kevlar and foam to protect against shrapnel and blast waves, but were extremely bulky and difficult to work in. Doug had trained countless hours in them. Microphones allowed him to document his findings and to keep the rest of the team informed in real time.

Roberts coordinated from the ground floor, "Take it slow and steady. We have plenty of time before the expected deadline."

"The mirror shows a device attached to the underside of the table. It's about six by six inches and three inches deep. A cell phone is attached with tape and wires from the phone to the box. Are we sure the cell service is blocked in here?"

A technician confirmed cell service blockage, and multiple team members at the top of the tower reconfirmed that no service was available. Doug proceeded. "I don't see anything attached to the tablecloth, so I am going to lift it for better exposure." He slowly lifted the tablecloth and bunched it on top of the table to expose the underside. "I'll circle around to give a 360 view. Confirm you are receiving images."

"Images are clear," Roberts responded.

The EOD suit contained a high definition camera that allowed other team members to evaluate the device and also preserved information in the case of detonation. Several monitors were set up around the command center, and other experts closely examined the video.

Roberts scanned the images himself, "This looks pretty basic to me. Anyone see something I'm missing?" The team returned a chorus of negative responses.

"Doug, we're not seeing anything fancy."

"I concur. Unless he has a surprise inside, this looks fairly straightforward. Want me to cut the wires?"

"Negative. Bring the robot in."

"Bringing in the robot. For the record, I'm happy to do this one."

"I will make sure the record reflects your courage. Now get out of there. Your wife will let me have it if something goes wrong when the robot could have done your job."

"Roger that, sir. Running away meekly to let a robot do my job."

. . .

Lana, embedded with other journalists behind the barricades, listened through an ear pod connected to her burner phone that gave her near real time access to what was happening in the control room. She anxiously followed the arrival of the robot, when her main cell phone rang, and she held it to her other ear.

"I'm kind of busy, Doc. What do you need?"

"I'm worried y'all might be at the wrong place. A choir of predominately black children will sing to honor a black race driver at noon. That's too close to the poem for comfort."

"Relax. They found a device in the restaurant and are defusing it now. This is the right place."

"Okay, stay safe and keep me informed. Love ya."

"Love ya, too. Gotta go."

.   .   .

The robot approached slowly, controlled from downstairs by an impossibly young looking technician. In her free time, she competed for money on streaming video game platforms. No one could control the robot as well as she. She advanced it until its entire frame fit below the table to give everyone a detailed image of the device.

Roberts commanded, "Get a closer view of those wires." Elise complied. Roberts turned to the assembled team members. "What do you think?"

After only a quick view of the image of four wires connecting the phone to the device, the experts unanimously agreed that while the color of the wires was important in commercial wiring, bomb makers rarely followed any protocol. The red, white, black or yellow wire could be responsible for completing the circuit when cut.

"No way to tell which wire to cut. I think we need to drill the device and look inside. Anyone else have a better idea?" Roberts asked. No one did.

Using an appendage with a small drill, Elise picked a spot on the side of the device away from the wires. The drill easily advanced through the shell of the device. When resistance fell, she withdrew the drill, and advanced a small, flexible scope with a high detail camera and LED light on the end.

A murmur arose from the gathering of bomb experts. The four wires entered the box, but were not connected to anything. The box was empty, except for a metal object laying on the bottom. Elise advanced the camera and focused it on the object from above.

"What the fuck is that thing?" Roberts asked.

"Sir, it looks like a silver medal," Elise responded.

"Son of a bitch. We're in the wrong place." Roberts looked at his watch, as he reached for his radio. It read 11:56 a.m.

CHAPTER NINETEEN

Thursday, 11:50 a.m.

I watched as an award ceremony concluded on stage with an announcer enthusiastically calling out the winners. "The gold medal of the 2023 Young Entrepreneurs Award goes to My Courseway from Frisco, Texas! Esha, Casie, Akshaya, and Megan, congratulations!" The impressive high school kids hugged each other, as they were hustled off stage to usher in the choir.

The excited musicians began with "God Save the King." The talented choir consisted of about a hundred kids of all ages. Their families and fans had gathered in front of the stage. Banshee and I stayed on the perimeter, enjoying the music in the shade.

Lana called and spoke before I could say hello. "The bomb over here was a fake. The real bomb is still out there. It may be near you. Clear the area."

I looked over the crowd of at least a thousand people. "There is no way to move all these people safely."

"You have to do something. It's almost noon."

I glanced at my phone and saw the numbers switch from 11:59 to 12:00, and the bomb exploded. My distance from the epicenter and the mass of people between me and the bomb muffled the force, but it still rumbled through my chest. Screaming broke an eerie moment of silence, and people stampeded from the stage.

With Banshee by my side, I wove through the fleeing crowd toward the still intact stage, where the stunned choir kids appeared terrified, but unhurt. The My Courseway teenagers assisted the choir director in gathering them together and leading them off the side of the stage. As the crowd thinned, I counted seven adults writhing in pain on the ground around a hole about three feet wide and deep in the front of the stage that evidenced the power of the blast.

"Banshee, search," I ordered. He dutifully sniffed the area in widening arcs, as I turned my attention to the injured. I knelt by the nearest victim, a young lady holding her hands over a bloody thigh wound.

"I'm a doctor. Let me take a look at that. What's your name?"

"Mallory," she replied, struggling to hold back tears.

The deep wound, about five inches long, was not life threatening. I opened my backpack and removed some gauze. "Don't worry, Mallory. It looks bad, but it didn't hit any arteries. You're gonna be fine."

I gently packed the gauze in the wound and wrapped it around her leg. It oozed and needed someone to hold pressure on it. I looked up to see a young man wearing a backpack. A breeze rustled his red hair as he watched. Most importantly, he was calm.

"Are you a medical person?" I asked.

"No. I'm a writer, but how can I help?"

"I need someone to hold pressure on this bandage until paramedics arrive."

He took off his backpack and knelt by the patient, and I placed his hand in the correct position on her leg.

"Thanks for helping. What's your name?" I asked.

"Chris."

"Chris the writer, I'd like you to meet Mallory. Why don't you tell her about your book to distract her?"

Chris began an animated discussion with her, as I moved to the next patient. More people had arrived to help the injured, but one woman cried alone. "My son. How's my baby? He was on stage."

I laid a reassuring hand on her shoulder. "The staff got the kids off stage, and it didn't look like anyone was injured up there. My name is Doc. I'm an ER doctor. Let's take a look at these injuries."

The blast had blown pieces of wood out from the stage, sending slivers in all directions. Multiple cuts bled down her legs, but fortunately, without evidence of arterial bleeding. I took some bandages out of my backpack and wrapped the largest wound. "Stay right here. Help is on the way."

The first police officer showed up, and I told him what happened.

"Looks like the bomb was under the stage. We have seven wounded, all leg injuries, none critical. We're gonna need seven ambulances, and call Sunrise to let them know they're headed their way." With a nod of thanks, the policeman got on his radio to report the information.

I felt good about the situation of only seven injured, none critically. It could have been much worse, I thought, when Banshee gave a single, crisp bark. I turned to find him seated next to a trash can. We made eye contact, and he barked again with a nod toward the garbage container. Things were about to get worse.

·   ·   ·

"Damn this traffic. How long to get there?" Roberts asked.

"About eight minutes, sir," the driver replied.

"I can't believe we fell for that shit. We went for the obvious target and wasted time on a fake bomb, while the real one blew people up. The press is gonna eat us alive."

The driver wisely kept silent.

Roberts spoke on the radio. "Listen up, team. We're too late to stop him, so let's focus on evidence collection. Let's get this right."

· · ·

I ran to Banshee who thumped his tail, as he remained seated next to the trash can. I led him a short distance from the trash can and had him sit. He looked at me with excitement. "Find bomb." Trained to sniff out common explosives, among his many other talents, he put his nose to the ground and headed straight back to the trash can. Once again he sat next to it and gave a single bark.

About a hundred people remained in the area, with more trickling in. A second explosion would be catastrophic. I ran to the policeman and pulled him aside.

"My dog is a trained police dog and alerted to a bomb in that trash can. We need to evacuate everyone immediately."

He turned to the crowd. "Listen up! There is a possibility of another bomb nearby. I need everyone to move away from the stage in that direction. Help the wounded if you can. Let's move people!"

The crowd responded quickly. I scooped one woman up into my arms, as the officer lifted another. Chris and a few others helped the wounded stand and limp away. An apparent soldier in shorts and a black t-shirt with "Fuck Cancer" emblazoned across his chest threw the last man over his shoulder and rushed away. I whistled for Banshee who bounded to my side. With the area cleared, I set the injured woman down as gently as I could, as the first ambulances arrived with the cop directing them. More cops had arrived, and EMS took over the patients' care.

I gave Banshee a vigorous neck scratch as I told him what an amazing good boy he was, and the bomb squad arrived in their truck. A short man leapt out before it fully stopped and yelled orders as he advanced on us.

"Who the fuck moved all these people?" He asked as he looked at the injured being treated by EMS.

"I did." I stepped forward.

"The famous fucking Doc, again. Who the hell are you to be further injuring these people by moving them?" He asked as he moved into my personal space.

I calmly, but sternly faced the angry man. "I moved everyone back because there may be a second device in that trash can over there."

"How could you possibly know that?"

"My dog is a former police dog and has been through the bomb detection training. He alerted to that trash can." I pointed to it.

"How sure are you?"

"One hundred percent."

Roberts turned to shout to his team. "Make sure we have a safe perimeter and send in the robot to check out that garbage can. Evidence collection will need to wait until the scene is secure. In the meantime, start grabbing videos from anyone who was recording. Check social media. Some videos are probably already uploaded."

Elise rolled the robot toward the trash can, as a transfixed crowd watched anxiously from two hundred feet away. The trash receptacle abruptly burst, propelling deadly shrapnel in every direction. The second blast was much larger than the first, and would have injured anyone within a one hundred foot radius. Fortunately, the area was empty except for the battered robot, which lay on its side. Elise lowered her controller. "We need a new robot."

I scratched Banshee's ears. "Good boy. You did good today."

CHAPTER TWENTY

Thursday, 1:32 p.m.

Tim Roberts, still seething over being duped, scanned the debris field. "What do we have so far?"

Bertrand responded. "The first device was relatively small and shaped to blast outward instead of upward. It doesn't look like the kids on stage were targeted, and it doesn't look like it was meant to kill anyone. It did send some wooden debris into the front of crowd, though."

He turned to point at the second blast site. "More concerning is the much larger second device, designed to kill. The force of the blast was angled toward the stage where rescue workers would have been if the area hadn't been evacuated. The shrapnel from the trash can would have torn through the rescuers. As it turns out, the only casualty was the robot."

Everyone turned as one to look at the mangled mass of metal that remained. "How were they detonated?"

"They were on timers this time. No phones, but we found evidence of small clocks on each. Looks like one was set for noon, and one was set for twenty minutes later."

"Tell me we got something on camera."

Sergeant Krug spoke up. "Five security cameras cover the area. Unfortunately, yesterday they were all disabled, like someone shot high power lasers at them and fried the lenses. There's no video to show placement of the devices."

"He's a clever son of a bitch," Roberts commented, as he chewed his lower lip. "He suckered us to the wrong site, then set a perfect trap. Do we have anything to work with?"

A chorus of silence and eyes gazing at the ground answered his question.

"This is unacceptable. This guy is two steps ahead of us, and we still have the race this weekend. We need to get ahead of this guy. Finish up here, and find some answers."

.   .   .

Stillman and Roland fared no better. The site had no security, relying only on the cleverly disabled cameras. Roving security guards had noticed nothing unusual, not surprising given that thousands of people passed through the area each hour.

Roland threw down her notes. "I got nothing. Chief is gonna be pissed."

"Along with the mayor, the Senators, the race director and a few billionaires. We gotta solve this soon, but we can't make nonexistent evidence appear. We're lucky that dog was there today, or it would have been much worse," Stillman said.

"Wasn't luck. He's dating that reporter I talked to, and she fed him almost real time information. She's got better sources in the police force than we do."

"We have to finish interviewing the victims, but that won't lead us anywhere. We can make a plea to the public for anyone that saw anything unusual in the area last night to contact us, but given that almost everyone is either drunk or stoned or looking to fight supporters of other race teams, I don't expect anything. We need to hit the street and roust people. This is getting big, and someone has to know something."

"I want to know where all the members of the bomb squad were last night and see who doesn't have an alibi. I'm gonna ask the Chief for surveillance on these guys to see if anyone is acting funny. We need a break."

Roland scrolled through her contacts looking for the most promising source to contact first.

.   .   .

Banshee and I headed for the ER after an interview with the cops. I didn't have much to say beyond the obvious. Lana gave me a heads up that this was the second most likely site, and Banshee found the second device. They had my contact information.

"Jen, how are the bomb victims doing?" I asked.

"Really well. Four broken bones and a bunch of lacerations. The residents will be sewing them up for the next couple hours."

Rick joined the conversation. "That's a bullshit move to make more work for us on your day off."

"Actually, we saved you some work. Banshee found a second device, so we could evacuate the area before it exploded. Without him, you would have had a full trauma bay and some fatalities."

"I didn't know that dog could detect bombs," Rick noted.

"In all fairness, it's not exactly a skill he can show off regularly."

"Damn, Banshee may be smarter than me."

"Correction, Rick. All dogs are smarter than you." Jen quipped.

I turned my back as Rick and Jen argued over whether Rick was smarter than most dogs. Lana approached with a huge smile. "There's my hero," she said with open arms. I stepped forward to hug her, and she moved past me to get down and greet Banshee. "Such a good boy today," she said, smothering him with love.

I stood impotently with my arms out waiting for her to finish lavishing praise on Banshee. Finally, she acknowledged me. "I want an exclusive. You talk to another reporter and you'll be a patient in here."

"Yes, ma'am. Have you learned anything yet?"

"Looks like it's the same guy, but the secondary device has them all freaked out. That's a classic terrorist move and escalates the danger. The race director and drivers have grave concerns about a bomber on the loose during a race weekend. They're tightening security, but with 300,000 spectators and another million wandering the Strip, no way they can police everyone."

I pulled her to the side and lowered my voice. "What about those cops? Any more leads on them?"

"Krug is still the most likely. They're trying to nail down alibis for everyone without alerting them. I should hear if they discover anything."

"Someday you'll have to explain to me how you have that many sources."

"It's because I'm charming and damn good at my job, and most men are suckers for a pretty lady. A little bit of attention and a thank you gets me most of what I need."

"Are we really that simple?"

Lana motioned toward Rick, who was trying to juggle three empty urine containers. "Yes, you are."

"Not much to argue with there. C'mon, let's go check on Dr. Williams and her baby."

I left Little Mac in charge of Banshee. Word of his heroics had spread, and Little Mac basked in the spotlight as he proudly paraded Banshee around the ER.

Upstairs in the ICU, we found Mr. Williams at his wife's bedside. I knocked lightly on the open door. "Mind if we come in and say hi? This is my girlfriend, Lana. She's helping me look for the guy who did this."

Lana extended her hand and smiled radiantly. "I'm so sorry this happened. How's she doing?"

I looked over her monitors with a clinical eye. Her vitals were good, and her color was much better.

"A little better each day. They got that breathing tube out this morning. It hurts to talk, but she said a few words earlier. Still pretty drowsy from all the pain meds."

"That's great news. How is the baby doing?"

Before he could answer, Dr. Williams opened her eyes and motioned for her drink. Her husband held the straw to her lips, and she sipped slowly. She laid back in bed and tried to focus on the room. A small smile appeared at the corners of her mouth. "That looks like Doc."

"The one and only. You're looking good."

"I'm pretty sure I look like shit."

"You're looking way better than you were a few days ago. You actually had us worried for a little while."

She reached out for my hand. "Thank you for saving my baby."

I squeezed her hand. "It was a team effort. I'm sorry they couldn't save your leg."

She held her hands up. "Don't worry about the silly leg. I still have these two hands, and that's all I need to hold my baby." Dr. Williams closed her eyes and fell back to sleep.

I turned to her husband and spoke softly. "Is your son doing okay?"

"He's doing great, feeding well and gaining weight." He turned serious. "I heard there was another bomb this morning. Anyone hurt?"

"It was actually two bombs, but we got lucky, and there were no serious injuries this time."

"Someone needs to stop that guy."

Lana responded. "The police are throwing everything they have at it, and we're doing what we can to help. You just focus on taking care of your family."

"Will do. Thanks."

Lana and I left quietly. "I'm gonna get Banshee and head home, provided Little Mac let's me have him."

"He's really attached to that dog, isn't he?"

"He's about the most loyal and kind person I've ever met. What are you up to?"

She held up her phone. "Gonna call some people and see if I can break the case, and I need to get my story filed in time for the evening shows." She gave me a quick kiss on the cheek before walking away.

"Good luck with that."

CHAPTER TWENTY-ONE

Thursday, 7:28 p.m

Detective Chambers slapped a piece of paper down on the desk in front of Roland and Stillman. "We got the warrant. Electronic surveillance on all four and round the clock surveillance on Krug. If he does anything suspicious at all, we can pick him up. I'm gonna need some people to help. Who do you trust to keep this quiet?"

The three detectives devised a schedule to watch Krug constantly. The electronic surveillance would be handled by a separate team, but they would be notified immediately of anything unusual.

.   .   .

The bomber seethed, as he paced in his living room. His setup had been flawless. The police went to the wrong location and found the fake device as planned. The second scene was perfectly timed to cause maximum harm to responders, but it had all been ruined by that obnoxious doctor and his dog. Worse, he had heard that he and that reporter nipping at his heels were dating.

He made spaghetti and meatballs for dinner as he calmed down and thought through the problem. Everything had gone so well until now. He was so close to the finish line. The interference at the bombing earlier today was unexpected, but not catastrophic.

Further interference couldn't be tolerated. He spent another hour meticulously planning his next steps. He wouldn't act until his plan was analyzed from all sides to eliminate any more surprises.

Finally, he cut a new burner cell phone from its packaging. Discovering Lana Hearns' cell phone number was easy. As an investigative reporter, she listed it and encouraged people to send tips, pictures, and video. The bomber fired his first text.

I have information about the bombing. You interested?

Lana's phone dinged, as she changed into her favorite soft pajamas. She read the message with a lack of enthusiasm. All sorts of quacks texted her with crap, but she always responded.

What do you know?

I know you're looking for a cop.

Lana sat up, riveted now. The possibility of a cop's involvement had not been publicly reported. She wanted more.

Do you know who the bomber is?

Pretty good idea. But it can't come back on me. This guy don't mess around.

You can remain anonymous. Let's meet.

Okay. Not in the city. He has too many friends.

Where?

A long pause worried Lana that he had changed his mind, but he finally responded.

Tomorrow. Hoover Dam. Take the 10 am tour and follow my texted directions. Come alone.

I'll be there.

Lana threw her hands up in the air and did a brief happy dance. Stories were made by contacts like this, but no way would she go alone.

•   •   •

The bomber turned off the burner and pulled out a new one with internet access. He figured that IA had electronic surveillance on him by now, but they could only surveil what they knew about. After multiple security protocols, he was back on his trusted murder for hire site on the Dark Web. He typed furiously, hoping for an immediate response, which he got.

I have another problem. Urgent.
Details?
Lana Hearns. Reporter. She will be on the 10 am tour for Hoover Dam tomorrow.
Will she be alone?
Probably
$7500 wired to this link.
She will be awaiting texted directions at the number below
On the schedule

The bomber disconnected and wired the bitcoin. At the other end of the transaction, its receipt was acknowledged and a text sent to his chosen assassin, "Time to chat?" Five minutes later on a secure site, the hitman agreed on a price of $3500 for the job. The mediator returned to his movie, $4000 richer for only a few minutes work.

•   •   •

Mr. Zhang and his entourage prepared for another night on the town. He vowed to take it easy and be back by midnight. He wanted to be well rested for the race. His valet had laid out six outfits to choose from, and he selected a white shirt with a black satin jacket. His valet had set out his watch collection for his review, and of the thirty-seven he had brought, the billionaire chose a Patek Philippe Titanium model that he had commissioned last year. It was a unique piece that had set him back over six million dollars, not his most expensive watch, but he felt it best complemented his outfit.

His four companions in another room, busy picking out jewelry and outfits as well, giggled as they tried on various necklaces, earrings, and bracelets. After Mr. Zhang and his companions departed, the valets restored the jewelry to locked cases, and security returned them to the hotel vault.

CHAPTER TWENTY-TWO

Friday, October 20
8:26 a.m.

"Tell me again what the plan is," I said, as I drove east to Hoover Dam, about a forty-five minute drive from the Strip and easily accessible from Interstate 11.

"I'm going on the 10 a.m. tour and then waiting for this guy to contact me. You're going as my backup."

"So I'm supposed to join the tour and keep my eyes open for trouble?"

"Yep, pretend you don't know me, but keep an eye out. I don't expect trouble, but you never know."

"Is it normal for a contact to want to meet out in the middle of nowhere?"

"It's not the middle of nowhere. It's one of the biggest dams in the world, and these guys are usually paranoid enough to pick exotic locations. Makes them think their information is more important than if they just shared it at a Starbucks."

"What if his information sucks?"

"Then you get to cross a tourist trap off your list of interesting places to visit."

I had to admit that I was interested in Hoover Dam. Built in the 1930's during the height of the Great Depression, the dam spans over twelve hundred feet across the Black Canyon of the Colorado River. It impounds Lake Mead, the largest reservoir in the United States. Years of drought had lowered the water level, but the dam was still a marvel of engineering, providing water and power for Las Vegas, Phoenix, and much of Southern California.

"Did you know over a hundred men died building it?" I asked.

"So you're saying it's haunted?"

"No. I'm saying it's dangerous. I don't want you added to the body count."

"Don't worry about me. Banshee has my back, don't you?" Banshee thumped his tail and gave her a kiss at the mention of his name. Dressed in his full tactical gear with a service dog patch for the day's excursion, Banshee was ready for anything. Unarmed, other than the cameras and a microphone attached to his vest, I still felt prepared for trouble.

Security waved our vehicle through without a search, and we made the final switchbacks to the parking garage. The Mike O'Callaghan – Pat Tillman Memorial Bridge dominated my initial view of the area. The long bridge, spanning two thousand feet, towered nine hundred feet over the Colorado River flowing below and allowed traffic to cross the river while avoiding the dam itself.

We rounded the corner for our first full view of the dam and Lake Mead. Only forty-six feet wide at the top, the dam plummeted over seven hundred feet to the base of the valley, where it widened to six hundred feet thick. The huge wall of concrete held back millions of gallons of fresh water.

"That's quite the project," I said.

"Agreed. The amazing thing is that they completed the whole thing in only five years."

"I'm rarely impressed with governmental efficiency, but that would take twenty years to build today."

"And they brought it in under budget."

"Definitely built by aliens. Let's check this thing out."

"Okay. Remember, from this point on, we keep the phone lines open, but we proceed separately."

"Enjoy the tour. Banshee and I have your back."

We waited a few minutes for Lana to clear the area, then rode the escalator down to the visitor's center. After another security check, we entered the lobby with displays about the construction of the dam. We mingled with a growing crowd, as I looked for our informant, a useless task, as I had no idea what an informant would look like, but I didn't see anyone scary or paying attention to Lana.

I climbed the stairs to the observation deck, which provided a stunning view of the dam and of the valley below. The ER doctor in me was appalled by the merely waist-high wall that prevented a seven hundred foot fall to the canyon floor. Safety glass to prevent falls by social media users tempted to sit on the wall for the perfect picture was definitely indicated.

Our tour assembled on time, and the guide gave us the rules, including sticking with the tour at all times, before leading us into the elevators to descend five hundred feet into the dam itself.

We exited into an arched tunnel that led off into the distance. Fluorescent lighting illuminated the tile as we walked, our voices echoing down the broad hallway. All sense of direction was lost as our tour guide explained how the dam was built and how it produced power. The power plant housed fifteen enormous generators that were turned by water pressure to produce electricity. I got caught up in the tour and had to refocus on watching Lana. So far I hadn't seen anyone suspicious.

Lana received a text about fifteen minutes into the tour and nodded at me. At the next tunnel juncture, she held back to tie her shoes, allowing the group to proceed around the corner. She motioned to a door marked for employees only with a keypad on the side and punched in a number. The lock clicked, and she entered, holding the door open for Banshee and me.

"I'm supposed to meet him in room NV 428 at the end of the hall."

"We'll be right behind you."

Lana smiled and proceeded down the hall, as we trailed silently behind. I told Banshee to be on alert, and his ears perked up as he scanned the area.

Lana entered room 428, and Banshee and I crept to the doorway and peered in. It appeared to be some sort of large storage room filled with tools and parts used to maintain the dam. Lana advanced further into the room and called out.

A man stepped out from the shadows. "Are you Lana Hearns?"

"Yeah. Who are you?"

"Did you come alone?"

"Yes. Do you have information about the bomber?"

He reached into his pocket and pulled out a six-inch knife. "I don't know anything about any bomber, but I do know someone wants you dead. I can do this quick and painless, but if you try to scream or fight, I'll take my time."

CHAPTER TWENTY-THREE

Thursday, 10:37 a.m.

I entered the room silently, as the man slowly advanced on Lana. She backed up with fear radiating from her eyes, holding her hands up in front of her. She implored the man to stop, but he continued his advance.

I entered the room behind the man, who was now walking away from me. I stepped forward to close the gap, then lunged the last two steps for a roundhouse punch to his temple. It was a solid strike and the man collapsed to the floor, dropping his knife. We turned to exit, and saw another man across the room pointing a pistol at us. He fired, and the suppressor masked the sound of the shot, but not the sound of the bullet hitting something metal near my head. We instinctively ducked and headed deeper into the dam with Banshee.

"Where are we headed?" Lana asked as we ran.

"No idea. Let's keep moving and find somewhere to hide until we can find an exit."

We took random turns in the tunnels and soon were completely lost. The concrete maze stifled any sense of direction. Lana slowed as we entered a large equipment room, gasping for breath with hands on her knees. She wasn't going to last much longer.

"Go hide over there while I lead them away and find help. I'll leave you Banshee for protection."

"No. We stay together."

"You're winded and need to rest. Head over there and settle in. I'll find help." I turned my attention to Banshee and commanded, "PROTECT, ALERT."

Banshee stood beside her, ears up and eyes scanning the room for threats. Lana was in good hands. I exited the room through a door, making sure to slam it closed. The metal door could probably be heard through the entire dam. Time to find an exit.

· · ·

Tommy Casper, unhappy about being cold cocked, aimed his rage at George Sinclair, who felt equally furious that he had missed the shot as well. George rushed to Tommy's side and helped him up.

"Do we leave or go after them?"

"We go after them. I need the money, and he needs to pay for that cheap shot."

"The contract is only for the girl."

"The guy is personal. We do him for free. The dog can live. Come on."

George and Tommy ran after the reporter and her defender. Sound echoed and traveled well in the tunnels, but was difficult to localize. They could hear their targets running ahead of them, but couldn't figure out their direction. Soon, they were lost, too.

"Let's split up," Tommy suggested.

"We have only one gun."

"I can take care of them with this," Tommy brandished the knife. "No more than fifteen more minutes down here, then we split. If you hear the authorities, ditch the weapons and act scared. Good hunting."

· · ·

Lana and Banshee settled behind a large metal piece of machinery of unknown usage. Lana closed her eyes and slowed her breathing, as

Banshee watched the room. Lana couldn't believe this was happening. It would make a hell of a story if she survived. In the distance, she heard Doc running away and slamming doors. She hoped he would be okay.

Banshee tensed and emitted a low growl. Lana put a hand on his back to calm him and felt his hackles rise. She peered around the corner of the machinery. They hid within deep shadows and would be almost impossible to see. She gasped, as she watched one of the men enter the room, leading with his suppressed pistol. He paused to search the room visually, as this was one of the few places to hide that he had come upon. He circled the room, peering into the shadows.

As he approached, Banshee tensed, lowered his center of gravity, and prepared to launch. Banshee recognized the gun as a threat and focused on it.

George had no chance to react. One moment he circled the room, and the next, a dark shadow hurtled at him with a fierce snarl. The gun flew from his hand, as teeth clamped on his wrist and wild white eyes bored into him. George screamed and fell hard to the floor, as Banshee let go of his arm and stood over the cowering man.

Lana picked up the gun and called Banshee to her side. He sat obediently next to her, eyes locked on George. Lana pointed the gun at George. "Don't move." George sat still, cradling his injured arm and watching Banshee, much scarier than the woman with the gun.

• • •

I heard the distant scream of fear and pain from the man and smiled. Banshee had taken down at least one of the bad guys. Only Banshee could make a man scream like that. I slowed to consider whether to return to Lana or to move forward for help, when my decision was made for me.

The second assailant, the one I had punched earlier, rounded the corner with his knife in hand. A cruel smile crawled across his face, as he blocked the hallway, leaving me nowhere to run.

"I'm gonna kill you for that sucker punch."

About my height, but probably thirty pounds heavier, his well-muscled frame displayed his comfort with his weapon, which, along with his crooked nose, proved his proficiency at fighting. He slowly advanced with the knife hovering ahead of him. I settled with my left leg forward and weight on my back foot. He continued his slow advance, flicking the knife erratically in front of him.

He lunged at my chest, then quickly reversed direction and swiped at my scalp. Incredibly fast, blood streamed down my face before I realized I had been cut. He stepped back and laughed, as I processed the fiery pain searing my forehead. I reached up to find a steadily oozing gash at my hairline that already affected my vision.

I resumed my stance and prepared for his next attack. I had to close on him. If I stood toe to toe he would cut me over and over without sustaining damage himself. I launched at him. My offensive move caught him by surprise, and I was able to get my left hand on his wrist before he could bring the knife into play. I continued forward and threw my right elbow at his temple.

He turned at the last moment and caught my elbow on his jaw. The hit, although powerful enough to stun him, failed to knock him out. He stumbled backward, and I pressed my advantage. I swept at his legs, catching his right ankle, and he fell to the ground. I drove him into the hard floor, as we landed, never releasing my grip on his wrist. His breath exploded from his chest as I landed on him.

I raised my right arm to drive my forearm into his temple, but he was not out of the fight. He threw a quick left jab up at me. The punch didn't hold much power, but it was enough to disrupt my shot to his head. I landed only a glancing blow to his skull, as he took a deep breath and raised his hips to throw me off. Imbalanced because of my grip on his knife wrist, I tumbled to the side. He leveraged one leg off the wall and continued the roll until we had switched places with him now on top of me.

His rage and superior bulk gave him the advantage, and he slowly turned the knife point toward my chest. He pinned my right arm down and laughed, as he methodically pushed the knife toward my chest. His strength and leverage were greater than mine, and I couldn't let go of the wrist holding the knife. It was only a matter of time before his strength won, and the knife plunged into my chest.

I screamed, "BANSHEE!"

CHAPTER TWENTY-FOUR

Thursday, 10:44 a.m.

Back in the room, George pushed himself against the machinery, keeping an eye on Banshee at all times. He cradled his injured wrist as he sat on the floor.

"Who are you and why are you trying to kill me?" Lana asked.

"Fuck you, bitch."

"Would you like to see what else this dog can do? Maybe after he uses you for a chew toy, you'll change your mind."

George reconsidered his position. "Lady, it's a job. Nothing personal. Someone wants you dead."

"Who?"

"How the hell should I know? It's all anonymous online. How many people want you dead, anyway? So many you can't figure it out?" He stood up against the machine.

Lana stepped back and pointed the gun at him. "Don't fucking move. I swear I'll shoot you."

"Relax. I'm not going anywhere, and you won't shoot me. You're not a killer. I just don't want to sit by that wolf."

Lana relaxed her grip on the gun, but kept it pointed in his direction. "Doesn't it bother you to kill people?"

George shrugged. "It's just a job that pays well."

They stood in silence for a moment until sounds of a fight reached them. "Looks like my partner caught up with your boyfriend. I doubt this will end well for him. Tommy was pissed about that sucker punch and is handy with a knife."

Lana chewed her lower lip as she worried about what to do amidst the noise of the escalating fight. Her decision was made when Doc screamed for Banshee. He rocketed away at the sound of his distressed owner's call. George straightened and smiled at the dog's departure.

"We both know you won't shoot me, so why don't you put down the gun and leave." He shuffled closer as he spoke.

"Stay back. I'll shoot if you come closer."

"No, you won't." He slithered closer.

Lana kept the gun pointed at him, backing slowly until she was against the wall.

"Nowhere for you to go. You shoulda shot me when you had the chance."

George rushed at her and Lana pulled the trigger twice before he ran into her.

. . .

With the blade only a few inches from my chest, the goon smirked, as he pressed harder, his foul breath toxic in my face. "Don't worry. It'll all be over soon."

I heard the clattering of nails on the floor as Banshee rushed down the hallway. With the knife tip now touching my shirt, I yelled out a command I had never uttered before. "NECK!"

Banshee didn't hesitate as his training kicked in. He launched from five feet away and ignored the knife, focusing on the neck of the man assaulting his owner. The man didn't see him until the last second. Banshee opened his jaw wide and clamped into the lowest part of the neck, puncturing the trachea and sinking into the major blood vessels of the neck. The man swung his knife at Banshee, but the blade bounced harmlessly off his vest. The wounds were potentially survivable, but Banshee shook his head vigorously side to side, turning punctures into tears.

A stream of blood blanketed me, as the man was thrown to the side. He dropped the knife to bring his hands up to try to push Banshee away. I called Banshee off, and he let go to sit at my side with blood soaking his fur. The man lie on the floor, choking on his blood entering his airway, as more blood pooled around him on the floor. His hands futilely attempted to slow the flow of blood. I held his hand as he died on the floor of the tunnel.

I sat back against the wall and scratched Banshee. "Thanks buddy. Sorry you had to do that." Banshee thumped his tail with the attention. Let's go check on Lana."

I stood up, as two gunshots and a scream reverberated through the tunnels.

I commanded Banshee to "FIND LANA." He led the way, confident at each turn. I staggered into the room expecting the worst and found Lana standing over the other man, bleeding on the floor and cursing at her. His eyes widened at the sight of Banshee, but not as wide as Lana's eyes when she saw me.

"Oh my god. What happened to you?"

I looked down at my blood stained arms and shirt. "Don't worry. Most of it isn't mine."

"Where's Tommy?" the assailant on the ground asked.

"If you're referring to your friend, I'm sorry, but he's deceased. He came at me with a knife and lost."

The assailant laid his head back on the ground and closed his eyes. "What happened here?" I asked.

"He snuck in here, and Banshee took his gun before he knew what was happening. I was pointing it at him and told him not to move. When Banshee left, he lunged at me, and I shot him twice."

I turned my attention to the man on the ground. "Where are you hit?"

"My fucking leg and hip. And my wrist is killing me where that damn wolf bit me."

I leaned over to examine the wounds. The hip was a graze of the hip bone. Painful as hell, but not serious. The other shot went through the thigh. Blood seeped out, but it appeared to be venous bleeding, not arterial, which would have killed him already. I removed my belt and placed it above the wound. "I need to put a tourniquet on to slow the bleeding. It's not horrible, but it's gonna take a while to get you out of here, and we have to do it. Okay?"

The man nodded, and I tightened the belt until the bleeding slowed to a trickle. I commanded Banshee to guard, then hugged Lana. "You never shoot for the leg. You should have aimed for the chest. You were lucky to stop him."

She held me tight as she whispered in my ear. "I was aiming for the chest. The damn gun is too heavy with the silencer, and I shot low. Let's take a look at that head wound."

I had forgotten about the scalp laceration with all the excitement, but the adrenaline was wearing off and the pain returned. The blood had slowed, but still dripped down my forehead.

Lana took off her sock and used it to clean some of the blood away, and took a picture of the wound for me with her phone. It was about three inches long and a clean cut at the hairline, all the way through the scalp to the bone.

"Is it bad?" she asked.

"Not really. Biggest worry will be infection from using a sock as a bandage," I said as I held the sock over the wound to slow the bleeding.

"Does it matter if I have extremely clean feet?"

"They aren't that clean. Nothing some antibiotics won't take care of. Now we need to figure out where we are, and how to get help."

Lana pointed to the far wall. "How about we see if that phone works."

I staggered to the phone that welcomed me with a dial tone. I was even more relieved to see a button labeled "emergency." A bored voice answered. "Security, Officer Hopkins. How can I help you?"

"Good morning, Officer Hopkins. I am a tourist, and my companion and I got separated from our group and were assaulted by two men. We need medical help, and I'm afraid we don't know where we are."

"I have your location from the phone. What are the injuries?"

"I have a laceration to my scalp from a knife wound. Bleeding is under control. A second man has been shot in the thigh and hip by a 9 mm pistol. Bleeding is also under control. A third gentleman is in a hallway near here. He is deceased from neck wounds."

"Please repeat that. You have a knife wound, a gunshot victim and a dead guy down there?"

"That is correct. One of the bad guys is deceased, and the other is on the floor with the gunshot wounds. The scene is secure, and I have unloaded the pistol."

"Stay on the line. Help is on the way."

I sank to the floor with the phone in my hand. Banshee and Lana sat down next to me, with Banshee relentlessly watching the man across the room.

CHAPTER TWENTY-FIVE

Friday, 10:53 a.m.

Officer Hopkins switched to the radio to broadcast to the forces around the dam. "Attention all units. We have a code red. Repeat, code red. Tourist reports he and his girlfriend were assaulted by two men. One man deceased and second man injured with gunshots to the leg. Tourist reports a knife injury to the scalp. Location is Engineering NV 481. Repeat, location is Engineering NV 481. Security response force to respond."

Hoover Dam is a jurisdictional nightmare. Half of the dam is located in Arizona and the other half in Nevada. Contracted security guards patrol the tourist areas. Unarmed, they respond to minor problems, such as falls, unruly behavior, and traffic control. Mostly, they answer questions for tourists.

The Hoover Dam Police are actually Bureau of Reclamation security guards. Although unarmed, they have the power to arrest individuals and control access to critical areas of the facility.

The Bureau of Reclamation Security Response Force, the highest level of law enforcement for the dam, consists of highly trained and heavily armed officers who constantly patrol against terrorist threats. They train for many scenarios, including a possible hostage situation in the dam with armed perpetrators.

The SRF responded immediately to the red alert call. Forces inside the dam converged on the room where the call originated and took strategic positions in the hallway to lock down the area, but waited to move forward. As they called in their locations, the commander marked positions on a map and directed some officers to new positions. The dam was a maze inside, but officers could find their way to any location quickly. Within two minutes, a secure perimeter isolated the area of the dam where the call originated.

On the surface, all officers rushed to the two elevators closest to the affected areas. Team A used the Nevada elevators and Team B the Arizona elevators. About the time the perimeter was established inside the dam, the two teams of eight officers descended into the dam.

In a well rehearsed movement, officers advanced on the room quickly. Lead officers peeled off at each intersection to cover intersecting hallways until the team passed and then joined the rear of the line. Five minutes from the initial alert, both teams stood at the perimeter ready to assault. The commander confirmed everyone's positions and gave the order to go.

Team B led the assault into the room, entering with rifles up, pointing front left and front right, screaming for hands up. Officers behind peeled off as they entered, each taking a sector of the room. In seconds, eights officers covered the entire room. They were met with one man lying on the floor in a pool of blood with his hands above his head, and across the room, a blood covered man and a woman sitting against a wall with their hands up. Strangest of all was a dog standing on his back legs with his front paws in the air.

Shouts of "clear" echoed from each officer, and the order came for weapons to be lowered.

•   •   •

Medics bandaged my wound, replacing Lana's sock with sterile gauze, and saw to the gunshot wounds, as we waited for the Commander to arrive. I pointed out the gun we had left on a table across the room, and pointed officers to the blood trail leading to the body in the hallway.

Officers secured both areas, then continued a sweep of the entire dam for any other victims.

Commander Toomey arrived a few minutes later. In his early fifties, he had the physique of a man in his prime. His eyes slowly scanned the room before settling on me. "Can you two walk?"

"Yes, sir."

"Follow me."

He led the way confidently with a measured step through a series of hallways and then invited us through an open door into a break room. "Have a seat at the table. Can I get you anything to drink?"

"Water, please," I said.

"Vodka," Lana replied.

The Commander cracked a brief smile. "Two waters it is."

We sat at the table while he appraised us. "Are you okay to talk? Looks like you lost a lot of blood."

"Fortunately, most of it is not mine."

"Care to tell me how my dam turned into a war zone today?"

"It all began with the bombing at the hospital a few days ago." Lana summarized what we knew about everything that had led up to today's meeting. He listened without interruption as another officer recorded us and took notes.

"That is quite the story. And you think these two men were sent here to kill you?" the Commander asked Lana.

"Yes, sir. The man I shot admitted that he was hired to take care of us, but said he had no idea who hired him. He was pretty casual when he talked about it, like it was just a job to him." She grabbed my hand and squeezed as she repeated their conversation.

"This story gets better with every detail, especially with a dog who disarmed one man and killed another. Forensics will have to confirm everything, but for the moment I believe you."

"What happens now?"

"Let me make some calls, and I'll be back."

Lana leaned over for a hug.

"How are you?" I asked.

"A bit traumatized, but okay. I've never shot anyone before."

"He didn't give you a choice. If you didn't shoot, you would have been lying under a sheet instead of sitting in this lovely room."

"How are you doing?"

"A little conflicted. The guy was about to stab me in the chest with a knife, and calling for Banshee to go for his neck was a desperation on my part. Never thought I would give that command. Feels like I killed the guy myself."

"Same story. Without the command, you would have been under a sheet yourself. You did the right thing. How do you think Banshee is doing?"

We looked at him lying peacefully at our feet. "He's fine. As far as he knows, he followed a command just like any other command. He's probably disappointed he didn't get a treat for obeying."

"Wish it was that easy for us to process death."

"I often wish I had his life. That dog has it made."

We sat in silence with our own thoughts until the commandeer returned. "This occurred on the Nevada side, thankfully, so jurisdiction is either federal or local. Normally the feds would want the case, but this really doesn't have anything to do with the dam and everything to do with the bombings in Las Vegas, so they're happy to defer jurisdiction. Ma'am, one of my officers will escort you to police headquarters, where you can give a formal statement. Sir, you will go to the hospital with one of my officers as an escort. They will turn you over to the Las Vegas police for a statement after you're fixed up."

"Can my dog come with me?"

The Commander smiled. "Son, that dog can go wherever he pleases, and he's always welcome in my dam."

CHAPTER TWENTY-SIX

Friday, 12:11 p.m.

I dozed as we rode back to the city in the back of a police SUV. The combination of blood loss and plummeting adrenaline levels seemed to rock me to sleep. Sirens awakened me, as the officer threaded his way through the race traffic.

We arrived at Sunrise ER, and I politely refused a wheelchair and walked inside with Banshee. Little Mac met us at the door and joyfully took Banshee's leash. "Please make sure he gets some food and water. He's had a busy morning." Little Mac waved acknowledgment as he walked away, talking to Banshee about his day.

"Oh look, it's our hero bringing us more work. You look like shit." Jen said, noting my bloody scalp and crimson stained shirt.

"You should see the other guy. Where do you want me?"

"At another hospital, but since you're here, let's go to room six and take a look."

I settled onto the stretcher, and the team went to work. "Everybody needs to calm down," I said to Jen. "It's a scalp laceration, not major trauma."

Jen cleared most of the staff out of the room and gently unwrapped the gauze. A fresh round of bleeding commenced as she removed the last bandages. She gave a low whistle. "Impressive. How's the other guy?"

"He will be heading straight to the morgue."

"Seriously?"

"Unfortunately, yes. Banshee didn't like him trying to stick a knife in my chest and chomped him on the neck."

"Remind me not to piss off that dog. You got lucky. He cut some skin, fat, and muscle but nothing important. We can close it down here and avoid the OR. We'll give some IV antibiotics while we do it."

"Holy shit! That's awesome. Let me sew that bad boy up, and I'll give you a great scar," Rick, sporting his Spider-Man scrubs, exclaimed as he entered. Jen looked at me for an opinion, and I nodded. Rick was a goofball but an excellent clinician, and his energy would make the time pass easier. Jen left muttering about dangers of an over abundance of testosterone.

Rick set up his equipment, as the nurse started an IV for the antibiotics. I refused IV pain meds for the moment, but reserved the right to change my mind.

Rick now had a medical student watching him and gave a running commentary, pointing out the visible anatomy before addressing the closure. "This thing's about three inches long and deep, so we need to do some subcutaneous stitches to pull the deep tissues together. We'll use a 3.0 vicryl for that. Skin closure will be under a lot of pressure, so we can't do a simple running stitch, likely to burst. We'll do some 5.0 prolene stitches, and once we have the tension under control, a layer of skin glue. That should minimize the scar, but it is at the hairline, and Doc is so ugly anyway that no one will notice. First, we need to get him numbed up and irrigated. Infection is the most likely complication, and Doc will probably sue me if it gets infected." Rick was such an entertaining clinical teacher that I imagined his protégés would remember nearly everything, and they'd have Rick's humorous voice ringing through their minds throughout their careers.

I tuned them out and relaxed on the stretcher, knowing this repair would take the better part of an hour. Momentarily uncomfortable, the lidocaine injection blocked pain, and I drifted off to sleep. A hand gently shook my shoulder, and I awoke to see Detective Stillman's intense gaze. "Can you talk for a moment?"

Rick answered for me. "He can talk. I want to hear this story. I'll write an order for him to talk if that helps."

"Probably not necessary, but I'll let you know. Doc, tell me what happened." He turned on a digital recorder and readied a notebook and pen.

I inhaled deeply as I organized my thoughts, then ran through the series of events. I started with the text Lana had received the night before to explain our trip to Hoover Dam, the tour we joined, the text to separate from the tour, the attacks, and finally, the subduing of the two perpetrators and the call for help. Detective Stillman listened carefully without interruption.

Anger and excitement danced in Rick's stunned eyes. "That is fucking bad ass!"

Detective Stillman smiled and pointed at the recorder. "We're still recording." Rick refocused on his sutures, as Stillman asked a few minor questions to clarify.

"So, who were those guys?" I asked, when he finally finished.

"A couple of nobodies known to the Las Vegas justice system as occasional guests in our facilities, mostly for lower level stuff, like assault and extortion. They don't have any known association with white supremacists, but we'll check. Best guess is that it's true that they were hired for the hit through an anonymous website."

"I assume you mean to kill Lana."

"It looks that way, and they would certainly have succeeded, if not for you and Banshee."

"This is a real life Scooby episode," Rick exclaimed. "They would have gotten away with it, if it weren't for you meddling kids and that dog!"

We laughed, grateful for the tension release. "This the best doctor they could find for you?" Stillman asked.

"I'm the best doctor anyone could find," Rick proclaimed.

"If your skill level is anywhere near as high as your confidence that may be true."

Rick winked, as I turned the conversation back to matters at hand. "Detective, why do you think they went after her? It seems like a drastic step."

"It is, and it makes us think she's close to the bomber and knows something important."

"What does she know?"

"That's what we're trying to figure out."

．　　．　　．

Lana leaned back in a comfortable chair in Detective Roland's office and sipped a drink courtesy of a bottle kept in her desk for such occasions. Roland tipped her glass. "Cheers, and congrats on not getting shot."

Lana took a healthy swig from the glass. "What's the deal with guys trying to kill me?"

Roland set her glass down and got serious. "Two low level pieces of shit were hired for the job. We'll press the survivor, but I don't expect him to know much. Plus, bad things happen to snitches in his world."

"Bad things are happening in my world. You think it's the bomber coming after me?"

"Unless you have another big story brewing, I'm sure it's our friendly bomber. He already proved his willingness to murder and seems to have ordered the hit on Milly. He must think you know something important."

Lana silently stared at Roland, as she mentally scanned the information she had collected. "In journalism, we have off the record conversations with assurances that nothing will come back to bite the informant. What do the police have that is similar?"

Roland leaned forward. "I'll play along. We're desperate, and time is not on our side. We got a crazy bomber out there with a million race fans descending on us this weekend. So, this conversation is off the record. Tell me what you know."

"I think Krug might be the bomber. I did some digging after talking with Milly and couldn't find anything wrong in the financial records of the other three arresting officers, but Krug is in some serious debt with three hundred thousand owed to the casinos and probably more to private bookies. He's heavily leveraged and facing imminent bankruptcy."

"But this is a bombing based on ideology, not financial gain."

"I don't think so. I think the white supremacy is a red herring. No one has heard of this group; there's no chatter about them; and the established groups are pissed at the increased attention from authorities. The targets have been African American, but without strong statements. He's a talented bomb builder, but hasn't used them to kill anyone yet. This whole thing reeks of attention seeking behavior, not an actual hate based campaign."

"Why do you think this is about money?"

"Because people commit crimes for money, passion, or revenge, and I'm not feeling the passion or revenge."

"How does money tie into this?"

"No idea, but one of the guys who had an opportunity to acquire the explosives and has the knowledge to build bombs just happens to be near bankruptcy, and that's a lot of coincidence."

"How do you think he monetizes this?"

Lana threw up her hands in exasperation. "It's Vegas with money literally on every street corner. There're a million possibilities."

Roland stood up. "Thanks for sharing with me. I need to get your official, recorded statement, but I prefer that you leave out the information about Krug. Just stick to your facts about the investigation and the trip to Hoover Dam."

It took an hour to conclude her official interview. "I don't think it's safe for you to be at your home until this thing is resolved. We can put you up at a hotel."

"I love the idea, but I don't think there's a room left in Vegas with the race in town."

"There's always a room reserved for us. Which hotel do you want?"

"That's easy, Bellagio."

"Good choice. Give me a minute."

Lana checked her phone for messages, as she waited for Roland to return. Ten minutes later, she was back with a piece of paper. "You're all set. This will get you into VIP parking. Take the elevator to the VIP lounge where they will get you checked in. It's a junior suite, but they're charging you the regular room rate. Your name for check in is Linda Carter."

"Seriously? Wonder Woman?" Lana laughed, and Roland cracked a smile.

"Get out of here, Wonder Woman. We mere mortals have work to do."

Lana left for Sunrise to check on Doc, as Stillman returned to compare notes with Roland.

CHAPTER TWENTY-SEVEN

Friday, 3:49 p.m.

Lana walked into my room as Rick put the finishing touches on my bandage.

"What do you think?" he asked. Rick proudly showcased a pink bandage with a Barney sticker on my forehead.

"It brings out your inner child, very on brand for Rick. Does anything inside that head still function?"

I scrunched my forehead, causing Barney to undulate.

"Awesome, it's like a Barney dance party," Rick quipped. "Wait here for your discharge instructions."

"With all due respect to your wealth of knowledge, I think I'm good on the wound care instructions, but I do need my dog. Can someone please track down Little Mac for me?"

Lana leaned in for a hug and kiss on my cheek. "Sorry I almost got you killed today."

"I had no idea being a reporter was so dangerous. Are you okay? Shooting someone can be a burden."

Lana waved me off. "It was only a leg wound, and he was trying to kill me, so I don't feel too bad about it."

"You should have aimed center mass," Rick said.

Lana laughed. "I did. I had my sights on his chest, but apparently the gun barrel drifted down with the weight of the silencer on the end.

Detective Roland said it's pretty common to shoot low without training with a silencer."

Little Mac arrived with Banshee, who jumped on the bed to give me a kiss. His nose made a beeline for the bandage, as he thoroughly sniffed the wound. I checked his vest where the knife had struck him to find barely a scratch. "Buddy, you owe a big thank you to Stephanie Kwolek."

"Who's that?" Lana asked.

"A scientist at DuPont who invented Kevlar in the 1960's. Her creation saved Banshee's life today." I hugged him before sitting up in bed. "Let's get out of here."

Lana handed me a clean scrub top to replace my bloody shirt that she promptly threw in the trash. "C'mon, we need to pack some things."

"We got a vacation I don't know about?"

"The police don't want us in our home until the bomber is caught, so you and I are gonna spend some time at a hotel. They gave me a choice, so I went with Bellagio."

"Big surprise."

"I may need to recover in their spa, followed by dinner at Michael Mina's."

"I hate to be the bearer of bad news, but it's race weekend. No way we can get a room."

"Already taken care of. Apparently, the cops always have a room reserved, and we got it under an alias at regular rates for us, and they're aware you have a service dog, so let's pack for a few days and check in."

"What do you say, Banshee? Are you up for a vacation at Bellagio?"

Banshee thumped his tail.

· · ·

Stillman and Roland gathered at headquarters to compare notes. "Looks like Doc and Lana's stories check out. They got lucky today," Stillman noted.

"I would say they were prepared, not lucky. Bringing that dog was the best choice they made today. What do we have on the shooters?"

Stillman picked up two files and slid them across the desk. "George Sinclair and Tommy Casper, recently deceased, have been fine citizens of Las Vegas for the last twenty years or so, when they're not out at High Desert for a stay. Both have had multiple arrests for possession and assault and are suspects in a couple of hits."

"Let me guess. The witnesses suffered memory loss."

"Something like that. I say we offer George full immunity, if he flips on who hired them, and threaten him with federal charges, if he doesn't want to talk. He should be here soon. An ER doctor cleaned his wounds, sewed him up, and gave him some antibiotics and pain meds."

Mary grabbed a refill of coffee and entered the interrogation room to find George Sinclair chained to the table by his cuffs. His splinted left leg stretched out next to him. He stared at her defiantly as she sat, placed her steaming coffee cup, and skimmed the file. Finally, she looked up. "I'm Detective Roland, and you've been read your Miranda rights, correct?"

He nodded.

"And you're aware this session is being recorded?"

He glanced at the camera and nodded.

"Then I'll make this short and sweet, Mr. Sinclair. You're in a lot of trouble with attempted murder and weapons charges. Full immunity if you tell me who hired you."

George leaned forward in his chair. "I didn't do nothing. I was on a tour and that crazy bitch shot me in the leg. You should arrest her and put down that fucking dog who killed my friend."

Mary leaned forward to match his pose. "Mr. Sinclair, we have your prints on the gun and on its bullets. We have matching bullets with your prints found in your car, which was registered in your name and parked at the dam. And let's not forget, that dog you attacked, he had a camera system that captured the entire thing on video, which will persuade a jury to convict you in about sixty seconds. No more bullshit. Give me a name, and you get full immunity. Otherwise you go down for this, and we'll turn you over to the Feds."

Concern flitted across Sinclair's face for the first time. "Why are the Feds involved?"

"You may have missed the class in high school that explains that Hoover Dam is owned by the federal government. Crimes committed on their property can be prosecuted by them, or by us, if they're not interested, but they'll be interested in this. They'll convict you, and instead of doing time in High Desert with your friends, you'll be in a federal lockup with no friends. One last time. You want immunity or federal lockup? Give me a name, or it's bye bye Vegas for fifteen to twenty years."

Sinclair struggled mightily, and Mary hoped he would flip, but he shook his head and collapsed back in the chair. "I can't do it."

"You're willing to throw your life away to protect this guy?"

"If I snitch, I won't last twenty-four hours."

"We can protect you."

"Not from him. I'll take my chances in prison. No deal. Lawyer, please."

.   .   .

"Whoever hired them must be one scary motherfucker," Stillman said.

"True, but my best guess is that they were hired by cutout. He probably doesn't know who the actual client is. He would flip in a second, if he had something to share."

"He could give us the cutout, but that person has other hitters at his disposal. He doesn't know much, and what he does know won't give us the bomber, and will get him killed."

"I can't figure why he went after her. That's a big step."

"Bigger than blowing up Las Vegas? She and her boyfriend did interfere with the second bombing, and she got to Milly. She must be close to the identity."

"She still thinks it's Krug?"

"Yes. We need to tighten up surveillance on him. Do we keep up surveillance on the others?"

"For the moment, yes, but let's make sure the best teams are on Krug."

.   .   .

Lana and I stepped into the VIP lounge at the Bellagio via a private elevator from the garage, constantly manned by security. I gave a low whistle as we entered. "This is nice, although I do miss checking in behind a hundred tourists who can't find their registration confirmation numbers."

Lana ignored me and approached a woman smiling warmly at the registration desk. "Good afternoon and welcome to the Bellagio. Are you checking in today?"

"Yes, thank you."

"What is the name on the reservation?"

Lana looked at me nervously before replying. "Linda Carter."

"One moment Miss Carter."

I whispered in Lana's ear. "Linda fucking Carter. Are you kidding me?"

She gently stabbed her heel into my foot, as she studiously ignored me. The clerk handed her two room keys. "Your room number is on the envelope. It's a very nice suite with views of the fountain and race track. You can access it through the elevators to your left. Our concierge is available around the clock to help with any reservations you need for restaurants, the spa, shows, or any other services. If you need anything, please don't hesitate to call."

A bellman guided us to our room, pointing out all the amenities. Banshee hopped up on a chair with a view of the Strip outside and settled in for a nap. When the bellman left, I turned to Lana. "You know, I've never had a chance to sleep with a real life superhero."

Lana slowly stripped, as she made her way to the shower. "Better clean up then. Wonder Woman doesn't sleep with slobs."

CHAPTER TWENTY-EIGHT

Friday, 6;28 p.m.

"Why don't you rest like a normal person?" Lana asked.

"Because F1 races in Vegas only once a year, and I had to pull some major favors with a guy at Mercedes to get these passes," I replied.

"Is it really that big of a deal?"

I stopped her and held her shoulders. "F1 is the biggest sporting event in the world besides the World Cup. Mercedes is the most dominant team in modern F1, and Lewis Hamilton is simply the greatest driver in the history of F1, and I have passes allowing us into the paddock and pit lane areas, where we can see the cars up close and maybe meet a driver. Yes, it's a big deal."

"Maybe you can get him to sign that pretty pink bandage for you."

"Great idea! Let's go."

We filed through security into the crowded pit lane. On a short leash, Banshee wore his noise cancelling ear protection, but reveled in the attention and new scents. We politely wove through the excited crowd to the Mercedes garage, where the team prepared the car for the next practice run. I pointed out Lewis Hamilton talking with Toto Wolff and Bono, his race engineer, but Lana seemed more interested in the crowd than in the drivers.

I was talking with one of the mechanics when Lana nudged me. "Looks like someone has a better VIP pass than you do."

I followed her subtle gesture to notice a man in an impeccably well-tailored suit being led past the ropes and into the garage to meet the team. "Who is that?" I asked.

"Some billionaire from China here for the race. Apparently, he's a big fan and instrumental in bringing F1 to China."

"Quite the entourage he has with him," I noted, nodding toward the four bodyguards and five beautiful women waiting patiently for him to finish in the garage. "He must be doing something right to have those five hanging on his arm."

Lana punched me in the arm. "Those girls don't give a damn about that guy. They're here to make him look virile among all you alpha males, and it's apparently working."

"I'm perfectly happy with you, Wonder Woman," I recovered, hugging her. "Besides, I don't think I could afford all five of them."

"Honey, you couldn't afford one of them. Check out their jewelry."

I gave a low whistle as I appraised the necklaces, bracelets, and earrings adorning the women. "Maybe it's all fake."

"It's real and out of your league."

"I'll have to ask my boss for a raise. C'mon, it's about time to start hot laps."

"I still don't understand the wide appeal of this."

"Are you kidding me? A professional driver in a Mercedes GT Black Series is gonna drive me around the track at the limits of the car. It's not as fast as an F1 car, but we will hurtle down the Strip at 175 mph with 720 hp roaring through our ears, a once in a lifetime experience."

"Enjoy. Banshee and I will hang out with everyone without insecurities."

I kissed her on the cheek and hurried to check in. After a quick helmet fitting, an impossibly young Mercedes assistant led me to the pit area and introduced me to my driver. I held out my hand. "AJ Docker. Nice to meet you and excited to see what this beast can do."

The driver smiled warmly and pointed to his name tag. "Damn glad to meet ya. My name is AJ as well, and this is gonna be epic. Two AJs in a GT. Lets do this. What's up with the pink bandage?"

"Would you believe it if I told you it was a knife fight?"

"How's the other guy?"

"Resting in the morgue."

"I fucking love Vegas. Let's get you situated."

I climbed in and belted a five point harness that replaced the traditional seatbelt. AJ busily adjusted settings on the dash and finally got the thumbs up to enter the track. "Are we going fast or really fucking fast today?" He asked.

"I want the lap record in this car."

"Hell, yes! Let's do it." He hit the gas, and the engine roared, as the tires spun to accelerate immediately to 40 MPH, the pit lane speed limit. AJ's hands gripped the wheel firmly, as he gave a running commentary. "Pit lane dumps us out at turn one, a 180 degree left turn that is gonna be a major fight on race day."

He hugged the interior racing line and accelerated smoothly out of the corner. "Turn two is a little kink to the left that the drivers won't even notice." I felt it, as we accelerated hard into the turn, and I was pushed back into my seat.

"Three and four are high speed sweeping turns that head into the first straight. A good exit is important to carry speed all the way down the straightaway." AJ accelerated and moved through the gears, as we rounded through the turn, maxing out at 1.5G of lateral force. "The F1 guys will be pulling at least 4 G's on that turn."

The brief respite of the straightaway allowed quick acceleration past 165 MPH. "Hang on," AJ cautioned, as we approached the end of the straight. He pushed the brake pedal to the floor, and the ceramic brake pads screamed to slow the car, while the computer prevented the brakes from locking up. The violent deceleration slowed the car from 165 MPH to just 46MPH in fewer than a hundred yards.

AJ smiled, as he smoothly swung the car in a 90 degree right turn, hitting the apex of the corner, before drifting to the outer edges of the track. "This next series of turns is fun, and they lead to the real prize, the Las Vegas Strip straightaway."

AJ exited turn twelve near the Wynn Hotel and entered the Strip with the throttle wide open. "This straight is over a mile long, and we should hit close to 175 MPH."

We whizzed past onlookers behind the fences in front of the blurred majestic hotels, as we picked up speed. The Venetian on the left almost instantly gave way to Caesars on the right. The Bellagio, naked without its fountains, presented grandstands already half full of people instead.

Our speed hit 178 MPH. "Hold on. We got a hard left up ahead." With even more savage braking this time, he bled over 140 MPH of speed off the car, timing it perfectly to turn left smoothly into a small kink before the final short straight, slowing the car, as we entered pit lane.

"What do you think?" AJ asked.

"I think I need one of these cars and your job."

"We have to put up with a lot of bullshit from VIP's, but it's worth it for the track time. I hope you enjoyed your 3.8 mile trip around Vegas. They'll send you a video of the ride."

I unbuckled and shook his hand. "Thanks, man. Be safe out there." AJ gave me a thumbs up, as I hopped out, and the next person was buckled in. I returned my helmet and stretched, as I found Lana surrounded by a small crowd. Lana waved, "Doc, come over here. Banshee made a friend. Meet Roscoe."

I gently meandered through the small crowd to Lana's side to see Banshee and a bulldog sniffing each other with tails wagging. "Doc, this is Lewis. He works with Mercedes."

The man held out his hand. "Nice to meet you, Doc. Beautiful dog you have. I need to get Roscoe a vest like that."

I incredulously gripped his hand. "Nice to meet you, Sir Lewis. Good luck in the race tomorrow."

"It's just Lewis out here, mate. We have a good setup and hope to be on the front row. Cheers, mate. Gotta run. Enjoy the race." I grabbed a quick selfie with him before he hopped on his scooter and wheeled away with Roscoe happily jogging at his side.

I turned to Lana. "You do realize that was Sir Lewis Hamilton, seven time world champion and the greatest F1 driver of all time?"

"Really? That explains your fanboy reaction. How was your car ride?"

"You really don't give a shit about this racing stuff, do you?"

"No, but it makes you happy, so I'm glad to get to be part of it. I'm ready to return to the hotel now to enjoy the spa, though."

"Lead the way. A massage sounds like a perfect way to add to this amazing day."

CHAPTER TWENTY-NINE

Friday, 8:02 p.m.

Detectives Stillman and Roland sat at the table, joined by Detective Roberts from the bomb squad and Detective Chambers from Internal Affairs. Roberts glared at Chambers, rankled by the presence of internal affairs. Everyone stood as the Chief entered. "Please be seated. What's the latest?"

"Nothing new, sir," Roland responded. "Forensics is still pending, but we know that all of the parts are generic, and no prints have been found. Cameras in the immediate vicinity were incapacitated by lasers. Surrounding cameras show literally thousands of people, half of them carrying bags that could have contained the bomb. We questioned witnesses, and no one noticed anything unusual. The diversion device in the Stratosphere also gave us nothing. The restaurant uses no cameras, and we interviewed the staff, and no one remembers who could have had access to that table. A small amount of C4 under the silver medal alerted the dog, but it definitely had no detonator."

"What about the guys in the Dam attack?"

"Nothing, sir. The surviving perpetrator lawyered up and refused a deal."

The Chief leaned back in his chair. "Detective Chambers, I think it's time for you to share your investigation with the team."

Stillman interrupted, "Are you sure that's a good idea, Chief? There's risk with that."

"Right now, there's a crazy bomber hurting people and making us look like fools. It's about time to take some risks. Proceed, Chambers."

"Internal Affairs was notified on Tuesday of the possibility of a bomb squad officer's involvement in the bombings based on testimony from an inmate."

Outraged, Roberts stood and pounded the table. "This is fucking bullshit!"

Calmly, the Chief commanded, "Seat yourself, Detective, and listen."

Roberts sat back down, his unrelenting stare unsoftened, as Chambers explained. "As you all know, the explosives match those confiscated in an arrest months ago. The informant claimed to have had more than the amount we supposedly confiscated and suggested that a cop had to have stolen it and sold it or is now using it. Furthermore, the bombs show sophistication beyond what a YouTube video could teach an amateur. Our bomber clearly has training in explosives."

Roberts seethed as Chambers continued. "Four arresting officers had the opportunity to take some of the explosives. We have carefully investigated each of them. Armond, Bertrand, and Detective Roberts have clear financial records and are not considered suspects."

"That's great fucking news," Roberts said.

"Sergeant Krug, however, has a significant gambling problem with mounting debts that he has no hope of covering. Were you aware of this, Detective Roberts?"

Roberts calmed down despite all eyes focused on him. "No, I wasn't until you told me yesterday."

"Have you noticed any changes in Krug's behavior?"

"No. He's always been a loner as the only single guy in our group. He has his own group of friends outside our team, so I don't know much about his personal life. He shows up and does his job."

"What about this week? Has he seemed more stressed?"

"We've all been stressed. Do you really think he's the bomber?"

"Do you?"

"I don't see it. He's a good kid and a good cop. Of course, I didn't know about the money problems. That can drive people to crazy decisions."

"Does he have the technical skill to build those bombs?"

"All my guys have the skills to build those bombs. Anyone with formal training could do it. We have to know how to build them to defuse them."

The Chief spoke up. "Do we have enough to bring him in?"

Chambers responded. "No, sir. We can place him at the site where some of the explosives may have been stolen, but the only one who can corroborate the discrepancy is the inmate who was killed. He has the skill, but so do others. He has the financial issues, which will be a problem for him even if he's not the bomber, but nothing ties him to the explosions."

"So what's your plan?"

"We continue our surveillance. We can also try to get a warrant to hack into his home computer, but we can't be sure that a judge would give it at this point. No way we can get a search warrant for his house, and he's unlikely to have the explosives there, anyway. He probably has a second location to store the materials and build the bombs. We can track him from here without a warrant. If we get a sniff of his involvement, then we can bring him in."

"That's the best we can do. Go for the warrant and continue surveillance. I want it tight. No screw ups. Roberts, I want normal activity from the bomb squad. Don't let anyone else know what is happening, and don't even think about playing the hero. If you see or hear anything unusual at all, report it to Chambers, understood?"

"Yes, sir."

"I don't have to remind everyone that we've got a race tomorrow with half the world watching live on TV. This motherfucker will not hurt our people and embarrass this department. Dismissed."

They stood, as the Chief swept up his papers and left. Roberts scowled at the three remaining detectives. "If he's guilty, I will gladly nail his ass to the wall, but if he's innocent, you better apologize and make it up to him." Roberts turned and left the room.

"Think he'll cooperate?" Roland asked.

"Yes. No one likes it when we investigate someone on their team, but it doesn't reflect well on him if the bomber was operating right under his nose the whole time. He can be a hero if he helps catch the guy, and he can be full of righteous indignation if we're wrong. Either way, he's fine."

"What do you think the chances are that Krug is our guy?" Stillman asked

"Probable, but I don't understand the racial angle. Someone could be paying him to do it, but then we would see his loans disappearing. Keep digging. I'm gonna check on surveillance and try for a warrant."

· · ·

Lana and I curled up on the sofa in Bellagio's bathrobes to watch the night time qualifying session. Hundreds of thousands of people crowded the strip and packed into every available space. "You know, we could have been down there for qualifying this evening," I said.

Lana nestled into me. "The Strip looks like the most miserable place on earth right now. I prefer this air conditioned suite."

"It's definitely more comfortable up here, and it has been a bit of a stressful day."

Lana snorted. "Let's see. We were hunted by two killers; you were stabbed; and I had to shoot someone. You got stitches and raced around the track with your new man friend, and I had to submit a story explaining the mess at the Dam by the deadline. I think that's enough stress for one day."

"Don't forget you were promoted to superhero today."

"I'm sure you'll never let me forget. I'm going to bed."

"I'll be there in a few. I want to watch the end of qualifying." The cars raced down the strip at 220 MPH, as the TV announcers updated their times. Mesmerized, I couldn't imagine a better way to watch F1. Twenty minutes later, Q3 ended with Mercedes placing first and second. It would be an all Mercedes' front row to start the race the next day. Lana was already snoring softly, as I climbed into bed and Banshee took his place on the floor by my side of the bed. All three of us slept hard.

CHAPTER THIRTY

Saturday, October 21
8:11 a.m.

Sergeants Armond and Bertrand waited impatiently in the office. "I could have sworn Roberts said we were meeting at eight today. Where the hell is he?" Armond asked.

"Maybe he was out late last night, dancing with all the race VIPs."

"Unlikely. Maybe the Chief snagged him."

"What about Krug?"

"He was probably out late last night, but not with VIPs. Guy is starting to fall apart."

"I hear ya. Give him a call. I'll text Roberts."

Armond called Krug only to reach his voicemail after four rings. "Hey, dumbass, we're working today. Where the hell are you?" He hung up and texted him as well. "Where are you?"

Bertrand texted Roberts. "We're in the office. Let us know if we need to meet somewhere else."

Armond and Bertrand discussed the best bets on the race, as they waited for their teammates to contact them.

. . .

At Internal Affairs, the phone message and text to Krug were monitored in real time, and Chambers received an instant call. "Where is his phone located now?" He asked the surveillance team.

"Still in his house. Hasn't moved all night."

"Let me know of any other activity." He disconnected and called the officers monitoring Krug's house. "Any activity this morning?"

"No, sir. Lights went out last night around 10:15, and we haven't seen any activity since then."

"Please call me immediately if you do."

"Yes, sir. We got eyes on the front door, windows, and garage. We'll let you know if he leaves."

Chambers disconnected and called Roberts, but was sent to voicemail. "We need to talk, now." Next he texted "Call Chambers. 911." A bomb squad Detective would not ignore a 911 text, even if he was in a meeting with the Mayor.

After two long minutes of silence, he swore and called Stillman. "We may have a problem. Krug's team is looking for him, and he's not answering, and Roberts is off the grid. He's not responding to my 911 text."

"That's not good. Send me Roberts' address and have a black and white meet me there. Let's track him down first, and then worry about Krug. I got a bad feeling about this."

"Me, too. Call me when you learn something."

Stillman grabbed his gun and called Roland on his way out the door to update her.

"Do you need me there?" she asked.

"Hold for now. I'm closer and I'll see what we have and make a plan from there." He looked at his map to see twelve minutes to Roberts' home. With lights and sirens, he could be there in less than ten.

He arrived to find a patrol car parked out front. "I'm Detective Stillman. This is a detective's home, and this may be nothing, or he may be in trouble. Be alert, but no friendly fire." Stillman led the way to the front door, flanked by the two officers. He pounded on the door and shouted for Roberts, but heard only silence. He hit the door with a patrolman's baton, making enough noise to wake the dead, but the house remained quiet.

"Perimeter check. You go that way, and I'll go this way. You stay out front." Stillman crept along the house, peering through windows, but saw nothing suspicious. The patrolman went the other way and looked through each window. They rounded the house to the back yard at the same time and advanced on the back door. A quick glance revealed forced entry.

Stillman drew his weapon and motioned for the patrolman to get behind him. He took the patrolman's radio and called the officer in front. "The back door has been forced. We're going in. Stay outside and call it in. Officer in need of assistance. Friendlies inside."

The other officer acknowledged and contacted dispatch. A small army would arrive soon, but Stillman wouldn't wait. He turned down the radio volume and motioned for the officer to follow him inside.

They entered into the kitchen with Stillman sweeping right and the officer sweeping left, making sure not to walk in each other's lines. Nothing seemed amiss, and they advanced into a dining room, also unremarkable. Stillman advanced slowly around a corner into a living room. As his view of the room expanded, he held up his hand to stop. A body lay on the floor.

. . .

On the early shift at the ED, I scrambled to get as much work done as I could before the race started. A five-year-old boy colored a picture on my bandage, while I spoke to his mother.

"Are you sure it's okay for him to color on that, Doctor?"

"No worries. All my pediatric patients have been signing it. Makes it special. Now what other questions do you have?"

"Are you sure the fever won't hurt him?"

"Fever up to 103 degrees is common with strep and nothing to worry about. It might make him feel miserable, but it won't hurt him. We wrote the proper doses for his medicine on your discharge papers. Just follow those directions, and he'll be back to full speed in no time." I turned my attention to the drawing. "What're ya drawing on my head?"

"It's a bunny rabbit playing hockey in space. Do you like it?" the child replied.

"I think it's the best drawing on my whole head. Thanks for doing that. How about we get you a sticker, and you can head home?"

"Okay, can we take the dog with us?"

"Sorry, partner. The dog has to stay here to protect the emergency room. Let's get you going."

• • •

Stillman motioned for the officer to advance from the other side of the living room, and on Stillman's command, they slowly approached with no threats visible. They circled the couch until Stillman had a full view of Detective Roberts' entire body lying unconscious in a pool of blood surrounding his head. "Officer down! Officer down!" He called over the radio, as he rushed to his friend.

"Unlock the front door and let your partner in. Clear the rest of the first floor, and post someone on the steps. Don't go upstairs. Don't touch anything you don't have to. This whole house is a crime scene."

Fearing the worst, he knelt beside Roberts and felt his neck for a pulse, surprisingly strong, and he reached to check on his wrist. Zip ties held his hands bound together to the metal table. Stillman cut the ties with his knife, trying not to touch them to preserve evidence. The fingers were pink with a strong pulse in the wrists.

He gently shook his shoulder. "Can you hear me? It's Stillman." Roberts rewarded him with a groan and a little movement in his arms. "Relax. Help is on the way. Just stay still." He knew better than to move him before the paramedics arrived. A cacophony of sirens approached.

He opened one of Roberts' eyelids to check the pupils, and Roberts frantically blinked and briefly fought him. Most of the bleeding appeared to be from a nasty cut on his forehead. Stillman gently felt around and found no other injuries. He sighed with relief. It looked horrible, but head wounds could bleed a lot.

Stillman held his hand and murmured reassuring words as others arrived. Stillman barked orders. "I need a team to clear the upstairs, but try not to touch anything. I want the entire perimeter of this house secured with no one inside except paramedics and the evidence team. Get some officers knocking on every door for 500 feet in all directions to see if anyone heard or saw anything unusual last night. Get going, and get those paramedics in here."

The paramedics arrived quickly, and Stillman summarized. "This is Detective Roberts. I found him like this with his hands tied to that table. Unknown down time. He's got the nasty head wound, but no other obvious injuries. Good pulses."

"Have you moved him?" The paramedic asked.

"No, but he's been squirming."

The paramedics assessed his airway, breathing, and circulation and found them satisfactory. They placed a neck brace to immobilize his cervical spine and a bandage over his head wound. A paramedic leaned over and pressed his knuckles into Roberts' sternum, grinding them back and forth as he called out his name. "Detective Roberts, open your eyes!"

Roberts jerked, and his eyes flickered open. "That's great Detective. Now squeeze my hand." The paramedic held his hand but Roberts did not respond. He pressed down firmly at the base of Roberts' fingernail and repeated the command. Roberts squeezed his hand.

"That's a positive sign. He's responsive to deep stimuli and can move extremities. Let's get him loaded."

"I need to ask him one question. Can you wake him long enough for one question?" Stillman asked.

"I can try. Head injuries are unpredictable." The paramedic popped open an ammonium ampule. "Ready when you are."

Stillman leaned over. "Roberts, who did this to you?" No response. The paramedic waved the ammonium under his nose, and Roberts stiffened and opened his eyes. "Tell me who did this to you!" Stillman pleaded.

Detective Roberts' eyes focused on him briefly, and he whispered one word before closing them again, "Krug."

CHAPTER THIRTY-ONE

Saturday, 8:53 a.m.

"Heads up, Doc. There's a cop on the way," the charge nurse informed me, as I completed another chart in an endless line.

"Please tell me he didn't get shot."

"Nope. Sounds like he took a good blow to the head, though, stable and five minutes out."

"Okay, put him in Trauma One, and I'll be right there."

The ambulance pulled up, and the paramedics rushed the patient to Trauma One with their succinct report, "Forty-five-year-old male struck in the head. He's got a nasty cut on the forehead, but no other obvious injuries. Loss of consciousness for unknown period of time, but starting to wake up and answer questions appropriately. Moving all extremities. He's a Detective."

They transferred him to the exam bed, and the team hooked up his monitors and IV fluids. I leaned in and gave him a gentle shake. "Detective, can you open your eyes for me?"

He opened his eyes and blearily focused on me.

"That's good. Can you squeeze my hand?" He responded with a firm squeeze. "Very good. Now wiggle those toes for me." He wiggled toes on both feet. "You're doing great. Do you know what day it is?"

"Race day," he murmured.

"Damn straight it is. Most important question, who's gonna win the race?"

He gave a brief smile. "Hamilton."

"I think our patient is fully oriented and just about ready for discharge. Detective, we need to get some X-rays of your neck. If those are clear, we can get that brace off and get you off that board. We need a CT scan of your head to rule out bleeding inside the skull, and we'll get that cut sewn up." I did a detailed exam, including his back. Bloody head wounds require attention, but can distract from other less obvious injuries. It's always embarrassing to focus on stitching a head wound only to discover your patient had also been shot or stabbed in the back.

I stepped out to find a growing crowd of police in the emergency room. Detective Roland came up to me. "How is he?"

"Detective, you know I can't release information about a patient without his permission."

"Go get it. I need to ask him some questions."

"Is it important?"

"We think he may have been attacked by the bomber. That's Detective Roberts, head of the bomb squad."

"No shit. I didn't recognize him with the blood on his face. Wait here, please." I returned to the room and gently shook his shoulder. "Detective Roland has a few questions. You up to it?"

"Yes."

I asked a medical assistant to bring her in, as I cleaned the head wound.

Detective Roland held his hand, "Tim, okay if I record this?" He nodded, and she started the recording with her name, time, and location. "Detective Roberts, can you tell me what happened to you last night?"

He spoke slowly and confidently. "I was asleep in bed and woke up with a gun in my face and a hand over my mouth. Krug was leaning over me and told me to be quiet. He took me into the living room and sat me down on the sofa with his gun pointed at me. He said he noticed the cops following him and recognized one from internal affairs. He wanted to know why,"

"What did you tell him?"

"The truth. They were looking at everyone who has the skills to make the bombs, and he was getting extra attention because of his gambling debts. Krug became agitated and said he needed only one more day to finish."

"To finish what?"

"He didn't say, but clearly, he was talking about the bombings. I asked him why he did it, and he said I wouldn't understand."

"So he didn't deny being the bomber?"

"He didn't admit it, but he didn't deny it. It was pretty clear he was responsible and that it was ending today."

"Any idea what he has planned?"

"No idea."

"Then what happened?"

"He pressed me for more information, but I didn't have anything more to tell him. He was getting increasingly agitated. He seemed to come to a decision and told me he was sorry it had to end this way. I thought I was a goner. He approached with the gun in his left hand, and while I was focused on it, he hit me upside the head with my own baseball bat I keep by the back door. Next thing I knew, I was on the floor, gagged and zip tied to the table with the worst headache of my life."

"Any idea what time this was?"

"No. I was dead asleep when he woke me, and it was dark outside when I went in the living room. I don't even know what time it is now."

"It's just after nine. Get some rest and get your tests done. There'll be an officer outside. If you think of anything else, let him know, and he'll contact me." She turned to me. "Take care of him, Doc, and let me know his test results."

"Happy to do so, as long as the patient gives permission for me to share his information with you."

Roberts cracked a small smile. "You can tell her, Doc, or she'll probably knock you upside your head with my bat."

Roland had Stillman on her phone before she left the room. "He confirmed everything. I'll meet you at Krug's house."

. . .

A secure perimeter surrounded Krug's dark, silent house, and the residences within 500 feet had been evacuated. A SWAT team leader explained their plan.

"Normally I would say we go in hard and fast, but that prick may have booby trapped the place. First thing we need to do is see if anyone is in there. We're gonna stick microphones and cameras on every window. They're sensitive, and if he's in there we should hear him. Thermal sensors haven't detected anything, but those can be beat. Let's see what the microphones reveal."

Fifteen minutes later, the microphones and cameras revealed only silence without motion. The SWAT team agreed the house was empty.

"It's time sensitive we get in there and search the place," Stillman said.

"I'm not sending my guys through any doors or windows of a bomber's house. I suggest we cut a hole in the roof. We can enter the house from above and make sure it's empty, then your guys can clear it for booby traps."

Six SWAT officers climbed onto the roof. In a well-rehearsed maneuver, two officers turned on chainsaws and expertly cut a three-foot square hole in the roof. They dropped into the attic.

"Impressive." Stillman noted.

"They live for this shit." Roland responded.

"What do you think they'll find?"

"If we're lucky, he offed himself and is sitting on the couch with a hole in his head."

"Maybe we'll find a map with a big X on it showing his next target."

"We'll know soon enough."

The search didn't take long. The single story home was only about 2000 square feet with three bedrooms. The SWAT members exited the back door. "Dwelling is secure. No one is home, but there's a device on the front door. We took a picture, but didn't touch anything."

Armond and Bertrand, the remaining members of the bomb squad, looked at the picture and gathered their equipment. Bertrand entered first with their bomb sniffing dog. Slowly and methodically, they worked their way through the house. The dog alerted at the kitchen table where some supplies and debris were left, and at the front door, where an obvious device was attached. No other devices were found, and Armond stepped out the back door.

"The bomb looks rudimentary, like he was in a rush. The rest of the house is clear with some evidence on the kitchen table where he must have assembled the device. Let us disarm the front door, and the house is yours."

In his bomb suit, Armond returned through the back to the inside of the front door with his camera and microphone transmitting to Bertrand. "Are you seeing this? Looks simple."

Bertrand agreed. A small amount of C4 attached to the door frame connected to a wire secured to the door. If the door opened, the wire would open a circuit, allowing a charge to fire the detonator, which would cause the C4 to explode.

"Am I missing something, or is it really that simple?" Armond asked.

"He must have been in a hurry. Let's go over it one more time." They talked through everything again, following each wire from origin to insertion.

"I agree. Cut the wire to the detonator," Bertrand advised.

"Everything's simpler when you're the guy outside. Okay, I'm gonna cut the wire leading to the detonator. Wish me luck."

"Remember our motto."

"I know. 'Bomb squad. We only fuck up once.'" Armond quickly cut the wire and pulled the detonator from the C4, disabling the device. "All clear."

Stillman and Roland relaxed. "Kind of anticlimactic after all that build up," Roland noted.

"I'll take anticlimactic, but I'd be dead before I knew I had made a mistake, anyway," Armond said.

"You guys are wired differently."

"It does take a certain type to excel. The house is yours. We'll get the samples analyzed to confirm they match the others, while you collect the rest of the evidence."

Stillman addressed the evidence collection team. "Tear this place apart. I want to know where Krug is, and we need to know if there are any other devices out there."

CHAPTER THIRTY-TWO

Saturday, 10:27 a.m.

Detective Roberts finished his last sip from a juice box, as I stepped back into his room. "You're looking better," I said.

"I may look better, but I got a helluva headache."

"Understandable. You took a pretty hard hit. Good news is that your CT scan is normal with no evidence of fracture or brain bleed. The front of the skull is the thickest part, and an arch is one of the strongest structures in nature. It's actually a pretty good place to get hit."

"I'll recommend it to all my friends. What's next?"

"Now that we know your brains won't be leaking out, we can close up that wound. This is Little Mac. He's gonna get that wound washed out and all the equipment ready, then I'll be back to sew you up."

"Don't worry. Doc'll make it look pretty. Just relax, and I'll clean this up," Little Mac said.

"Thanks. Call me when you're ready."

• • •

Roland met Stillman back at Krug's house and shared her notes. "He's definitely our guy. Did you discover anything here to help us find him?"

"Not yet. We're going through his files, but nothing has jumped out. His car is in the garage, so he has alternate transportation that we don't know about. I just spoke to the Chief, who's calling a press conference to announce Krug as a suspect and to offer a reward for his arrest."

"Shit. Every junkie in Vegas is gonna call in a tip, hoping to cash in on the reward."

"His passport is flagged, so he can't fly. He's gotta be in a car. Question is whether he left town already, or whether he has unfinished business here. How's Roberts?"

"Nasty bump on the head, but he should be fine in a few days. He got lucky, all things considered. Krug would have been better off killing him."

"It's one thing to blow up a stranger, but killing a coworker in person may be a step too far even for him."

"I still don't get his play. He's never seemed racist, just broke. Why the hell would he blow people up and pretend to be racist? That ain't gonna get him out of debt."

"Maybe it'll make some kind of sense eventually. Let's roll. They'll let us know if they find anything useful. We need to coordinate the search and screen the tips about to come in."

.   .   .

"There you go. That's the last stitch. Number nineteen, if I counted correctly, and it looks pretty damn good. Little Mac is gonna get you bandaged up."

"Thanks, Doc. Can I go home now?"

"How are you feeling?"

"Still a helluva headache, but my brain is starting to function again."

"That's common with a concussion. You have a negative CT scan, and your mental status is improving after four hours, so I'm comfortable with your going home. You've got a significant concussion, though, and need to take it easy, which means strict rest around the house, nothing stressful, no exertion, and absolutely no work."

"Krug is still out there."

"And about a million other people will be looking for him. You are on strict rest, and I want you to see neurology on Monday for a follow up exam in their concussion clinic. Until then, you're off work. I wrote for some pain meds in case you need them, ibuprofen for mild pain and Vicodin for severe pain, just don't mix it with alcohol. Questions?"

"Can I watch the race tonight?"

"Absolutely. Watch for me. I scored a pit lane pass before the race."

"How'd you do that?"

"Easy. You give all your extra money to Mercedes over a ten year period, and they will hook you up with a pass. Get some rest. I'll make sure one of the officers drives you home."

"Thanks, Doc."

A few minutes later, Little Mac pushed him in a wheelchair to a waiting police car. I focused on finishing my charts. Race time quickly approached.

. . .

In his full dress uniform covered with a lifetime of earned ribbons and medals, the Chief addressed the media, including national and international figures in town for the race, the biggest press conference in Las Vegas history.

"Earlier this morning, our Detectives uncovered vital information which led to the identification of a suspect in the bombing case. His house was searched, but the suspect is on the run. We are asking for the public's help in locating Edwin Krug. Sergeant Krug is a member of the Las Vegas police force and should be considered armed and dangerous. Please do not approach or try detain him, but notify law enforcement if you see him."

Every member of the media shouted questions, and the Chief called on a local affiliate for the first one. "Chief, is there any concern that other members of the police force are involved in these bombings?"

"We believe that Sergeant Krug is acting alone."

"Is the Las Vegas police department racist?" the next journalist asked.

The Chief expertly avoided substantive answers, as the questions continued for a few minutes. Finally, the Chief concluded the press conference. "I repeat, he is considered armed and extremely dangerous. Do not attempt to approach or apprehend him. A $100,000 reward has been established for information that directly leads to his arrest. The number to call is on the screen. We will provide updates as they became available."

The Chief left the podium amid further questions hurled at his back. When he was out of sight and earshot, he turned to his deputies. "Find that motherfucker, now! I want his ass in a cell or in the morgue before the race starts." He stormed off, as the Deputies issued orders to their teams. Every officer had been called in to help with the manhunt.

· · ·

Lana had room service ready when I arrived back from my shift. She went with the salmon, and I with my usual grilled cheese and fries. Banshee tore into a chicken breast with gusto. "How was your day?" I asked.

"Frustrating. Between the race and the manhunt, all of my sources are too busy to answer my calls. I assume you heard that Roberts got beat up by Krug last night."

"As a matter of fact, I sewed him up in the ER this morning."

"I don't suppose you overheard anything interesting?"

I wrapped her tightly in my arms. "He laid out the whole story while I was in the room."

She pushed me away. "You better not hold out on me."

I pulled her close again. "Relax. I didn't hear anything that wasn't already mentioned at the Chief's press conference. Besides, you know I can't share patient information."

"I'm not asking for patient information. I'm asking about the case."

"That's a fine line I don't want to cross. Sorry your day was so frustrating."

"It wasn't all bad. Since my sources dried up, I treated myself to a massage at the spa, followed by a manicure." She held up her fingers for approval.

"Any reason you went with the silver and black?"

She kissed me. "Because my man can be superstitious and might think Mercedes will do well tonight because I have their team colors on my nails."

"I knew I made an excellent choice to hang out with you. Let's get ready."

·   ·   ·

At the southern end of the Strip, Mr. Zhang wore his most conservative suit, as he would be representing his country at the race. He added a Rolex, an official sponsor of F1. He would return to his room afterward to change into his evening clothes for a long night of celebration. His companions would not be joining him at the race, but would be ready to go to the parties later. The celebrations would last until dawn, no matter who won the race.

CHAPTER THIRTY-THREE

Saturday, 7:11 p.m.

I leaned into her ear to be heard over the noisy crowd. "What do you think?"

In response, Lana almost shouted to be heard. "I thought these pit passes were exclusive. It seems like everyone in Vegas has one."

The pit lane was extremely crowded. Professional athletes and VIP celebrities were everywhere, accompanied by their entourages. Friends and families of the drivers talked with each other, while the celebrities tried to look important. Media members competed for interviews with the A listers, while the B listers struggled for attention.

"What are we supposed to do?" Lana asked.

"Absorb the atmosphere. Appreciate those incredible machines and the drivers getting their focus amidst all this chaos. It's one of the great racing spectacles of all time."

"It's definitely a spectacle," a clearly unimpressed Lana conceded. "You need some bodyguards like Mr. Zhang over there."

I noticed the crowd part, as the billionaire made his way through the pit lane with four large bodyguards keeping people at a respectable distance. "He paid more for his pit pass than I did. Come on, let's head up to the suite and get settled in before the race."

"Great, I'm looking forward to the air conditioning."

. . .

The call to 911 came in at 7:30, and a heavily modulated voice gave a succinct message.

"I would spew some racist crap, but you know that's bullshit. You know who this is. You know I'm serious. Three devices are hidden downtown, which will be detonated at the end of the race. If you're competent, you'll find them. If not, boom!"

The call was relayed up the chain of command to the anxious Detectives Stillman and Roland. "Dammit. I knew he would do something during the race. What are our options?" Stillman asked.

"Nothing good. There's got to be 300,000 people downtown right now, and our forces are spread thin with the race and the search for Krug. I recommend we pull everybody we can downtown to start searching. If we don't find anything quickly, we'll have to start evacuating the area."

"This is a fucking nightmare. Let's focus on Fremont Street first. It's the most crowded and has the highest profile."

"When do we let the casino owners know?"

"I think we have to tell them immediately. They can help with the search, and they can make their own determinations on when to evacuate."

"You talk to the Chief. I'll get everyone moving."

A system had been designed years ago to alert casinos of potential threats. The first communication about the bomb threat was sent fourteen minutes after its receipt. Each casino had a policy to deal with threats. They were all on heightened alert with the race, but the downtown resorts went to their highest alert level. The casinos on the Strip elevated their alert statuses as well.

. . .

"It's lights out and away we go for the Las Vegas Grand Prix. The Mercedes get away beautifully and lead into turn one, followed closely by LeClerc and Norris. The Redbull dropped two spots and is running fifth," came the call from the announcer. I didn't hear much of it due to the howl of twenty race cars accelerating at the same time. The incredible view from the suite above the paddock featured the race's first turn. Oversized screens showed the progression around the track. The mood elevated in the suite, as Mercedes settled solidly into the first two places.

Ninety seconds later, the lead cars hit the start/finish straight with the Mercedes comfortably in the lead. Only 49 more laps to go.

. . .

Downtown, a quarter of the way through the race, the bomb squad had no luck identifying any devices. Augmented by federal resources, five separate dog teams still frantically searched the most crowded locations for a bomb.

"What are the chances we find the three devices soon?" Stillman asked.

"Not good. We've covered less than five percent of the total area down here. It would take us a full day at least to cover this area," Armond responded.

Stillman got the Chief on the line and shared the update. "What do you think, Chief? Do we evacuate?"

A frustrated Chief waited to reply. "Clear the public areas. Alert the casinos, and let them make their own calls. Let's try to avoid a panic, but move people away from the center of downtown as quickly as possible. I want Fremont Street cleared."

They sent the emergency update to all the casinos, advising of the recommendation to evacuate all public areas. Top personnel at each casino debated options.

Police cars moved along Fremont street and blipped their sirens while announcing over their speakers, "Attention, this area is now closed. Please clear the area immediately."

A confused crowd walked away from the streets, many heading for the nearest casino. Binions and the Golden Nugget chose to remain open, while Four Queens, Circa, and the Fremont Hotel decided to close their doors. People already in the casinos were unaware of the closures outside. Confusion grew as people struggled to leave and enter the casinos at the same time. Combined with a lot of alcohol and a significant amount of drugs, tensions rose quickly. Two drunk race fans outside the Golden Nugget threw the first punches. Chaos and panic spread quickly.

.   .   .

Lana monitored the chaos in real time on her phone. She tapped me on my shoulder. "Something strange is going on downtown. They're starting to evacuate."

"Something strange is always going on downtown. Enjoy the race, only twenty laps left," I advised, riveted by the action.

Lana ignored me and headed for the back of the suite to make some phone calls. Soon, she had her notebook out, hurriedly scribbling notes, as she alternated between calls and checking her phone for messages.

CHAPTER THIRTY-FOUR

Saturday, 9:24 p.m.

A panel truck, painted black with "Las Vegas Bomb Squad" stenciled on the side, held seven men dressed in full tactical gear, including visored helmets and vests identifying them as bomb squad members. The truck approached Mandalay Bay at the southern end of the Strip and entered the lower level ramp that granted VIP private access to the casino. At a discreet drive camouflaged by plants, the truck turned right and pulled up to a metal gate. The driver punched in a six-digit security code, and the gate rose to welcome them to an underground garage filled with security vehicles and the private cars of casino executives. In a utilitarian space rarely viewed by the public, they approached an unmarked door with no handle on the outside.

A passenger approached the door and pressed the intercom. "Bomb squad. We just got a tip and need to speak with your head of security immediately."

"Authorization code?" The intercom responded.

"Delta. Tango. Five. Charlie. Mike. Three. Seven."

"Confirmed. One moment."

The door buzzed, opened by an armed security guard. All seven members of the team entered in full gear, following the guard down a hallway to the security control room. A second armed man guarded the door and badged the heavy metal door open as they approached.

The team filed in, greeted by a balding man in an impeccable blue suit. "I'm Anthony Rigetti, head of security for Mandalay Bay. What's this all about? Is there a bomb threat to the hotel?"

The lead officer removed his helmet and held a pistol to Anthony's head. "Just the man we're looking for. The good news is there's no bomb threat. The bad news is you're about to get robbed."

The security chief looked on incredulously, as his men were swiftly disarmed and restrained by the remaining members of the bomb crew. "Wait a minute. You're that guy who's been on tv."

The bomber smiled. "That's me. Tim Roberts, head of the bomb squad. Now, let's talk about that vault."

CHAPTER THIRTY-FIVE

Friday, October 20
5:38 p.m. (28 hours earlier)

"Let's call it a day. Keep those phones on in case anything happens, and take it easy tonight. I want everyone rested for tomorrow. We got a big day with the race. It's a perfect opportunity for this guy to cause some chaos. Everyone back tomorrow at 8 a.m. sharp," Roberts said.

A chorus of "yes, sirs" rang around the team as they packed up their gear.

Roberts subtly motioned for Krug to wait behind the others. After the last man left, Roberts motioned for him to have a seat. "We've got a problem. Internal Affairs is watching us."

"What the fuck are those guys looking at us for?" Krug asked.

"It seems that due to the sophistication of the bombs, they think one of us may be the bomber."

"That's bullshit, man."

"I know. I don't like it, either. Unfortunately, while looking at us, they looked at our finances and some worrying issues came up with you."

Krug stood and paced. "Aw, shit, man. It's just a run of bad luck. Just because I lost some bets doesn't mean I'm the bomber."

"I agree, but to prove your innocence, we need to find the actual bomber."

"How are we supposed to do that?"

"I've got a plan, but I need your help. One of my informants says he has a solid lead, including a sample of the C4. He wants to meet tonight, but he won't go anywhere near headquarters. I'm meeting him at eleven, but I want someone watching my back in case he brings friends. You in?"

"Hell, yes. Tell me where to meet you."

"It's a little more complicated. IA is following you and has your phone bugged."

"Fuck those guys."

"I know, but we can get around it. They have only one unit watching your front door and garage tonight. You can easily sneak out the back. Act normal, like you're going to bed, and turn the lights off at about 10:15. Dress in dark clothes, leave your phone, go out the back, and meet me over at Ridge Park and Independence. Bring your gun in case it gets messy. Hopefully this guy will have the goods, and we can tie this thing up tomorrow."

"Okay. I can do that."

"No funny stuff. Don't go looking over your shoulders for followers."

"I get it, but when this is done, some people are gonna owe me an apology."

"Truer words were never spoken."

. . .

Roberts waited anxiously in his car and sighed with relief, as Krug came around the corner right on time. He looked casual, as he strolled down the street, quickly opened the door and climbed in.

"Any problems?" Roberts asked.

"Nope. They never saw a thing. Who're we meeting tonight?"

"Guy goes by Squirrel, which is appropriate given his occupation. He's a thief and a con man and runs in lots of circles. He trades information for get-out-of-jail free cards."

"Is he violent?"

"No, but he's street smart. He'll probably have someone watching his back, which is why I need you watching mine."

"Where's the meet?"

"Out near Whitney. It's an old abandoned gas station that's now a junk yard and crack house."

"Sounds pleasant."

"It should be fine. We'll be in and out real quick. Squirrel doesn't want to be seen with me anymore than I want to be around him."

They drove in silence the rest of the way, the neighborhoods becoming darker and grimier as they progressed, revealing a side of Vegas that the tourism teams never shared with the public. They arrived at the gas station and pulled around back. A dilapidated fence refusing to submit to gravity provided some measure of privacy from the streets. Piles of discarded debris lined the perimeter.

They exited the car and surveyed the area. "Where you want me, boss?"

Roberts pointed to the darkest corner. "Lets set you up there. It's dark enough where no one will see you, but you should have good sight lines of the whole area."

Krug led the way to the back corner. He never felt Roberts' bullet that entered his brain. The .22 caliber slug packed enough power to penetrate the base of his skull, but not enough to punch through his face. The bullet ricocheted inside his skull, destroying every vital structure. Although catastrophic, the fatal injury displayed surprisingly little external evidence. A small hole at the base of his skull leaked a minimal amount of blood, and despite his instant death, he looked as if he merely slept.

Roberts felt surprisingly little emotion. A gambling addict, Krug had dug himself into a hole way too deep ever to climb out. Eventually, he would owe money to the wrong people, or he would resort to illegal activities to pay for his habit. Although gruesome, the quick death supplied by the bullet to the base of his skull was probably the least stressful ending to his story that Krug could expect.

Roberts scanned the area for anyone who may have alerted to the sound of the gunshot, suppressed, but not silent. He counted on the low, quick burst being dismissed by anyone who may have heard it. After sixty seconds of silence, he felt confident that his presence remained unnoticed.

No prints on the gun, suppressor, or bullets would offer evidence against him. He had handled it only while wearing gloves. The untraceable parts had been seized from a crime scene two years before. The serial number would confirm the weapon as previously stolen. With no way to trace it back to him, he laid the gun on Krug's back.

Roberts hurried to the car, changed his gloves, and removed a small bomb from the trunk. He brought it over to the corpse and ran Krug's hands over it to transfer his prints. He carefully sealed it in a bag and set it aside. He found Krug's keys in his pocket and placed them in his own. He left his wallet in place.

He lifted a car hood to reveal a small space that he had cleared out earlier in the week. He grunted as he struggled to force Krug's body into the space, throwing the fallen gun on top of him. After replacing the car hood over Krug's crude grave, he swept the ground with his foot to erase evidence of dragging the body. Roberts glanced at his watch and noted that it had taken less than seven minutes to kill Krug and temporarily dispose of his body. He had a lot to do tonight, but he was on schedule.

He drove normally, headed to his warehouse in south Las Vegas. He had rented the 6000 sf building two months ago with a fake ID and a disguise. The owner had been happy to do a cash deal off the books for a one-year lease, and no paperwork on the lease existed. Most importantly, no security cameras pointed at the building or to any of the surrounding streets. Roberts opened the garage door and pulled in.

The interior consisted of one big open space with a single bathroom and office in the back corner. Roberts donned a fresh pair of gloves. He had never been in the building without gloves. He turned on the lights and reevaluated the eight vehicles filling the space, a box truck painted as a replica of the bomb squad truck and seven yellow cabs that had seen better days. He had bought them over the last few months with cash while *wearing a disguise, and none of the vehicles were registered. Stolen license plates adorned their dented bumpers.*

He carefully removed all of his current clothing and placed it in a bag. Although Krug's wound had been fairly clean, microscopic spray could have landed on his clothing. Roberts dressed in clean clothes and placed the bag in the truck for later disposal. He double checked readiness for the next day. Satisfied, he locked up and left.

He drove to within a block of Krug's house and parked his car in a dark area near a house for sale. He stepped out of the car dressed in his dark clothes with a backpack slung over his shoulder. He walked casually to the alley behind Krug's house and quickly entered using Krug's key. He opened the backpack and used his night vision goggles to avoid turning on any lights. He set the bomb on the table along with the tools and supplies used to assemble it, then walked the bomb to the front door, where he placed the device. He left silently, locking the door behind him. He dropped the keys and his gloves into separate drains on the way to his car.

He sat in the driver's seat and mentally checked off the tasks he had carefully planned for the night. Satisfied that he had completed everything, he drove home for one final task.

. . .

He took a long swig of whiskey, as he prepared for his final act of the evening. Like many cops, he kept a baseball bat by his back door for security. Normally, he loved the feel of the bat in his hand. He had owned this one for over thirty years, since his high school days. It held sentimental value, and today, it would play a major role in his deception.

The first step was to make it look like a break in. He stepped out back and locked the door, then put his shoulder into it. It took three progressively violent hits before the lock gave way, and the door swung open. He left it ajar, an obvious forced entry.

He changed into the boxers and t-shirt that he normally wore to bed and made sure everything was put away. He sat on the living room floor with the bat at his side. Taking a deep breath, he tied a gag around his mouth. He picked up the heavy duty zip ties and secured one around his left wrist. The other one he left dangling for the moment.

He dreaded this necessary part of his plan, and had mentally practiced it for hours. The hit had to be hard enough to be convincing, but not hard enough to do any real damage. He finally decided on a strategy of blindfolding himself first, and then moving his head forward as he brought the bat back toward his head. He took a few deep breaths and some practice motions. Finally, with a muffled roar, he threw his head forward and the bat backward at the same time.

His roar quickly escalated to a scream, as the bat connected with his skull. Pain exploded and lights flashed in his eyes despite the blindfold. Blood poured from his head and soaked his blindfold, as dizziness led him to fall to his side. He reached blindly for the heavy coffee table and slid his hands in the heavy metal opening of one of the table legs, fumbled for the zip tie, and managed to secure his right hand in the remaining tie. He collapsed on the floor and passed out, wondering if he had hit his head too hard.

· · ·

He awoke an unknown time later, the pain in his head overwhelming the increasing soreness in his body from his lying awkwardly positioned on the floor. Relieved to be alive, he hoped he would be found soon. He needed to stay on schedule. The fog in his mind slowly dissipated, and he reviewed everything that needed to happen for his plan to work.

Finally, he heard the knock on the door and people calling his name. He relaxed into stillness and pretended to be passed out. After no answer, he heard muffled voices at the door, then silence. He assumed they were checking the perimeter, verified, as he heard people enter through the broken back door. Deadly still, he waited.

He recognized Stillman's voice and followed along as they cleared the house. Finally, Stillman came to his side, removed the gag and blindfold, and tried to wake him. Roberts played the helpless victim, but gave a small, genuine cry when his eyes were exposed to the light after being blindfolded for so long. Stillman gently shook him and asked the question Roberts knew was coming.

"Who did this to you?"

Roberts held back a smile, as he muttered, "Krug."

Roberts progressively perked up during his brief hospital stay and was relieved to find that he had not seriously damaged himself with the baseball bat. It genuinely hurt, and he had a concussion, but he was functional. By discharge, he felt well enough to go home, but hurt enough to require prolonged rest. With the pain meds, he would be expected to sleep all night. His perfect alibi solidified.

· · ·

Roberts assured the officer who drove him home that he was fine and entered his house. Crime scene had finished their collection of evidence. A large blood stain remained on the living room carpet, but someone had already repaired his back door. You can always count on cops to take care of their own. Roberts laughed to himself, as he imagined what they would think if they actually knew everything.

Roberts looked in the mirror as his shower warmed up. The stitch work was good, but would leave an ugly scar on his forehead, all the better to remind everyone that he was a victim in all of this. The bruising was significant and at least one black eye was in his future. All in all, the perfect injury.

He showered, slid into his sheets, and set his alarm for two hours later.

· · ·

He awoke at five o'clock and reheated some spaghetti. He threw two of his Vicodins down the disposal. He didn't think anyone would check, but he wanted to be thorough. He left his phone at home, but had message forwarding set up to a burner in his pocket. GPS on his main phone would show him at home all night, but he would know if anyone tried to reach him.

He pulled on a baseball hat and locked his house, leaving through the back door. Walking casually, he travelled two blocks to a residential parking area for motorcycles. Anyone was free to leave a motorcycle in the slots, and a majority were always occupied. His ten-year-old bike attracted no notice, unused for a week, after its purchase for cash from Craig's list. This would be only the second time he had ridden the bike.

He rode it to the warehouse and nodded to his assembled team. Like him, they had arrived on untraceable motorcycles that would soon be abandoned. Palpable excitement electrified the air as they prepared for the evening. The plan had been in the works for months and was about to pay off.

Timmy Lemkins, a sociopathic leader of the six men and a disgraced ex-cop, had been kicked off the Las Vegas police force after multiple excessive use of force charges. He had expensive drug and gambling habits and no qualms about how he earned money to support those habits. His steroid infused mind and body made him the perfect pawn in Roberts' game.

"What the fuck happened to your face?" Timmy asked.

"Don't worry about it. It's all part of the plan."

"I feel like I don't know the whole plan."

Roberts squared off, "All you need to know is if you and your men follow the plan, each of you will have about three million dollars in the next hour. We good?"

"We're good, for now, but if you fuck us over, I'll bury you myself."

"I have no doubt. Load up. I have one more thing to do."

Roberts pulled another burner phone from his pocket and made the 911 call about the three bombs downtown.

The team loaded their gear and reviewed the plan and contingencies one more time, as Roberts monitored the police scanner. When the call to evacuate downtown went out, he ordered his team to load up for the twelve minute drive to Mandalay Bay. By the time they arrived in the security center, chaos and gridlock overwhelmed the downtown area.

CHAPTER THIRTY-SIX

Saturday, 9:37 p.m.

Roberts put his arm around Rigetti's shoulders, as his men quickly zip tied and gagged the other workers. "Mr. Rigetti, we want in that vault, and you are one of three people who can access it. We're on a tight schedule and want you to open that vault without raising any alarms. Can you do that for me?"

"Fuck you!"

"Maybe this will change your mind." Roberts held up an iPad and shared the image. "You may recognize these folks. Looks like your wife is reading night time stories to your two children. I think the girl is five and the boy is three, right? You should know that next to that camera is a block of C4 strong enough to blow up your family into little tiny pieces. So unless you want their caskets to be filled with plastic bags, I suggest you cooperate. Now, are you ready to open the vault?"

A visibly shaken Rigetti nodded. "Good. Before we go, I need you to log into the computer here, so my associate can update your security system."

Rigetti sat in the chair, entered his password, and confirmed log in with a retinal scan. One of Roberts' thugs sat next to him and took over the keyboard to upload a program to erase recorded images of the last several minutes. Another member of the team guarded the restrained employees. The remaining thieves gathered behind Rigetti and Roberts. "Remember, no drama, or the family explodes. Walk nice and calmly to the vault, and we'll be gone in ten minutes. Relax, it's not your money."

Rigetti and the fake bomb squad members exited the control room and turned right down a hallway. At the elevator, Rigetti punched in a code and again scanned his eye. The team entered the elevator and rode to the bottom floor, exiting into a lobby containing the vault door and two armed guards.

Roberts advanced toward the vault. "Bomb squad. We believe there may be an explosive device in the vault, and Mr. Rigetti is here to open it." Neither guard noticed the tasers that stunned them. They dropped and were quickly zip tied and gagged.

Roberts turned the iPad to Rigetti. "You have thirty seconds to get this door open, or the family is going to be spread over the lawn." He tapped a button, and a thirty-second countdown began. Rigetti approached the door and placed his palm on the reader and his eye in front of the scanner. When they both clicked green, he carefully entered twelve digits on the keypad, which also turned green. The locks disengaged with a clank.

Roberts stopped the countdown. "Impressive, you still had six seconds to spare." Roberts spun the wheel and pulled on the massive, steel door with titanium plates inside, and swung it easily and silently open. Roberts and his team crowded forward and stared at the open vault.

• • •

Downtown, the ten block area surrounding Fremont street had degenerated into total chaos. Word of potential bombs had sparked panic, as the crowd moved senselessly in all directions to avoid an unidentified threat. Casinos across town moved security personnel to the main floors to protect their assets.

A few troublemakers, fueled by alcohol, used the opportunity to cause more chaos. Fights broke out among strangers who jostled each other, and other strangers joined in just to taste the violence. Within fifteen minutes of initial efforts to clear the area, an orderly and profitable evening for the casinos had turned into a security nightmare.

The police were flooded with 911 calls, and units on sight worked to separate combatants. Internal police radios were overwhelmed with calls for assistance. The Chief reluctantly ordered all remaining personnel downtown in riot gear to restore order and to reroute traffic approaching downtown. The race was ending soon, and no one needed a few hundred thousand more people downtown.

.   .   .

With five laps to go, Hamilton held a comfortable six-second lead over his Mercedes teammate, George Russell, who closely battled for second with Charles LeClerc. Separated by less than a second, they exchanged positions on almost every lap, as the race neared the end. I was completely mesmerized.

Lana, engrossed as well, but with the drama unfolding downtown, played her police scanner app, as she scanned social media for the latest details. All of the media was at the race, and the only word coming out of downtown was from social media. Videos and reports of violence flooded Twitter, Instagram, and Facebook. Lana documented everything she could find for her developing story.

.   .   .

Sturdy, steel, tall shelves lined the perimeter of the square, thirty-foot vault with a two story ceiling. The left wall contained chips of different denominations, from one dollar to $250,000. The back and right walls organized cash and coins, neatly packed in shrink wrap.

"Where're the hundreds?" Roberts asked.

Rigetti pointed to the back wall, and three of the team members advanced on the wall, opening their canvas bags. The fourth zip tied Rigetti, then dragged the two guards into the vault. Roberts strolled around the vault, scanning its contents.

The team transferred stacks of hundreds into their bags. The bills, wrapped in groups of $10,000, each contained a hundred new bills. A million dollars consisted of a stack of 10,000 hundred dollar bills, weighed about twenty-two pounds, and measured forty-three inches high. Neatly stacked, each bag could hold about $3.5 million in cash, and they had brought eight bags, hoping to carry at least $25 million out of the vault.

While the men stuffed the bags and joked with each other, Roberts searched until he finally found four leather briefcases embroidered with the seal of China on a bottom shelf on the left side. They had no locks, as no one would dare to touch jewels belonging to an important representative of the Chinese government.

Roberts opened the first case to see beautifully displayed necklaces of diamonds, emeralds, and other jewels. He emptied the jewelry into his backpack and opened the next case, which contained rings, bracelets and earrings. He greedily dumped those into his bag as well. The next case contained watches, thirty-seven added to his growing stash.

The final case contained small velvet bags, each weighing about a pound. He opened one, dazzled by the glitter of diamonds. Mr. Zhang, notorious for impulsive purchases of expensive items like jewelry and cars, was rumored to travel with diamonds that he used as payment to avoid paperwork and taxes. Roberts smiled, as he imagined the amount of wealth in this one case.

Ten little bags went into his backpack. He stood up and urged the men to finish. None were even aware that he had loaded his own backpack.

When the last bag was filled with cash, one of the men reached for the $100,000 chips. Roberts batted his hand away. "Those things have microchips in them. They can trace them. We take only the cash and get out. You ready?"

Each adrenaline-fueled man lifted two bags weighing seventy-five pounds apiece and carried them to the vault lobby. Roberts looked regretfully at all the money they were leaving behind, but all the cash was simply too heavy and bulky to carry.

Rigetti and the guards anxiously appraised him, as he stepped to the vault door. Roberts shrugged and said matter-of-factly, "Sorry, this is the way it has to be. For what it's worth, your family is safe." Then he pulled the pin on three grenades, threw them into the vault, and closed the door. After three muted bursts, Roberts swept away thoughts of what the inside of the vault now looked like, as they boarded the elevator.

At the control room, their hacker confirmed that he had disabled the cameras and erased any images back to the time of their arrival, including the cloud images. No images of their arrival or departure would exist. Roberts nodded to Lemkins, and his eyes lit up, as he pulled his pistol, attached the suppressor and advanced on the ten frightened employees. He methodically shot each one three times, twice in the chest and once in the head. When one tried to roll over, he calmly rolled him on his back and shot him in the chest. He calmly reloaded his Glock after the fifteenth shot. Roberts shuddered as he watched the psychopath's killing spree. When he was done, he casually threw the gun on the top of the pile.

The men put on their helmets and marched to their truck. They loaded the eight bags in back and quickly drove away. They had been at the hotel for a total of sixteen minutes.

·   ·   ·

"Lewis Hamilton takes the checkered flag for the 110th time in his career. The battle for second will come down to the last turn, but it's Russell edging out LeClerc for the final two podium positions. What a race! Thank you Las Vegas for an unforgettable night!" the announcer said.

I stood and cheered along with the others in our suite and with a few hundred thousand people who lined the course. The cheering sang through the drivers' cool down lap, then crescendoed, as they pulled into pit lane and climbed from their cars.

I turned to Lana, still seated in the back of the room, scribbling hurriedly in her notebook. "You missed a great finish," I said.

"I absorbed the emotion through all the testosterone permeating the room. Take a look at this. Downtown looks like a war zone."

She turned her phone to me and showed videos of crowds streaming through the streets, occasional fights, and the inevitable vandalism of at least one police car. "It looks like the LA riots from years ago," I noted.

"Not that bad yet, but the cops are getting ready to enter in full riot gear. They've locked down all the streets between here and downtown to prevent anyone else from entering the area. It's complete anarchy."

"Any bombs go off?"

"Nothing on the scanner yet."

"We need to get you back to the hotel, and I need to get to the ER."

"I thought you were off tonight."

"I am, but they're about to get inundated with injuries, even worse if the bombs go off."

"Can we make it to the hotel?"

"There're about a quarter million people between us and the Bellagio, but we can make it. You need to sit tight in the hotel tonight. Streets aren't going to be safe."

"What about you?"

"I'll have Banshee."

· · ·

Unlike downtown and along the strip, traffic still moved south of the hotel. After an uneventful return drive, they hid the truck back inside the warehouse. The trip had taken only sixteen minutes, and the police scanner indicated no knowledge of their heist.

"Make it fast. All your gear comes off and goes in the truck. Keep your gloves on. Everyone grab one bag. Let's go," Roberts ordered. They joked as they changed and argued over which bag contained the most money. Eventually, the six men were in regular clothes with a bag at their feet.

"Let me stress this to you one more time. You lay low. No flashy purchases. No drunken stories. Don't go partying. My guy will contact each of you in a month to help you launder the money. Each of you has over $3 million in cash. You don't get to spend it if you get caught. If anyone does get caught, stay silent and take the rap. Anyone talks, and everyone they have ever loved will be dead, and I'll find a way to make your death last as long as possible. Each of you has a cab to drive. No one will notice you. We leave one at a time, and you travel to your designated area and switch to your secondary vehicle. The cabs are clean. Leave the windows down and the keys in the ignition. With any luck they'll be stolen by morning. Car number one get going."

CHAPTER THIRTY-SEVEN

Saturday, 10:14 p.m.

Tina Wright had joined security at Mandalay Bay four months earlier after a seven-year stint in the army. Centered on helping tipsy guests to their rooms safely, the relaxed pace of her work made for a refreshing change from her time in the army, particularly the two years she had spent in Afghanistan. Experience in theater had taught her to recognize potential trouble. Perpetually alert to her surroundings, Tina mitigated problems before they became bigger ones, which was why she was the first officer to suspect an issue.

"Why the hell aren't they answering?" she asked her partner, Johnny Lanier, who tended to behave as her exact opposite. A former collegiate athlete, he outweighed her by a good 150 pounds. While he had a size advantage, he had a deficit of motivation. Johnny liked to do the bare minimum to get by on his shift. While his bulk could be useful to intimidate people, most of the time, he only occupied space.

"Don't know. Don't care," Johnny replied. His catchphrase could be his epitaph. "Here lies Johnny. He didn't know, and he didn't care."

Tina clenched her fists in frustration. "They should be answering. I'm gonna check on them."

Johnny shrugged and turned his glazed expression back to the crowd on the casino floor. Tina raged inside at his indifference, which in her experience, got people killed. She left him and marched to an unmarked door at the periphery of the casino. Her badge accessed the secure corridor, and she sped to the security center. She rounded the last corner and halted.

The unguarded security center door alarmed her. She reached futilely for a sidearm that was not there. Security personnel did not routinely carry guns in the casino, a sacrifice for her. A 9 mm had been her constant companion in the army. She approached the door and found it locked. Her badge did not allow access to the room, so she knocked. With no response, she banged louder and called out, but was met with silence.

She clicked on her radio. "Wright calling for floor supervisor."

"Go for supervisor."

"Sir, I'm at the security center, and no guard is outside, and no one is responding to my knock on the door."

"On my way."

Tina paced impotently, as she waited for the supervisor. Several members of security, alerted by her radio call, arrived. Nick Pasterno, the night supervisor and a competent leader, pushed his way to the door.

He badged the door and made it one step into the room before he exclaimed, "Oh, fuck!"

Tina peered around him to see dead bodies piled in the corner. Again, she reached for her nonexistent gun, as she scanned the room for threats. Seeing none, she quickly advanced to help any survivors. Like all army personnel in active war zones, she knew basic first aid and that immediate medical attention increased the odds of survival. She realized that no amount of medical technology could help. All had been professionally assassinated.

Pasterno regained control and ordered his officers to access the security videos to see what had happened and to issue firearms to all qualified officers. The security center supplied a small armory, and Tina quickly acquired a 9 mm Glock.

Pasterno kept trying to reach Rigetti and ordered officers to search the entire casino for him. "Sir, Rigetti has access to the vault, doesn't he?" Tina asked.

"Shit. Pull up a camera of the vault," Pasterno ordered.

An officer clicked on different images, then pulled up a camera from the vault, and put it on the big screen. Everyone leaned closer to comprehend what they were seeing. The blurry image showed dust and debris floating in front of the camera lens. The shelves were intact, but towered over a deep pile of debris scattered across the floor.

"Sir, I'm afraid we might have found Rigetti," Tina pointed at an object in the bottom corner of the frame. "If I'm not mistaken, that's an arm." The implications set off a series of gasps from the assembled officers, and one vomited violently into a trash can.

"Holy fucking shit," Pasterno sighed. He called 911, then the Casino owners.

. . .

Roberts sent each cab out of the warehouse at one-minute intervals. Each had a different planned route and dispersed nicely. Roberts looked at the two remaining bags of seven million dollars in cash. It would be a shame to leave it, but fresh from the central bank, the serial numbers were sequential. The missing serial numbers would be in the system by morning, and any attempt to use them would be flagged. The cash was useless, as were the morons driving away in the cabs. He had needed them, but he knew they would fail to lay low and keep their mouths shut, an intolerable risk.

He pulled a burner phone from his pocket and texted "boom" to six different phones.

Timmy Lemkins, in his cab on the Bruce Woodbury Beltway headed for Summerlin, where he would change out his vehicle, clutched a stack of $100 bills that he kissed, as he sang loudly and poorly to a country western song on the radio. He mentally replayed the excitement of the robbery and killings, when the text message arrived to the device hidden under his seat. Roberts' bomb detonated perfectly. One moment Timmy sang about a dog retrieving a beer, and the next, he ceased to exist.

The explosive force blasted the roof off of the cab, and Timmy's body shot upward in a thousand tiny pieces. His head remained largely intact, thrown two hundred feet from the blast. While many of the bills disintegrated, many rained on the scene. An Uber driver caught the explosion on a dash camera three cars back and quickly went viral.

Across Las Vegas, the other five cars similarly exploded, leaving unidentifiable drivers and cash confetti. Traffic halted, as people stopped to rubber neck and to collect the money raining from the sky. Videos from each scene were uploaded to social media, creating more chaos in the city. The overwhelmed 911 system could offer only delayed help for bystanders injured in the blasts.

Roberts smiled, as he listened to his police scanner. Moments later, the robbery and murders at Mandalay Bay dominated the conversations over the scanner. With the evacuation downtown, the end of the race, the exploding cars, and the violence at Mandalay Bay, chaos ruled Vegas and crippled transportation. Roberts had one more scheme to add to the confusion.

· · ·

Lana and I weaved through the multitude to the Bellagio. The emotional crowd, already hyped from the race, learned about the problems downtown, as they checked their phones, and anxiety brewed.

Banshee greeted me with a kiss, as I entered the room. "That's a good boy. Did you enjoy the race?"

He thumped his tail vigorously.

"Well, get ready. We have another adventure tonight."

"Do you think it's a good idea to go back out there?" Lana asked.

"Not really, but the ER is probably already overrun. I would sure appreciate the extra help if I were working." I loaded my backpack with clean scrubs and my stethoscope and badge. I threw in an expandable baton, since the hospital had banned guns.

"Expecting trouble?" Lana asked.

"Always. That way, I'm not surprised and unprepared. What are you gonna do?"

"Stay here and build a cohesive story from this chaos." She paused, as her scanner lit up again with frantic calls. "New plan. I'm headed to Mandalay Bay."

"What's happening at Mandalay?" I asked, as I tied my running shoes and reached for Banshee's vest.

"Sounds like a group robbed the casino and killed a bunch of people," she said, as she rushed to gather her things.

"That's fucking brilliant."

"What?"

"This whole thing was about a robbery. He built up the tension to divert the police downtown during the race and then hit the casino at the other end of the Strip, sure that the cops would be preoccupied and unable to respond quickly. Krug's smart. Ruthless, but smart."

"You really think Krug created this entire mess to rob the casino?"

"Think about it. He knows how to build bombs and had access to the material. He needed the money badly. He knew exactly how the police would react. You don't just waltz in and rob a Vegas casino, but it's a hell of a lot easier if downtown is rioting, and the Strip is paralyzed by the race. Love you. Be careful out there."

I gave her a quick kiss and led Banshee. With over three miles to the hospital, the roads were shut down, but Banshee and I could jog there in less than thirty minutes.

·   ·   ·

Police headquarters had the emergency operations center fully staffed. Information evolved rapidly, but coalesced into a coherent picture.

"Let's break this down into workable sections. What is happening downtown?" the Chief clarified.

A deputy chief summarized. "No reports of explosions downtown. Units on sight are controlling the streets, and the casinos report only mild disturbances at this time."

"Does everyone agree the threats downtown were just a diversion?"

A series of nods and "yes, sir" came from the force.

"Okay. Put out a message to the casinos that bomb threats were likely a diversion and that no further danger is expected. Open the roads to allow normal activity downtown. Maintain a heavy presence, but we have to allow those race fans to get back to their hotels. Someone get the word out on social media that downtown is safe and that the threat is neutralized."

"Sir, that could bite us in the ass if a bomb explodes over there," one of his deputies warned.

"So noted. For the record, it's my call. This old ass has been bitten many times. Right now, the panic is causing more damage to more people than the bomber has. What's the injury tally?"

"Unknown. Lots of fights and falls, so the ER's will get hammered with cuts and broken bones. We have one report of a heart attack and another of a woman who went into labor early. We're moving them to hospitals as quickly as we can."

"Okay. How is the Strip?"

"Relatively good. We still have an overflow of people, and we expect the partying to last until dawn, but no unusual activity."

"Not sure of the last time someone reported that the Strip was the least chaotic part of Vegas," the Chief observed to some mild laughter. "What's the latest on Mandalay?"

"Not good, sir. The entire team of ten in their security center was bound, gagged and professionally executed with two in the chest and one in the head. Someone hacked into their system and erased all cameras around the time of the robbery. The system works fine, now, but we have no images from the time in question. Mandalay is working on it, but they're not hopeful that they can recover the images."

"And the vault?"

"A camera still works in the vault and shows evidence of an explosion and of at least one body in there. We assume it's their security chief, as no one has been able to find him, and he is one of three people with access to the vault."

"How soon can we get that door open?"

"Should be soon. The casino owner is on his way back to the hotel from the race."

"Are we sure it's a robbery?"

"We have early reports that a bomb squad vehicle and officers were on site at the time of the incident. None of our officers were anywhere near Mandalay at the time. There are also unconfirmed reports of officers leaving the building with large duffel bags."

"Could Krug have done this?"

"He knows our procedures and how to access the casinos. All of our bomb guys do. He could do it."

"Are Roland and Stillman on site?"

"Yes, sir. They arrived within the last few minutes."

"And the casino is continuing with normal operations?"

"Yes, sir. Fortunately, the violence was contained in the secure area of the building. We took over the VIP entrance and garage and have locked down that part of the building. Mandalay is working with their sister casinos to move cash and chips in if needed."

The Chief rubbed his eyes, as he leaned back in his chair. "Anything else happening we need to know about?"

"A few cars are burning around town, likely part of the celebration. The fire department is handling those."

"All right, people. Let's focus on restoring order to downtown, dispersing the race crowds safely, and focusing on Mandalay. We need to know what was taken, and we need Krug in custody. Let's go."

CHAPTER THIRTY-EIGHT

Saturday, 10:22 p.m.

Roberts walked away with his backpack full of jewels. The panel truck in his warehouse held everything else related to the robbery. Two blocks away, he texted another burner phone, and three thermite grenades exploded in the truck housed in the warehouse. They burned at over five thousand degrees, incinerating the truck and its contents.

Only a surprisingly quiet "whump" confirmed that the grenades exploded. He waited for a full minute to allow the truck to be reduced to a slag of molten metal and sent his last text of the night. The remaining C4 placed throughout the warehouse detonated with a roar and lit the night sky.

Roberts smiled as he eyed the truck he had parked in an industrial lot nearby. Wearing gloves, he drove it to within five blocks of his home and left it in a strip mall with the windows down and the keys in the ignition, likely to be stolen by the morning. Roberts whistled quietly to himself, as he walked home, not even noticing the weight of the backpack.

. . .

Forced to use side streets far to the west to bypass the race traffic, Roland and Stillman finally arrived at the Mandalay Bay entrance after a frustrating journey from downtown. Nick Pasterno met them outside the security center. "I'm acting security chief at the moment. We believe Rigetti is among the dead," he explained.

"What do we have?" Roland asked as they pulled on gloves and booties.

"Nothing good." Nick led the way into the security center, where three men worked at computers.

"What are they doing?" Stillman asked.

"One of them is transferring security systems to our back-up site. He should be done in a few minutes. The other two are trying to figure out what their guy did to our systems. Right now, all of the images are irretrievably erased."

"They can stay, but only at their stations. No one else enters until crime scene has cleared the area, and I don't need to tell you that is gonna take a while," Stillman said, as he shuddered at the pile of bodies and blood in the corner of the room. "Nothing else we can do here. When can we access the vault?"

"Mr. Hedenfeld should be here any moment."

Charles Hedenfeld III, the most successful of the Hedenfelds, made his first billion by the age of forty. Now sixty-three, his empire had grown to over fifteen billion dollars. Mandalay Bay was a prized possession.

At the vault elevator, they donned fresh booties and gloves before entering. The vault lobby appeared unremarkable with no obvious damage.

"Two armed guards are always stationed here. The men on shift at the time of the robbery are missing and presumed to be in the vault."

"How exactly is the vault accessed?" Stillman asked.

"It's protected by a retinal scan, palm print, and digital code. The retinal scan and palm print scan for body temperature and pulse, so the TV trick of severing the hand or eye won't work."

"Who has access?"

"Only Mr. Rigetti, our security chief, Mr. Hedenfeld, and the security chief of our sister casino."

"Roger, we need to get prints on those areas before Mr. Hedenfeld accesses them," Roland said.

Stillman called to send a crime technician to the vault. They were waiting impatiently, when Mr. Hedenfeld arrived, flanked by four personal security guards. He ignored the others and swiftly reached the vault door. Roland stepped in front of him and held up her hand to stop him.

Hedenfeld jerked back in surprise. It had been years since anyone had impeded his progress and never at one of his properties. "Who are you and why are you here?" He demanded, towering a good ten inches over her. His guards closed in. Roland held her ground.

"I'm Detective Roland, and this is Detective Stillman. We're overseeing the investigation. This is a crime scene, and we need to print those surfaces before you touch them."

"That is my vault, which contains items of significant value. I will enter when I please." He tried to move past her, but Roland blocked him with her arm.

"Sir, our technician is on the way and will be done in only a few minutes. I understand your desire to get in. We need to get in there, too, but we have only one chance to collect this evidence. If you want us to figure out who did this, please trust us."

Hedenfeld stepped back. "Forgive me. The news of an attack on my hotel has been most stressful. I understand there is significant loss of life."

"Yes, sir. Ten members of your security team are deceased upstairs, and more may be inside the vault."

"We will do it your way, but understand that I do not tolerate failure. You will find the men who attacked my hotel and killed my team." He moved to a corner to speak with his security team in hushed tones.

The technician arrived, dusted for prints, and swabbed for DNA on the surfaces needed to enter the vault. A full examination of the area would be carried out later.

Hedenfeld removed his glove, placed his palm an the reader, and centered his eye on the camera. Green lights lit up, and he entered his twelve-digit code. With a thunk, the locks disengaged.

Stillman asked them to step back, as he pulled the massive door open. Despite the earlier explosion, it slid easily in silence. Debris and dust littered the room. Scattered bills, chips, and containers were covered with bits of blood and soft tissue.

Hedenfeld stepped forward. "Let me in there."

"No one is going in there until our team has collected the evidence," Stillman countered.

"I demand to see it."

"Please don't go inside."

Hedenfeld pushed his way to the entry and scanned the vault. His anger shifted to horror, as he realized the thick liquid splattered on everything was bits of people. He paled and turned to vomit on the lobby floor.

"Let us do our job, sir. After we have everything collected, your team can get in there."

Hedenfeld dabbed at the corners of his mouth with a handkerchief. "Very well. Do your job, Detective. Find the men who did this." He motioned to one of his guards. "Josef, one of you is here at all times until we get a full accounting of what is missing from that vault." He turned and left with his three remaining guards.

Roland glanced at Stillman. "Gonna be a long night. Let's get started."

．　．　．

Mr. Zhang arrived back at the hotel to change after the race ceremonies. "I'm sorry, sir. There is a problem with the garage. We will have to use the main entrance," his driver said.

The billionaire ignored him, as he contemplated his plans for the evening. His security formed a tight cordon around him and cleared a path to a waiting elevator. In his room finally, his valet had several outfits laid out for him. Mr. Zhang chose a red silk shirt to go with his dark jacket and pants.

"Where are my watches? I wish to change for the evening."

"I'm sorry, sir. The hotel has a security lockdown and cannot access the vault at the moment."

Mr. Zhang waved him away. "Please make sure the hotel is aware of my displeasure." The billionaire put his Rolex back on and focused on the evening ahead. He had seven hours until dawn and he planned to enjoy every one of them.

．　．　．

Lana threaded her way through the boisterous crowds to Mandalay Bay. She expected to find a huge police presence, but everything appeared normal on the outside of the building. Customers walked in and out, laughing too loud at stories only they found funny. The inebriated stumbled back to their rooms, while the younger crowd was just getting started for the evening.

Every table on the crowded casino floor was full of gamblers, alternately bragging about their luck or cursing it. Drink attendants made their way through the crowd with trays loaded with colorful drinks. Keeping customers tipsy with low inhibitions seemed an effective casino marketing strategy.

Lana, watchful for anything out of the ordinary, finally saw what had been in front of her the whole time. Many more alert casino security personnel occupied the floor. Dressed in dark suits, they blended into the background and looked more like concierges than security. Usually low key, even bored, they gave directions and calmed the occasional belligerent drunk. This much larger, vigilant group was determined to miss nothing.

She looked for a good prospect who would likely talk to her, choosing a petite woman standing alone to guard an unmarked door. "Excuse me, are you with security?"

"Yes, ma'am. How can I help you?"

"My name is Lana Hearns. I'm an independent journalist trying to get more information about the incident that occurred here this evening."

The guards eyes turned cold and looked away. "There are no incidents here tonight, ma'am."

Lana held up her phone with the scanner app open. "It's all over the police radios. There have been some murders of the security team and a possible robbery. I'm just trying to get the facts out to the public."

The icy stare focused on her. "You looking to sensationalize this or report facts?"

"Just facts. The talking heads on TV will focus on the drama, but I report real news."

"Are we off the record? I'm not supposed to speak about this."

"We are off the record."

The guard sighed. "A group breached our security center and vault. It's presumed that they robbed the vault, but we haven't got a count yet. In the process, they murdered thirteen of our security team."

Lana was saddened and stunned. "Thirteen? Are you sure?"

"I saw the bodies in the security center. Ten of them with double taps to the chest and one to the head, piled like garbage in a corner."

"That's horrific."

"The vault is horrific. Rumor has it they set off an explosive device with people locked in there."

"Do they think the Las Vegas Bomber is responsible?"

"They gained entry by driving up in a bomb squad truck and wearing bomb squad uniforms, and they blew the vault. Odds are pretty good it was our bomber. They better hope the police get them before we do, or the Chinese."

"The Chinese?"

"One of their billionaires is staying here and stored his jewels in that vault. Best case scenario is that he will need to get them cleaned. Worst case, they're missing. Listen, I gotta go back to work. Hopefully, this information will help find these fuckers."

"I hope so, too. So sorry about your friends. If you hear anything else, please call me, off the record." She handed her a card, which the guard pocketed. Lana headed out to find a billionaire.

· · ·

I arrived at the hospital thirty-two minutes later. Not my best time, but fighting through the crowd slowed me down. The hospital ER was packed. While many establishments slowed down or closed every evening, a Las Vegas ER would never be one of them. I badged my way through security to the nursing station.

"What the hell are you doing here? Did you get stabbed again?" Jen asked.

"No, I figured this was a good time for a wound check and bandage change."

She scoffed with a flicker of a smile.

"I figured you could use some help. Where do you want me?"

"If you could take over the minor trauma bay and monitor the residents, that would be great, lots of lacerations and fractures to clear out."

"Let me change into some scrubs, and Banshee and I will go clear the board."

A visibly relieved Jen smiled, probably for the first time that evening. "Thanks, Doc."

CHAPTER THIRTY-NINE

Saturday, 11:24 p.m.

Roberts lounged across his couch in the dark with a cold beer in his hand and with the backpack slouched next to him, as he reviewed every step he had taken that led to this point. Finally, he allowed himself a relaxed smile, not of joy, but of contentment. He had planned a perfect crime and had executed it flawlessly.

The idea originated in his childhood, that like so many, had been dominated by an abusive, alcoholic father. He had been a successful, respected engineer, but a failure as a parent. His first drinks began in the car on his way home and ended when he passed out at night. Vodka was his drink of choice, but beer sufficed.

A brilliant man, exacting in his attention to detail, he expected the same from his only child. He required precision in his every action, from how he made his bed to how he placed his utensils at the table. Failure of any kind was addressed with a demeaning lecture. His father never raised his voice, but calmly told his son how worthless he was and how he would amount to nothing. Later in the day, when the alcohol kicked in, he punctuated his insults with slaps, kicks, and punches, never in anger, but with emotionless attacks necessary to hammer down his point.

The resulting child had learned to disassociate feelings from actions. Violence was expected and necessary to meet a noble end. In his father's case, the noble end was to raise a child who respected attention to detail and who incidentally normalized violence.

Roberts was driven by a perpetual inability to please his father. No matter how well he did at school, or how clean he made his room, or how perfect he performed chores, he always failed in some small detail that his father accentuated.

By the time he left for college, he functioned as an organized sociopath. Outwardly, he appeared to be another obsessive, high-performing college student, gunning his way to the top of his class. Inwardly, he felt empty. Emotions and friendships were irrelevant in his hierarchy of needs. He wanted to focus only on completing his projects.

His sophomore chemistry class set him on his path. The organization and precision of molecules fascinated him. They always reacted precisely the same way, and if mixed in the right proportions, reacted predictably. He immersed himself in this universe of precision. The realization that exothermic reactions created energy sealed his career choice. He would devote his efforts toward mastery of devices that created exothermic reactions, bombs.

With his focus and intelligence, a career with the bomb squad was never in doubt. He easily passed the tests. When it came time for the real life experience of defusing bombs, his ability to disassociate proved his greatest strength. Where the minds of others clouded with nervousness, Roberts remained calmly sharp. He understood the complexity of each device and what would happen with each decision. Emotion played no part for him. He became known as the coolest diffuser on the bomb squad, unflappable no matter the situation.

Despite his success and his rising to the top of his department, he knew he was a failure. The beatings had stopped, but the alcohol-fueled lectures ran in a continuous loop in the background of his mind.

Roberts realized his dad had been right. Although at the top of his game, he rarely got called to a real bomb scene, and even those few featured rudimentary devices, unworthy of his time. He regularly got to experiment with various explosive devices at the range as part of his training, but he needed to do something extraordinary that would capture the attention of the world.

His idea firmly rooted when the F1 race in Vegas had been announced. The world's media would focus on the city. His first thought was a bomb to disrupt the race, sure to garner attention, but unsophisticated and uncomplicated. He needed something more elegant that would be talked about for a hundred years. Las Vegas symbolized money and greed, but no one had ever successfully robbed a casino. Sure, some idiots had stolen some chips from a table, but no one had ever robbed a vault. He would do it during a high profile sporting event that hosted the wealthiest targets.

He began with updating communications to all of the casinos about the potential for bomb threats, a reasonable preventive action in times of terrorism. He met with the larger casinos and established plans for his team to respond quickly to such threats. He reviewed security strengths and weaknesses of each resort and made recommendations. He collected information and solidified his plans.

Eight months before the race, as part of the security review, the bomb squad planned protection for the Chinese billionaire's attendance at the race and stay at Mandalay Bay. Roberts learned that he normally traveled with large amounts of jewels and would require space in the main vault to store them. Roberts targeted the jewels. Cash was too bulky and easily traced, but jewels stolen from a Chinese billionaire would be remembered for centuries.

The laborious planning had been done entirely in his head with nothing written, and he made sure to pay for everything in untraceable cash or bitcoin. When he had to meet with people, he used shoe lifts and a padded suit that added three inches and forty pounds to his frame, along with makeup and glasses. No one he met could identify him.

Racial supremacist groups, established in Las Vegas and known for violence, offered a convenient distraction. Police would see through the ruse eventually, so Krug was a necessary sacrifice and perfectly framable. They would waste time searching for him, while Roberts moved freely with a perfect alibi.

Lemkins and his band of misfits comprised his biggest risk, but played a key role, their deaths a forgone conclusion. His murdered and injured victims didn't factor into his calculations at all. Only success of the robbery mattered.

The only hiccup had been that reporter getting to Milly so quickly, but he had planned for that contingency. The only unsuccessful part of the operation was the failure to kill the reporter at the Dam, something his dad would have been sure to point out, but she was no longer relevant. The game was over.

Roberts planned to stay on the force for a few months before he retired, due to the stress of Krug's betrayal, and to liquidate some of the free diamonds to support his quiet retirement to the Caribbean. The jewels would remain securely hidden, unseen by any other human. He would write his story, sharing the details of the crime. When he died, his lawyer would mail copies to media outlets as well as to the FBI. Thirty years from now, the story of the greatest unsolved robbery of all time would finally be shared, and Roberts' name would live into eternity.

CHAPTER FORTY

Saturday, 11:38 p.m.

Lana found the boisterous craps tables in the middle of the casino, as bettors celebrated each winning roll of the dice. The center table hosted a small crowd watching a single man playing on half the table. The five beautiful women cheering for him and the four bodyguards insulating him left little doubt of his princely identity. Dressed in a silk jacket and an open collar shirt, he maniacally focused on the game.

Fascinated, Lana watched him roll the dice and place his bets mechanically, appearing to receive neither pleasure from big wins nor sadness from losses. She waited for a break in the action to call to him. "Mr. Zhang, do you have any comment about the robbery of the vault downstairs this evening?"

His dark eyes turned and pierced into hers, his game temporarily forgotten. Lana held his stare. "Are you concerned that any of your property may have been stolen?"

He held her gaze, as he indicated for one of his bodyguards to approach him. He whispered briefly in his ear, and then turned back to his game. The bodyguard approached Lana and asked her to move away from the table for some privacy.

"Mr. Zhang would like to know what you are talking about."

Lana handed him a card as she spoke. "My name is Lana Hearns, and I'm a reporter. I have been following the story of the bomber, and apparently, he broke into the vault, robbed it, and set off an explosive device earlier this evening. My understanding is that Mr. Zhang stored valuables in that vault. Does he have any comment?"

"We have not been informed of a problem with the vault."

"Then I suggest you walk down there and ask to see his jewels."

Concern flitted across the bodyguard's countenance. "Will you please remain here for a moment, while I check with some people?"

Lana agreed, and the man walked directly to the secure area of the hotel. Lana wandered closer to the table to watch the billionaire in action. He had a generous stack of chips in front of him with the smallest worth $5000 and the largest $100,000. By her quick count, he had over four million dollars in chips at the table. The dealers knew his preferences, and after each roll, they asked if he wanted to increase his bets on the table. He responded with single word answers, his eyes constantly focused on the chips in play. During brief breaks inherent in the game, he surveilled the crowd, and again, his intense gaze fell on Lana. She felt like he was reading her DNA, although without malevolence.

A few minutes later, the bodyguard returned and whispered into the ear of his boss. He nodded and continued to play. When he rolled a seven to end that round, he abruptly turned and left the table. He gave a quick order, and the women accompanying him remained in place, as his guards cleared a path for him. The original bodyguard approached Lana. "Miss, if you would please follow me. Mr. Zhang would like a word."

She followed his entourage, as she glanced back at the table with four million dollars worth of the billionaire's chips. The guards led the small group to the VIP area, where a table for two awaited them. As he was seated, a drink was placed in front of him and food was brought to the table. Mr. Zhang sampled the seafood platter before turning his attention to his guest. "Feng has confirmed an incident in the vault this evening. Why am I learning this information from you?"

"Sir, it's my job to collect information. I've been following the story all week, and things heated up this evening. The story led here. Did you lose anything in the robbery?"

Mr. Zhang ate a piece of crab leg before responding. "I entrusted several items of value to the vault. Unfortunately, we are unable to access it at the moment. Your police are investigating, and an explosion in the vault has left a significant mess."

"My sources tell me three people were closed inside the vault when at least one grenade exploded."

"Your sources are better than mine, it appears."

"You are a guest here, and I work as a reporter. It's my job to have sources."

"Miss Hearns, Feng will give you a phone number. Please share any information you discover regarding this robbery. I hope the authorities will keep me well informed. In the meantime, please call Feng immediately at any hour with any information you collect."

The billionaire pushed his chair back to stand, but Lana leaned forward and touched his arm. "One more thing, please, sir."

Mr. Zhang acknowledged her hand on his arm, and his guards leaned forward, but the billionaire held up his other hand. He pulled his chair back in and focused on Lana. "In my country, a woman would not touch me uninvited and most certainly would not ask a favor of me." Lana held his gaze and said nothing. "But my country has many faults, not the least of which is our treatment of women. America raises women to be strong and confident, a strength we might emulate. Please, ask your favor."

"If you have any statements or information you would like to share with the press, either officially or off the record, please consider calling me. Feng has my number, and I can also be reached at any time."

Mr. Zhang smiled for the first time, showing a perfect set of white teeth accentuated by his dark complexion. "It was a pleasure to meet you, Miss Hearns. Please, feel free to enjoy whatever you want here. Feng will take care of the bill. I must return to my vices. I have a long night ahead of me." The billionaire stood and swept out of the room with his guards surrounding him.

Lana leaned back in her chair, elated at acquiring the billionaire as a source. She realized she was famished and went to work on the seafood tower.

.   .   .

Detective Roland was the first to put everything together. Bombarded with information, her team processed the two crime scenes at Mandalay, but she kept one ear on the scanner registering everything else happening in town. The notable number of cars on fire around the city had been written off initially as secondary to the chaos.

Increased chatter from one of the scenes reported money scattered across the ground near the burning car. Another burst of appalled disgust from another scene reported a human head found on the shoulder of the freeway near a burning car.

Roland called dispatch to speak to a supervisor. "This is a Roland. What's going on with these car fires?"

"We have eight reported car fires. Two are downtown and have been extinguished. The other six are spread around town."

"Anything unusual about them?"

"Crews report significant destruction at a couple of them, like the gas tanks blew."

"I don't think it's only gas tanks. I need someone at each of those sites to text me a picture of each scene immediately."

The supervisor acknowledged the order and ended the call. Roland paced for a minute before the first text arrived. The photo showed the remains of a cab with significant damage burning on a side street in a wide debris field. Her phone dinged with more messages, and she opened them to see other cabs that had sustained similarly massive damage.

Roland found Stillman and showed him the photos. "These don't look like mere gas tank explosions to me. These look like the work of our bomber," Roland said.

"Agreed, but why? Maybe to create more chaos for us?"

"Possibly, but an officer from one of the scenes has reported hundred-dollar bills on the ground near the explosion. What if these cabs are part of Krug's team, and he's eliminating them? Six taxis exploded at the same time, all headed away from the Strip."

"I agree that's too coincidental. Let's get someone out to each of them to secure evidence. With cash on sight, we need to make sure no one has sticky fingers and further destroys evidence."

"Where are you with tracking the fake bomb truck?" Stillman's team had been trying to identify the path of the truck from traffic cameras.

"We know he came from the southeast and left to the southeast, but there aren't any cameras on the side streets. He got off the main roads quickly. We'll keep looking, but there're a lot of places to hide."

Roland called the supervisor at dispatch again. "Thanks for getting those photos so quickly. The car explosions are now our crime scenes. Anyone has any problem with that, tell them to call me."

"Yes, ma'am."

"One other question. Anything unusual happen southeast of Mandalay?"

The supervisor chuckled. "All's quiet except for a warehouse that had a gas explosion. The fire department is on site."

"A gas explosion?"

"Presumably. Witness said the building just blew up."

Roland closed her eyes and took a deep breath. "Let them know that scene is ours, as well."

Stillman watched her end the call. "Gonna be a long night," he said.

CHAPTER FORTY-ONE

Sunday, October 22

7:04 a.m.

"Thanks for your help last night, Little Mac. You got a ride home?"

"Yep. My friend is over there. Do you guys need a ride?"

"Thanks, but we're gonna walk. It's not far. Get some sleep. You earned it."

"You, too, Doc. Good night."

Little Mac rode away with his friend, as Banshee and I leisurely walked toward the hotel. I savored the quiet of the morning after the chaos of the previous twenty-four hours. The alcohol that had led so many people to the ER had finally led them to seek sleep. A few stragglers meandered home through the nearly vacated streets, as the occasional health nut jogged past. Folks who made their living on the streets slowly returned to their daily haunts.

As we approached the Strip, crews were hard at work disassembling the barriers around the racetrack to restore normal traffic patterns. Evidence of the enormous crowd was everywhere. Las Vegas never claimed to be the cleanest city even at its best, but it would take a few days for crews to make the Strip presentable for Vegas's standards.

Banshee explored new scents off leash, and I clicked it back on before we entered the Bellagio. The subdued casino floor still hosted a smattering of hopeful gamblers searching for a lucky hand.

I stepped into the suite surprised to find Lana asleep on the couch with her notepad and phone on her chest, still in last night's clothes. I had guessed wrong that she had gotten a decent night's sleep. Obviously, she worked long hours, too.

Banshee kissed her hand, and she opened her eyes and stretched. "What time is it?"

"Just after eight."

"How was your night?"

"Busy. Vegas didn't disappoint with the number of people showing bad judgment last night. How do you feel about breakfast? I'm starving."

"I had a late dinner with a Chinese billionaire, but I could use some eggs Benedict. Why don't you order some room service, and I'll warm up the shower."

"Did you say you had dinner with a Chinese billionaire?"

"Yes. Order breakfast and meet me in the shower, and I'll tell you all about it."

One phone call later, Lana shared her story, as I washed her back. I had received no news in the ER and was amazed to hear it. Breakfast arrived, and minutes later, all three of us slept.

. . .

The Chief called the meeting to order. Coffee pots littered the table, as the group struggled to stay focused after the all-nighter. Dark circles under eyes, disheveled hair, and wrinkled clothes combined with a deficiency of deodorant and toothpaste permeated the room. Detective Roland led the summary.

"The 911 call indicated the presence of bombs downtown that would explode after the end of the race, and the majority of available forces were dispersed to that area. At 8:30, the decision was made to evacuate the major public areas, as no devices had been found. In addition, many casinos elected to evacuate their public areas. This led to generalized chaos in a ten block area downtown that required more officers to respond.

"No devices have been found, and we now believe that the threat to downtown had been only a diversion. About twenty minutes before the end of the race, with maximal chaos downtown, a truck with 'bomb squad' signage entered the underground lot at Mandalay Bay. The guard at the entrance to the garage waved them through, but did not talk to them. He saw two officers in the front seat in full tactical gear and cannot provide a description.

"They parked in front of the secure entrance and had authorization codes to get the door open. Krug would have had access to those codes. In the security room, they restrained the guards and personnel and wiped any security images from the computers. They proceeded to the vault where Rigetti, head of security, let them in. They restrained Rigetti and two guards inside the vault, and after helping themselves to the vault's contents, they threw three grenades in there and closed the door. They shot everyone else three times, before the entire group left in their truck. Guard timesheet indicates they were on site for sixteen minutes. No one alive talked to them or saw them without their gear, so no witnesses."

"What is missing from the vault?" the Chief asked.

"Final accounting will take time due to the mess in there, but it looks like they focused on hundred-dollar bills. Early estimate is that they carried out about twenty-seven million."

Murmurs and whistles resonated around the table. "That's a heavy load of cash," someone pointed out.

"About six hundred pounds of bills. They left a lot of cash, but we think they took what they could carry. Other than the horrific loss of life, the most expensive loss is the Chinese billionaire's jewels. Apparently, Mr. Zhang travels with an extensive jewelry collection as well as with a significant number of diamonds to use as currency. All four of his cases were emptied."

"And the value of this jewelry collection?" The Chief asked.

"North of a quarter billion dollars."

"We followed them on traffic cams heading southeast, but lost them after they turned onto side streets. About twenty-five minutes after they left Mandalay, a series of six cabs exploded at about the same time, all high order detonations that instantly killed a lone, male driver. The cabs were completely destroyed, but each contained a canvas bag full of hundred-dollar bills.

"Fifteen minutes after the cabs blew, a warehouse in southeast Vegas exploded. Initially thought to be caused by a gas leak, we now know that C4 caused the explosion with thermite used on a truck inside. Bags of charred money were found on this site, too. We're still sifting through the debris, but we don't expect to find anything else meaningful.

"We're thinking that someone, presumably Krug, eliminated his crew and sacrificed the cash for the jewels. Everything else was a distraction for him to get the jewels. So far, every single person who had contact with him is dead, except Roberts. I hate to say it, but so far, he hasn't made any mistakes. We just need to hunt him down."

"That is some cold-blooded shit. Is Krug really good for twenty murders and a bunch more injuries? Killing his own crew?"

"Hard to say, sir."

"Have we ID'd the crew yet?"

"No, not a chance at dental records, and we haven't found any intact fingers."

"I want Krug found and in a cell or in the morgue, but we need him found." The Chief left, and the remaining officers divided up responsibilities for the search.

•   •   •

Mr. Hedenfeld called Feng to invite him to his office. They sat on sofas across from each other, and Mr. Hedenfeld leaned forward as he spoke, his nervousness a rare emotion.

"Thank you for coming so quickly. We have completed a preliminary inventory of the vault."

"What is missing among Mr. Zhang's property?"

"It looks like everything in his cases is missing. We are working with the police to find the men responsible and to return his property."

Feng stood quickly. "I expect you will hear from him shortly."

CHAPTER FORTY-TWO

Sunday, 10:54 a.m.

Roberts awoke with a splitting headache, worsened by movement. He sat up slowly in bed and felt gently around his bandage. The doctor had warned him that the pain and inflammation would maximize one or two days after his injury, and he appeared to be right.

Roberts stumbled to the kitchen and dry swallowed some ibuprofen, while his Keurig brewed a cup of coffee. He preferred something stronger, but he needed to be clearheaded. He sipped as soon as it finished, ignoring the burn, and the caffeine energized him.

He picked up the papers from his front porch and turned the TV to a local news network. His masterpiece had been dubbed the Great Vegas Race Heist, and every channel featured the same information. Roberts smirked at the scenes of chaos his threats had produced downtown and at the utter madness of the race crowd's dispersal. A few of the names of the dead security officers had been released, but he could find no evidence that the six co-conspirators had been identified yet. He imagined that at least one of them had been identified, but the police apparently withheld the information.

They prominently displayed Krug's picture. Mandalay Bay had offered a $250,000 reward for information leading to his arrest.

Heightened security at the airports and along the Mexican border watched for him. Road blocks slowed cars leaving Las Vegas, and any holding single males were briefly pulled over for further inspection, causing nightmarish traffic delays. Roberts knew the casino's private security would tackle the problem as well. Every snitch and every fence of stolen goods had probably been threatened. They knew nothing.

Roberts retrieved the backpack from his closet and laid the ten bags of loose diamonds on the coffee table. He left the watches and other jewelry in the backpack. Beautiful, but too distinctive, they couldn't be sold without attracting attention. He would save them as an ace in the hole, in case he ever got caught and needed to bargain his way out.

The untraceable loose diamonds, on the other hand, would be sellable as soon as he got away from Vegas. He poured the contents of one of the bags into his hands, admiring the way the faceted light reflected and the fact that their value was more than he could spend in a lifetime. For now, he needed to hide them.

He carried ten large candles contained in six-inch glass jars out of his closet and placed them on the coffee table. He had previously heated the glass and melted the majority of the wax out of each candle, leaving large cavities in their centers. He poured the first bag of diamonds into the first candle, creating a layer two inches deep. He inserted three fresh wicks into the candle to mimic the original design.

He retrieved another glass jar that contained the lavender candle wax he had previously removed. He set it on a hot plate to liquify. While waiting, he emptied the remaining bags into the other nine candles. He carefully poured the scented wax over the three lavender candles until he had an even layer at the original level of the candle. When it dried, it appeared identical to a new candle.

He repeated the process for the remaining candles and soon had ten perfectly new candles in front of him. The diamonds were invisible, and the weight felt the same as an authentic candle. He scraped off a corner of each label, minor imperfections to remind him which jars contained diamonds.

Hiding the candles would have to wait. Seventy-one-year-old Judy Akins had lived next door to him for the last five years. A widower who lived alone with her poodle, Ruby, Judy enjoyed having a policeman next door and had given Roberts a key to her house to watch it when she was out of town. Roberts also walked Ruby whenever Judy asked.

Roberts had been in her house several times over the years and noticed the fragrant candles she always burned. Judy took advantage of sales and stored extras. Given their size, it would take years for her to burn them all, and she was sure to add more.

A devout Catholic, Judy met with her church group every Sunday for dinner and cards. Tonight, she would leave at five fifteen and wouldn't return until after eight. Roberts would let himself in and place his candles in the back of her closet, accessible whenever he needed them.

He cleaned up and placed his backpack with the jewels back in his closet. He would hide them tomorrow. He sat down on the couch with a beer and turned on an NFL game. He would call to check in at the station in an hour. After all, he was on medical leave.

•   •   •

Lana finally awakened, as I read the latest news on my iPad. She yawned, stretched, and scooted under my arm to snuggle.

"I assume you slept well," I said.

"Yes, I needed that. Anything new happen while we slept?"

"Nope. No explosions, robberies, or deaths, and no sign of Krug."

"Looks like we picked a good time to sleep. Order some lunch while I get cleaned up, and then I have some work to do."

"Do we need to stay at this hotel any longer? Krug is on the run, and all that other BS was a distraction. It's probably safe to return home."

She leaned over to kiss me on the forehead. "Of course it's safe to go home, but we're already past checkout time. One more night here won't be too bad."

. . .

An exhausted Stillman skimmed the paper handed to him and straightened in his chair. "I don't fucking believe this. We got our first ID on one of the cab drivers. Want to guess who it is?"

Roland shrugged her shoulders. "Is it someone I know?"

"As a matter of fact, you do know him." Stillman tossed the paper across the desk. "The pride of the Las Vegas police force before Krug took his place, Timmy fucking Lemkins."

"That's gonna make the Chief happy, a former cop working with a current one. How did they ID him?"

"They found an intact ring finger on a nearby car. Apparently, it was driving by when Lemkins' cab blew up. Some debris hit the car, and they went to wash it this morning. They found the finger and called it in."

"Let's focus on his known associates and see if we can prove he and Krug knew each other. Lemkins ran with a steady crew most of the time, and maybe we can figure out the other five."

"Okay. Rock, paper, scissors to decide who gets to inform the Chief?" Stillman asked.

"Hell no, that's on you. You've got your twenty in already, and I need another two years to get my pension."

Stillman straightened his tie and took the paper to the elevator.

CHAPTER FORTY-THREE

Monday, October 23
10:03 a.m.

Roberts saw a neurologist to follow up on his concussion. He didn't even have to lie about his symptoms of bad headaches and relentless fatigue. The doctor reassured him and told him that he could return to light duty later in the week, if he continued to improve.

After his doctor's appointment, he drove by the highly active station to check on the case. The other five members of Lemkins' crew had been tentatively identified, and investigators scrutinized each of their lives, dissecting their cell phones, computers, and financial information. Family, friends, and known associates had been extensively interviewed. They sent word to informants that a lifetime get-out-of-jail-free card for anything short of murder was available to anyone with information on Lemkins' crew or Krug. Coupled with the reward, now up to a half million dollars, everyone vied to produce critical information.

Roberts inwardly laughed at the futility of the efforts. They would find no connection between Lemkins and Krug, because none existed. Roberts' only contact with Lemkins had been one meeting out of town, six months ago. The rest of their communications had been by dedicated burner phones, now little piles of melted metal and plastic in the demolished warehouse.

Roberts sauntered to the Detective's area and found Stillman at his desk. "How's it going? Any leads?"

Stillman threw down the file he was holding. "Not a damn thing so far, but it's not for lack of trying. How are you feeling? I thought you were still out on medical."

"I'm doing better. Saw the neurologist this morning, and I should be cleared for light duty later this week. Just wanted to stop by and see how everyone is doing."

"Tired and frustrated."

"So, normal for a Monday. Let me know if you get him. Embarrassing to have a guy like that wearing a badge."

"Will do. Go get some rest."

"That's my plan. Just need to return a file to storage."

Stillman opened his own file, as Roberts headed toward the elevator to take him to the basement. As usual, Murphy nested at his desk, guarding the entrance to the secure area. Sergeant Murphy had taken the responsibility eight years before, after a car wreck on duty left him with a bad hip. Unable to meet the physical requirements of active duty, he took the desk job in the basement.

"What's up, Murph? You look like the only one not working on the Krug case. It's busy up there."

Murphy smiled. "That's why I like it down here. It's always quiet. You're looking a little rough," he pointed to his forehead.

"Yeah. Krug smacked me with my baseball bat."

"That's some bad shit. He's got a lot of bad karma headed his way. What can I help you with today?"

Roberts pointed to his backpack. "I need to return a file on the Kepler case and check out one more. Might as well get something done while I'm resting this week." The Kepler case was a recent bust for selling dynamite. Kepler was in jail, but the source of his explosives was still unclear and an open investigation. Roberts had been gathering files on the case a few times a week over the last month.

Murphy struggled to get to his feet, but Roberts waved him off. "Sit down. I know where the file is. Rest that hip while I change this out." I handed him a file from my backpack, and he noted it's return date on the computer. He gave it to Roberts to put away.

"Thanks, man. I appreciate it. Let me know if you need help with anything." Murphy pressed a button to unlock the door with a buzz. Technically, no one was allowed in the secure area without an escort, but Murphy let trusted people in, especially for simple requests. Roberts made his way through the endless shelves and quickly switched out the file for a new one.

He moved down the row to a box labeled "Adkins, Matthew, 2008." He removed it from the shelf and set it on the floor. He opened the box full of evidence. Mathew Adkins lived on the street and had been fatally stabbed during a fight. One of thousands of cold cases, with no known family, no witnesses to the crime, and no useful evidence collected at the scene, no one would care to reopen it, but with no statute of limitations on murder, the evidence would be stored for at least seventy-five years.

Roberts unzipped his backpack and removed the jewelry, neatly contained in a generic black cloth bag. He tucked it under the existing bags of evidence and returned the box to its original location. He walked to the door with the new folder in his hand, and Murphy buzzed him out.

"Find what you were looking for?" He asked.

"Yes, sir. Everything was exactly where it should be. Here's the new file."

Murphy logged the new file into the system and handed it back. "Aren't you forgetting something?"

Sheepishly, Roberts opened his backpack for Murphy to inspect. It contained only a notebook and computer. Murphy zipped it up and handed it back. "Sorry, sir. You know the rules. Need to make sure nothing disappears from evidence."

"You're the right man for the job, Murph. Have a good day."

Murphy waved and went back to his newspaper, as Roberts left the building. The jewels were secure, as his seventy-million-dollar bargaining chip in the unlikely event he needed it. Otherwise, they would be rediscovered in sixty years, when the evidence was finally purged.

CHAPTER FORTY-FOUR

Tuesday, November 7 (Two weeks later)
2:37 pm

"Thanks for bringing the pizza. It's my favorite kind," Rick said, as he took another huge bite of his supreme pizza, making sure not to spill any on his Deadpool scrubs.

As he devoured his third piece in under a minute, Lana watched him incredulously. "You know it's okay to pause and chew your food before you swallow it."

Rick replied between bites. "It's part of the training. Statistically, the worst cases arrive when hot food arrives, so if you want to enjoy hot food, you need to eat fast." I nodded, as I bit into my second piece of pepperoni.

"How's the investigation? It's gotten boring over the last week," Rick said.

"Tell me about it. No sign of Krug or the diamonds and jewelry. It's like he vanished. A lot of angry people are searching for him. He better hope the cops find him before the casino guys do, or maybe even worse, the Chinese."

"The Chinese are still looking for him?"

"Yes. Feng is still here with a team. He calls me everyday to remind me that his boss is unhappy and to ask for new information. Unfortunately, I have nothing to share."

Rick responded while tearing into a fourth piece. "Well, I enjoyed my time as a reporter and made some swell friends at that white supremacy bar, but I'm off the case until something happens. Besides, I need to go wash crayon shavings out of a kid's ear."

"Why would he do that?" Lana asked.

"He thought it would help him hear the sound rainbows make. Thanks, again. See ya."

Rick left and the room seemed larger, empty, and quiet. "He certainly is something. Does he ever slow down?"

I shook my head, as I finished my last piece. "Nope. He's like that one hundred percent of the time. He should probably have his thyroid checked. Is it time to move on from the great race heist story?"

"Not yet, but close. I have no one left to interview. My guess is that he got out of town somehow and is on the run. This city has been torn apart looking for him, and with the reward at a million bucks now, even the tourists are looking for him. I'm afraid I've filed my last story on this unless something changes."

"How does it feel to disappoint a billionaire?"

"He has plenty of money. He'll be fine. It would have been a great story to return his jewels to him, though."

She stood to leave, and I gave her a hug. "Thanks, again, for the lunch. I'm done at six, so I'll see you tonight."

"See you soon."

$$\cdot \quad \cdot \quad \cdot$$

An afternoon storm blew in, and although it brought only a smattering of rain, wind gusted to 45 MPH, strong enough to dislodge the metal hood that had sheltered Sergeant Krug's body. The occasional patrons of the parking lot had noted the smell, but assumed it was just a dead animal. Bad odors were hardly unusual in that part of town.

For the scavenging coyotes that lurked in the area, the scent offered an invitation to a buffet, unreachable until the metal hood dislodged. They feasted on the partially decayed body and dragged it out of the enclosed area for easier access.

Two hours later, a group of teenagers parked to share some weed and blast their music. The occupants of the first vehicle immediately noted the smell.

"Damn, Juan. Did you shit yourself again?"

"Fuck you, Raul. It's probably just your momma pissing out here."

The good natured ribbing continued until Juan pointed at the corner of the lot. "Looks like the coyotes killed a dog over there."

"That's a pretty big dog," Raul said, as he approached with his nose covered. "Holy shit, man. That's a body."

"No way. Let me see."

The two advanced slowly, although obviously the man had been dead for a long time. "We need to get out of here," Juan said.

"Yeah, but we should tell someone."

"Fuck that. I ain't talking to no cops."

Raul thought for a moment. "Let's split. I'll call from my cell while we're driving, but we'll be long gone."

The boys left and made the call anonymously, a decision that would cost them the million-dollar reward.

Officers dispatched to the scene confirmed the presence of a body, called the crime scene technicians and detectives, and cordoned the area with yellow tape. Detectives Patterson and Nealy caught the case and approached with a lack of enthusiasm. A decaying body in this part of town would be a challenge to investigate with the unlikelihood of meaningful evidence left at the scene and of any witnesses willing to come forward.

The police photographer took dozens of photos from every angle. With the area well-documented, the crime scene techs dressed in full body suits advanced to collect evidence. The airtight masks failed to filter the stench of death completely.

"See if he has ID on him, would ya please? At least we can start doing something while you're working, if he does," Patterson said.

The tech checked the pockets and held up a wallet triumphantly. He handed it to Patterson, who accepted it with gloved hands. "Let's see who today's unlucky contestant is," he muttered, as he pulled out the license. "Fuck me!" The techs looked at him in confusion.

Wordlessly, Patterson showed the driver's license to his partner. "I'll call downtown and get Stillman and Roland out here. It's their scene now. I don't want any part of the circus about to descend here."

CHAPTER FORTY-FIVE

Tuesday, 3:27 p.m.

The circus started to build immediately, as word the discovery of Krug's body spread like wildfire. Roland and Stillman arrived within twenty minutes, along with the senior evidence team. Other officers arrived to help with the anticipated crowd. A police helicopter enforced a no fly zone, but media arrived like locusts, starved for information after two weeks of nothing.

"What do we have?" Roland asked.

"Deceased male who's been here awhile. Looks like some coyotes dragged him out and chewed him up." He held up the evidence bag containing the wallet and license. "We found this and expanded the perimeter."

"Good job. Cause of death?"

"No idea. Didn't get that far. I saw the ID and figured this was your case. Let us know if you need anything, but we're officially signing off."

"Thanks for the call. Get out while you still can. The media people are gonna block everyone in."

Roland and Stillman scanned the photos and formed a plan. The entire lot would be searched for trace evidence. Technicians began the tedious process of walking back and forth in small increments, observing everything, and bagging anything unusual. Each item was photographed in place, it's location noted on a digital map of the area, and bagged. It took over an hour to clear the lot. The collected debris would likely amount to nothing. Tire tracks were measured and photographed to compare to a database.

Finally, they approached the body. Clearly, it had decayed in a small depression behind the car hood and been dragged out recently. The animal bites looked fresh, but everything else was rotten. A .22 caliber pistol was found under his right leg, where it had been dragged with the body. Cursory examination revealed a gunshot to the back of the head.

"Looks like a contact wound. Someone was really close when he popped him," Roland noted.

"Someone he knew and trusted. No cop would let anyone else walk that close behind, especially in a place like this."

They were finally ready to transport the body. "Chief says bring him straight to the morgue, and they'll autopsy him tonight," Roland said.

"You want to go with him or stay on the scene?"

"I'll go. Let me know if you find anything out here."

Stillman evaluated the large pile of rusted debris lining the yard. Every single piece would need to be removed and searched, an effort that would take most of the night. "We'll get some more lights set up and get to work."

The search lasted most of the night, covered by every news outlet. The crowd swelled, as rumors of a treasure hunt for a quarter billion dollars in diamonds and jewelry was underway. Like most Vegas dreams of instant wealth, they evaporated into the bland reality of tedious work. The crew left at sunrise, dirty, tired, and no wealthier.

·   ·   ·

Lana received word of the discovery from her police scanner and was already on site when Roland and Stillman arrived. She stayed long enough to gather that Krug had been shot with a .22 and dumped there with no evidence of the treasure. The hunt for Krug had evolved into the hunt for his killer. She texted Doc to let him know she would miss dinner and called Feng. "I have some news for your boss…"

. . .

Roberts followed the news closely. He had expected the body to be found after only two or three days, and the delay was a bonus. The police had wasted enormous resources searching for Krug. Attention would now be diverted to who had killed him and taken the valuables. Roberts had no contact with Krug outside normal work hours. It would never be traced to him.

He would announce his retirement in another two weeks or so, blaming the stress of the investigation and his failure to notice a murderer on his team. He had his pension, and no one would think twice about his stepping away. He would retire abroad, citing the media for his desire to leave the country, somewhere in the Caribbean where no one would question his intermittent sale of diamonds, and where no extradition was possible. He could travel to Asia occasionally and sell some for cryptocurrency. He would carefully launder the money to remain untraceable.

Roberts went back to work, joining his fellow officers in the search for Krug's killer and feigning concern.

. . .

The Chief called the meeting to order that evening. "Settle down. Let's get through this so I can feed the media some lines for the evening news. Where are we?"

Roland gave the summary. "The body is confirmed to be Sergeant Krug by his wallet, fingerprints, and facial recognition. Autopsy confirms his death by a single .22 caliber fired at contact range into the base of his skull. Death would have been instantaneous and between twelve and fifteen days ago. The body's exposure to the elements makes a tighter window impossible, but we know that he was shot anywhere from immediately after the robbery up to two days later."

Roberts noted that the timeline allowed for Krug's shooting to have been before the robbery, but did not point it out. Even the best investigators could be blinded to the obvious by preconceived notions.

"The weapon left at the scene had been reported stolen four years ago and has not turned up since that time. The ammo is generic, and no prints were on the gun or ammo. The gun looks like a dead end."

"What about the caller?"

"The anonymous call came from an untraceable cell phone, likely some kids who happened on the body. That lot is a popular hangout for local teenagers. We're interviewing everyone within a five-block radius, but we're not hopeful. It's the kind of neighborhood where people like to forget what they've seen."

"Any good news?" the Chief asked.

"Not at this time."

"So right now, we have Krug organizing this, building bombs, diverting our attention, killing any witnesses, including his own team, and then he gets whacked by someone else. Do I have that about right?"

"Yes, sir."

"Where are we in identifying this mystery person?"

"Unfortunately, square one, sir. Our focus had been on finding Krug, as we assumed that he was in charge. None of our investigations so far have indicated that he was working for someone else. Frankly, we did not even know we needed to be looking for this person before this evening."

The Chief rubbed his eyes before he spoke, the exhaustion of the last two weeks seeping into his words. "What open leads do we have?"

"We are going back to the 911 calls to reevaluate voice recognition. Due to the modulation and accent, the FBI gave only a 70% chance of matching Krug's voice. If we can identify someone else from those calls, it would likely be the person above Krug on the food chain. We're still processing evidence from the scene, but unless we get lucky with some DNA, the voice is our best shot."

The Chief stood, indicating the end of the meeting. "Throw everything at it. We need answers, and we need to find the new alpha dog. I'm going to brief the press. Dismissed."

Roberts basked in the evident frustration of his colleagues. Like everything else, he kept his satisfaction hidden from his coworkers.

CHAPTER FORTY-SIX

Wednesday, November 8
12:11 p.m.

Lana brought a decorated cake into the conference room and gently set it on the festive table. "Looks like you guys have everything but a bar set up."

"The administration frowns on drinking while we're working for some reason, something about increased medical liability insurance rates," I mused.

"Even without the bar, I love what you're doing. Thanks for including me."

We celebrated Dr. Williams' discharge from the hospital that day. The Emergency Department had arranged a baby shower to celebrate her recovery, and a stack of colorful gifts awaited her arrival. "Rick, stop licking the icing."

"I just want to make sure it's fresh for our guest of honor."

She arrived with a bright smile at that moment in a wheelchair, pushed by her husband. Cheers sang from the crowd as she took her place at the head of the table. "Many thanks to each and every one of you for what you did for me and my baby, and what you do everyday for our patients. While I don't recommend getting hit by bomb shrapnel, if you're going to do it, this is the best place in the world for care."

Another round of applause resounded, and Rick called for cutting of the cake, graciously giving her the first piece before helping himself to the second, considerably larger piece. I sat in the back with Lana, as Dr. Williams opened her gifts to exclamations.

"She looks great. It's a shame about the leg, though." Lana said.

"It's not as bad as you think. With modern technology, a below-the-knee amputation will give her much better function than her traumatized leg would have. Once she gets used to it, she'll be able to operate like before."

"How's her boy doing?"

"Really well. They moved him out of the NICU and into a step-down unit. He'll be here another month to gain weight, but he's on the right track."

"What did she name him?"

"Alexander Joseph Williams"

"Another AJ?"

"He'll need to make a lot of bad life decisions before he becomes an AJ. The title is earned, not given."

The party lasted an hour before it finally broke up. The nurses had arranged for delivery of the gifts to her home, and Rick took care of the remaining cake. Dr. Williams stood on her good leg, supported by her husband, to give me a hug. "Thank you, Doc, for taking care of me and little AJ."

"It was a team effort. I'm so happy you're going home."

"Thank you, Lana, for your efforts to track these men down."

"You're welcome, but the suspect is still out there."

"If anyone can find him, it's you. Now, please excuse me. I need to get home and nap in my own bed."

The crowd dispersed as her husband wheeled her out, leaving Lana and I to clean up. Banshee fastidiously cleaned up all the cake crumbs that hit the floor. Little Mac came in to help and get some quality time with Banshee.

"Anything left to investigate?"

"They're reevaluating the 911 calls. They thought Krug had made the calls, but now that they know someone could have been the one, the FBI is trying their tricks to identify the caller. She pressed a recording saved on her phone of the first 911 call. "I could break the case if I knew whether Krug made this call."

Little Mac rubbed Banshee's tummy and offhandedly replied, "That's not Krug on the tape."

Lana looked at me, and I shrugged. "Why don't you think it's Krug on the tape?" Lana asked.

Little Mac scratched Banshee's ears. "Because Krug sounds different."

"Do you know whose voice it is?" I asked.

"Yeah. That's Detective Roberts' voice."

Lana looked at me with wide eyes, and I held up my hand for her to give Little Mac more time to express his thoughts. "Little Mac, how sure are you that voice is Detective Roberts?"

He looked up at us with innocent eyes. "I'm sure."

"Little Mac, this is important. Please listen to the whole tape." Lana played the recording as Little Mac focused on the sound.

"That's Roberts. I heard him when he visited the ER after the first explosion and when we sewed him up. He's not very friendly. That's his voice."

"But it sounds completely different than his regular voice," Lana insisted.

"Not to me," Little Mac replied simply.

I asked her to play the other 911 calls, and Little Mac stood firm that Roberts spoke on those recordings, too.

"Can I take Banshee for a walk?" he asked.

"Sure, but this is important. Please don't tell anyone that Roberts is the one who made the calls, okay? It has to be our secret for just a little while."

Little Mac held out his little finger. "Pinky promise. It's our secret." I wrapped my pinky around his, and he left with Banshee, leaving me alone with an incredulous Lana.

"Is it really possible?"

I considered for a moment. "Roberts could have built the bombs, and Krug would have trusted him. He was the one who implicated Krug with the attack, which also gave him an airtight alibi the night of the robbery. It's possible, but I just didn't see him as a psychopath."

"How well do we really know him? We gave only a cursory look at him before focusing on Krug. I think we need to do a deep dive on him."

"Do we let the cops know?"

"Hell, no. He's a senior officer, so we don't know who else might be in on it, and we are relying on the opinion of a twenty-three-year old medical assistant being more accurate than the full resources of the FBI. This stays between us until we get something concrete."

"Okay. What's the first step?"

"You go back to playing doctor and let me do my thing. By tonight, I'll know a helluva lot more about Detective Roberts."

"You're sexy when you play the bad ass reporter type," I said as I hugged and kissed her forehead.

"You'll have to wait. This sexy bitch has a new target and is on the hunt." She hustled out of the room with an extra swing of her hips, indeed a huntress on the prowl with her prey in sight.

.　　.　　.

I arrived home at nine to find Lana absorbed in a sea of papers on the couch, Banshee asleep at the far end. My entrance produced a one-eyed glance from Banshee, and no reaction at all from Lana. I leaned over to kiss her. "Looks like you've been busy."

She finished her markup of the paper in her hand before answering. "Sit down. You're not gonna believe this." She shoved some papers out of the way and patted the seat beside her. Words tumbled out, as she excitedly explained her findings. "Remember when your hacker friend got us those financials and the only thing we found was Krug's debt? Well, I went back and looked at Roberts again. The only thing abnormal was that $200,000 he withdrew to help pay down his dad's mortgage. I decided to take a closer look."

She shuffled through some papers until she found one highlighted. "Here's his check for $200,000 made out to First Prime Mortgage. You can see it was deposited into their accounts two days later." "Deposit to First Prime Mortgage, LLC" was stamped on the back of the check.

"Everything looks fine to me."

"But wait, I had your buddy get me the mortgage statements from his dad. You can see he has been paying it down regularly, but there was no $200,000 decrease at the time the check was cashed." She handed me the statements to review.

"So where did the money go?"

"It went to First Prime Mortgage, LLC, like it says on the back of the check."

I looked at the papers in my hand. "But it's not on these statements."

"Right, but you have to look at them closer." She smiled as she watched me look through the papers again.

"It's not here," I said in frustration.

"Read the company name."

"First Prime Mortgage, same as in the check," I said, pointing at the logo.

Lana leaned over and pointed at the end of the logo. "This company is First Prime Mortgage, Inc. The check was made out to First Prime Mortgage, and deposited to First Prime Mortgage, LLC. They're two different companies."

I looked back and forth between the pages. "Who the fuck is First Prime Mortgage, LLC?"

"That's the million dollar question. It's a Delaware LLC that was set up two months before the check was written and dissolved one week after the check was cashed. Address is a PO Box in Delaware. Corporate documents were filed by a law firm that files for half the LLC's in Delaware. The owners are ghosts."

"What about the money? It had to go somewhere."

"It did. The money was deposited in the corporate bank account of First Prime Mortgage, LLC, and two days later the entire amount was transferred to a cryptocurrency account, where it was presumably converted into various cryptocurrencies. Once in crypto, it's untraceable. He could buy things in crypto or convert it back to cash."

"You're telling me Mr. Nice Bomb Guy wrote a check for $200,000 that was converted into untraceable cash six months before all of this started."

"Yep, enough to finance the warehouse and vehicles used in this crime. Roberts had an untraceable war chest."

"No chance he used the money for something else?"

"Nothing I can find. No abnormal spending or trips in the last six months. On paper, everything was perfect, except for the stamp on the back of the check didn't match the name on the statement."

"How the hell did you find that in all of this mess?"

"That's my job, sweetie. Remember, I'm a bad ass reporter."

"So now we have a stamp on the back of a check which we obtained illegally and the testimony of a medical assistant with no formal training in linguistics. I'd say we have an airtight case against him. Are you gonna tell the cops?"

"Hell, no. First of all, we don't know who else may be involved. Secondly, half of my proof is based on material obtained from hacking banking records, which I'm pretty sure is illegal, and I love Little Mac, but explaining his talent to the cops is a long shot. Finally, if I share the info now I won't get a Pulitzer. I want to prove it and find the treasure, and then tell the cops."

"What about Feng? You gonna update him?"

"He'll have to wait. I think he would employ drastic measures on any reasonable suspect."

"So it's just the two of us. How do you know I won't share the story?"

She pushed me down and straddled me on the couch. "Because the pleasure you will receive from your silence is nothing compared to the pain you will feel from talking."

CHAPTER FORTY-SEVEN

Thursday, November 9
7:04 am

"I got an idea," I said, as I stuffed another bite of waffle in my mouth.

"Please share," Lana replied, as she leaned forward with her coffee cup in hand.

"What if we put a GPS tracker on his car? We don't have the manpower to follow him, but we can see where his car goes. Hell, it may even lead us to the diamonds."

"Not a bad idea, but highly illegal."

I pointed at the papers littering the couch. "A little late to worry about legal technicalities, don't you think? If it helps us, great. If not, we pretend it didn't happen."

"I thought you doctors were rule followers."

"You're thinking of internal medicine doctors. ER doctors have never met a rule they wouldn't break to help a patient. If the cause is noble, the means are necessary."

"Please tell me you didn't just make that up?"

"Not bad, huh? Might make a good tattoo across my shoulders. Anyway, what do you think about the tracker?"

Lana sipped her coffee. "Okay, let's do it."

"Good choice, especially since I ordered one last night. It should be delivered this morning. Now we need a plan to stick it on his car."

Lana walked away shaking her head and called over her shoulder. "That's your job, Mr. Bond. I'm gonna keep digging for information about Mr. Roberts."

. . .

The ER wasn't too exciting when I arrived for my shift. My first patient was a slightly inebriated tourist injured at an axe-throwing bar. Per his friends, the patient threw the axe, and it hit the wood wall backwards, and bounced back. He was laughing at the throw and not paying attention, when the axe slammed into his shin. His leg hadn't broken, but he would sport an impressive scar and leave with an entertaining Vegas story.

"What do you think about those bars where they throw axes at targets on the wall?" I asked Rick.

"I'm all for them. Let's go."

"Seems like alcohol and axe-throwing is a dangerous combination, and why do they need to be open for breakfast?"

"We should send them a thank you note. Their business model is good for our business model."

"What do you have after work today?"

"Big plans. I'm gonna get some pizza and play Call of Duty until I fall asleep on my couch."

"I need some help with something, and I'll buy your pizza."

"I'm in."

"Don't you want to hear what it is, first?"

"No, I'm in."

"It might be a little dangerous."

"Definitely in."

Rick took off to see his next patient without bothering with the details. He wouldn't mention it again until his shift ended, and then he'd focus only on my project. ER doctors are wired differently. I sat down to look up the billing code for an axe injury to the lower leg, initial visit.

· · ·

Lana researched the houses surrounding Detective Roberts' address and discovered that the house to his right was occupied by a widower in her seventies, a perfect potential interview. She likely spent much of her day at home, noticing activity in the neighborhood. She might welcome a visitor, especially a young woman eager to listen. Lana dressed conservatively in jeans and a button-down blouse, anticipating Judy Akins as an excellent source.

She parked in front of her house and admired the well kept, single-story house, freshly painted with clean windows and a pristine yard. As she scooped up her oversized tote bag from the passenger seat, she glanced at Roberts' house of the same size and age as Ms. Akins' home, but not as well taken care of. It didn't suffer from neglect so much as indifference.

Lana walked confidently to the door and rang the bell. A woman's voice commanded a small yapping dog to "simmer down." Ms. Akins opened the door wearing a sundress with her dog cowering behind her. "Hello, how can I help you?" A friendly smile accompanied her greeting.

Lana matched her smile and held out a hand. "Hello, Ms. Akins. Forgive me for not calling ahead. My name is Lana Hearns, and I am a reporter doing a story on your neighbor, Detective Roberts. Would you have a moment to answer some questions?"

"What type of story are you writing, young lady?"

"It's about his role in the recent bombing and heist."

"Of course, come in, please. Don't mind Ruby. She's a little shy around strangers."

Lana stepped into her foyer and bent down to greet Ruby. After a brief hesitation, the little dog sniffed her outstretched hand. With apparent approval, Ruby advanced for a scratch behind the ears.

"Come in, please, and have a seat. Would you like some coffee?"

"That would be lovely, thank you, with cream and sugar, please."

Judy sang to herself in the kitchen as she prepared the coffee, giving Lana time to explore the living room. The old-fashioned décor appeared perfectly preserved, clean, neat, and uncluttered. Two scented candles burned on opposite sides of the room, the distinctive vanilla scent present with every breath.

Lana sank comfortably into the couch, and Judy returned with coffee. "Thank you. These blankets are gorgeous," Lana eyed three sumptuous throws hanging over the back of the couch.

"Thank you. Sewing keeps me busy."

"You made these yourself? Do you sell them?"

"No, I donate them to a shelter that helps single moms. Every baby needs a warm blanket to snuggle in with her mom. What would you like to know about Detective Roberts?"

Their conversation lasted over a half hour, and Lana studiously took notes. The picture Judy painted of a kind, thoughtful neighbor who took care of her poodle and watched over her house contrasted with the killer Lana imagined, but her description could fit the profile of a psychopath. Many of them lived incredibly bland lives, successfully hiding murderous tendencies.

Judy walked her to the door. "Thank you so much for visiting. I'll let Detective Roberts know you came by next time I see him."

Lana leaned in to speak in a lower voice. "I would prefer if we kept this a secret between us. I really want him to be surprised when the article comes out."

Judy smiled, happy to be part of the conspiracy. "Your secret is safe with me. Take care. Stop by anytime."

Lana drove away pondering her next move. She hadn't learned anything crucial from Judy, but in her business, sometimes little details grew more significant.

.　　.　　.

"All right, what're we doing?"

"I need to place a GPS tracker on a car without getting caught."

"Cool. Whose car are we tracking?"

"You need to keep this quiet, but it's Detective Roberts' car. Lana wants to see where he's going as part of her investigation into the robbery."

"Sounds illegal. I like her more every day. How do we want to do this?"

"We're driving by to see where he's parked. If he's in the front in the driveway, I need you to jog by, stop to tie your shoe, and place the tracker, then keep jogging."

"That's boring. I was hoping we could trail him on a motorcycle and lean over to attach it on the freeway, or put it on a dart gun and shoot it into his wheel well as he drives by. Your plan kinda sucks. Why don't you do it yourself?"

"My plan is better, because it's simple, and I am not doing it myself, because he would recognize me from his ER visit. He's never met you."

"You're boring, and you still owe me a pizza. Let's go."

Parked in the driveway, Roberts' four-year-old black Accord had the license plate that matched Lana's records. "Nothing fancy, Rick. Keep it simple."

Around the corner, Rick stretched on the sidewalk, as I tossed him the tracker. "No worries, I got this. I am Mr. Simple."

I couldn't agree more. He jogged toward the corner, dropped and did ten push ups, and hopped to his feet to continue his jog. I turned the corner and parked across the street in fear of our risky endeavor.

Rick didn't disappoint. He dropped for ten pushups at each driveway and then sprinted to the next to do ten more. Roberts' house was the sixth on the street, and the fifty previous push ups hadn't winded Rick at all. He dropped next to Roberts' car and did his ten push ups. As he stood, his right hand slid under the bumper. To a casual bystander it would look like he was catching his balance. I hated to admit it, but he was pretty slick, not that I would ever tell him.

Rick made it to the corner and turned off the street. I pulled up behind him and told him to get in the car. Rick waved me off. "I'll meet you back where we started. This is a great work out and I want to see if I can make the whole block."

No point in arguing, I parked where I had originally let him out. He turned the last corner two minutes later, struggling a little, but still completing the pushups at each driveway. He finished his last set and slid into the car, sweaty, but refreshed. "I need to find a bigger block for more of a challenge. How did I do?"

"You earned your pizza. Thanks, Rick." I dropped him off and went home for some pizza myself. With Lana's tracking device in place, I needed some rest.

CHAPTER FORTY-EIGHT

Friday, November 10
10:41 a.m.

Detective Roberts knocked on the office door, and the Chief invited him in. "Have a seat. How are you feeling?"

"The symptoms come and go. The headaches aren't too bad, anymore, but the fatigue and memory fog flare up at the worst times. That's why I wanted to talk to you."

"What's on your mind?"

"I need to turn in my retirement papers. I don't think I can lead this department anymore."

"We can give you more time to recover physically, if that's what you need."

"That's part of it, but how can the team trust me when I had a mass-murdering psychopath working for me for three years, and I didn't even notice? I failed the entire force."

"You're being a little hard on yourself, don't you think? Krug fooled us all."

"But I was his commanding officer. I worked with him daily and never caught a whiff of how dangerous he was. I've enjoyed my time with the department, but it's time for someone new to take the helm. I have my pension, and I can recover on a quiet beach somewhere."

"I understand. The job takes a toll on you. I probably won't be far behind you, but I'm staying on long enough to close this case."

"I can't believe we have no leads on who killed all those people and took the jewels."

"It's unbelievable. We've talked to everyone Krug has ever met. Someone even tracked down his kindergarten teacher. We're running out of rocks to look under."

"I'm sorry to leave you, Chief, but if anyone can catch the guy, it's you. Thank you for everything, sir."

The Chief stood and held out his hand. "Thank you for everything, detective. Enjoy that beach and best of luck in your recovery."

Roberts smiled as he walked out of the office for the last time. He would need a week or so to get his affairs in order, and then he could concentrate on relocating to the Caribbean.

. . .

Lana received a text while we lunched. "Damn, looks like Roberts gave two weeks notice. He's retiring, claiming ongoing issues from the head injury and stress from his failure to recognize Krug as a threat. The bastard's bugging out."

I pointed one of my French fries at her to emphasize my point. "If he has the diamonds, he can't very well spend any of it here. He's too high profile."

Lana snatched the fry from my hand and ate it. "I bet he's gonna go to the Dominican Republic. No extradition."

"With the money he has he should go to the Maldives."

"We need to get him before he leaves town. With the money he has, he can buy a lot of protection."

"We still have the option of telling Feng our suspicions."

"I'm not throwing him to the wolves until we have proof. What does the tracker show?"

"It shows he has a boring life. He's been to work, a doctor's appointment, the grocery store, and a gas station."

"We need to panic him into making a mistake."

"Why don't we search his house when we know he's not home."

"Because he's a cop, and that's a crime."

"So add it to our list. If he's guilty, he won't report it. If we find anything, we can take some pictures and send them anonymously."

"Let me think on it. I'm gonna dig some more, and we can keep watching his tracker. He's got to make a mistake at some point."

I finished my fries, as Lana picked at the remains of her salad, each of us silent with our own thoughts. In the ER, when a patient's presentation didn't make sense, we had to look at the case from a new perspective. If we analyze data the same way every time, the same solution emerges. Unusual problems require unusual solutions. We had to think differently.

CHAPTER FORTY-NINE

Sunday, November 12
8:39 a.m.

"Eat up. Those waffles need to sustain you for the long day ahead."

Lana smeared a small bite in syrup before savoring it. "Are you sure this is a good idea?"

"I'm sure it's an idea. I'll tell you tomorrow whether it was good." Our plan had formed over dinner with details debated and refined until the early hours of the morning. We agreed to spook Roberts, drastically and quickly.

"You're the one in harm's way. It's your choice to call it off," I said.

Lana mulled it over while enjoying a few more bites. She set her knife and fork across her plate, looked me in the eye, and exclaimed, "Let's do this."

Banshee punctuated her raised voice with a small bark. He was always ready.

·   ·   ·

We waited for Roberts to leave the house. On a Sunday, he might stay home all day, and we would have to wait until Monday. The tracker showed his car moving at about two in the afternoon and parking at a sports bar fifteen minutes away, which was perfect. Whether he watched a game or only ordered a late lunch, he would likely stay for a while, and I would have a fifteen-minute warning before his return.

"Last chance. Are we doing this?" I asked.

"Go. Keep your phone line open. I'll let you know if his car moves."

·   ·   ·

Roberts settled into a seat at the bar and ordered a burger, onion rings, and beer. The Raiders fought a tight game with the Broncos early in the third quarter. He joined the rest of Raiders' nation to watch the second half.

·   ·   ·

I parked around the corner from Roberts' house and walked casually, despite the adrenaline flowing through my system. My baseball cap pulled low on my forehead did nothing to ease the itchiness of the bushy fake beard I wore, but its memorable distinctiveness might prove worthwhile. I kept Lana updated on my progress through my AirPods. She reassured me that Roberts' car had not moved.

I cut between houses to Roberts' back door. With gloves on, I knelt and pulled my lock picks from my pocket. I originally learned how to pick locks in high school, when an asshole of a chemistry teacher bragged about the difficulty of the next exam and made a big show of locking it in a filing cabinet in his room. He held up the key and taunted us that no one would pass without his key.

After spending a few dollars at the magic store, I had a set of lock picks and a book to teach me how to use them. I got into the file and took pictures of the questions, the only time I ever cheated. Even knowing the questions ahead of time, I made an 84 and was the only one to pass the test.

Most locks were pretty simple to pick, requiring a little practice and a good sense of touch. The skill had served me well. Ninety long seconds passed before the final tumbler fell into place and opened the lock.

I carefully closed the door behind me and listened for any noise at all. After a full minute of silence, I felt confident that the house was empty and no alarms had tripped. Lana confirmed that the car was still in place.

I searched the house. If we could find any of the stolen jewels I would take pictures, and we would send them to the cops. I had serious doubts that anyone smart enough to steal the jewels would store them in an underwear drawer or in a shoebox in the closet, but I had to check.

The small, neat house allowed a quick search. Roberts had already started to organize his move, but hadn't sealed boxes. I checked those, plus drawers and closets, under the bed and in the freezer, and found nothing. I didn't have time to tear out walls or floors. We had allotted only twenty minutes for the search, and time was up.

"That's it, Doc. Time to get out of there. Did you find anything useful?" Lana asked.

"He wears boxers. Otherwise, nothing. Do you want to proceed with the next step? We can still walk away from this. He'll know someone was here, but nothing will point to us."

"I want to see it through to the end."

"Me, too." I reached into my pocket and pulled out a cheap burner phone and a note. I placed them on the counter and locked the door on my way out. I walked around the block and drove away.

. . .

Roberts cheered with the rest of the patrons as the Raiders completed an eighty-yard drive for a touchdown with a minute left to take a five point lead, but the Raiders' defense had to hold for a minute. The Broncos drove to the twenty, but their last pass fell incomplete, handing the Raiders their tenth win of the season and a playoff spot. Roberts joined in the celebration, closed out his tab, and headed home.

He felt good, as he pulled up to his house. The Raiders were in the playoffs, and he had narrowed down his property choices in The Dominican Republic to three beautiful beach houses. His paperwork was ready for submission tomorrow. Tonight, he would pack.

He set his keys and wallet on the table by the front door and turned on the TV to catch the late game. He popped the lid off another beer and took his first sip before freezing. He put the beer down and pulled his Glock, falling silent, as he listened. Someone had been in his house.

He searched the small home and noticed small things out of place. His home had been searched, and no effort had been made to conceal it. Finding no one in the home, he turned his attention to the back door. He confirmed the back door was locked, but closer inspection revealed it had likely been picked. The lock was new since the staged break-in, but showed some scratches.

He picked up his beer and stared at the phone and note on the counter, "Answer me when I ring." The cheap burner phone rested on the simple note, written with a black sharpie in block letters.

As a bomb expert, no way in hell would he answer a phone left on his counter without examining it first. Although the charge would be small, if exploded right next to the ear it could decapitate a person.

He set down his beer, pulled out his bomb suit with the mask and chest plate, and approached the phone. He placed bricks from his garage on three sides of the phone to stabilize it, as well as contain an explosion. He used a long set of forceps to flip the phone over and pop the back off of the battery, wincing at a possible explosion. Met with silence, he leaned forward and saw a normal phone battery.

He sighed and took off his suit. He picked up the phone and examined it more closely. The cheap burner phone had no modifications or explosives. He put it back together and placed it on the counter, picking up his beer. Who the hell had been in his house? It couldn't be the cops. They would have arrived with a warrant and a SWAT team. He could run if he had to, but that would confirm his guilt. Someone wanted to talk. Roberts patiently waited for the call.

CHAPTER FIFTY

Sunday, 4:35 p.m.

Lana and I stared at the tracker anxiously, as Roberts parked in his driveway. We planned to notify police, if we saw evidence that he decided to flee immediately when he saw the phone, but after fifteen minutes of watching his stationary car on the tracker, we relaxed.

"I don't think he's gonna run," Lana said.

"I agree. How long do you want to let him stew?"

"At least a couple hours to build the tension. Also, we don't want to meet until it's dark, anyway. Let's get dinner and watch football."

"I feel like grilled cheese. Want one?"

"Gourmet food and football, an excellent precursor to this evening."

Banshee curled up with her on the couch, as I made the sandwiches.

. . .

The phone finally rang. With a sense of deepened dread, Roberts turned on the speaker and waited for the caller to speak first. A modulated voice, similar to the one he had used to call 911, slowly enunciated through the tinny speaker.

"I know everything," the voice said.

"No idea what you're talking about," Roberts responded.

"I'm talking about a robbery funded with $200,000 cash you laundered through First Prime Mortgage, LLC."

Serious concern spread through his tightening chest.

"I assume from your silence that you're not going to waste time denying it."

"What do you want?"

"Money. Turning you in is worth a million dollars. Letting you go should be worth a lot more."

"What assurances do I have that you won't turn me in anyway?"

"When I accept the payment, I am guilty, too. I can't spend my money in jail."

Roberts tapped his foot, as he considered his options. If they knew about the $200,000, they knew enough for the cops to justify a warrant. As soon as they focused on him, his story would begin to fall apart. "What exactly are you proposing?"

"We meet tonight. Come alone with twenty-million-dollars worth of the diamonds. I'm not interested in the jewelry. Hand them over, and we go our separate ways. If you deviate from this plan, my information goes to law enforcement and the media, and you'll never make it out of the country."

Roberts calculated his odds. The twenty million was not an issue, but he needed time to get out of the country. If his ID were circulated, he would have no chance to escape. Besides, he wanted to know who had his information. If a detective found his $200,000 check, he would be in a cell already.

"Where and when do you want to meet?"

"Palm Eastern Cemetery at ten tonight. In the back right corner, you'll find a statute of an angel reaching for the heavens surrounded by twenty tall palm trees. Come alone, bring the diamonds, and you'll never hear from me again."

Lana disconnected before he could respond. With trembling hands, she turned off her own burner phone and removed the battery.

"You gonna be okay?" I asked.

"Yeah. That was a lot more stressful than I expected."

"We have some time. Let's double check that everything is ready."

. . .

Roberts placed the phone gently on the counter and formulated his plan. He realized that he may be able to pay her off, but also that he may need to kill her. He suspected that bitch reporter, but he had to be sure. If so, the threat of her sharing the information was real.

He needed to get the diamonds. Fortunately, Judy would be playing her Sunday card game. Roberts used his key to access her home and grabbed one of the candles, arranging the others to hide the empty space. He didn't have time to melt them out of the wax. She would have to take it as is. Next, he packed a go bag in case he needed to run sooner than expected. Cash, clothes, and his passport went into that bag. All he would need to add was the rest of the diamonds, and he could grab those in minutes on the way out of town.

Finally, he holstered the Glock and sheathed his knife on the back of his belt. He had left one more car parked on the edge of town. If he could make it there, he had a good chance to escape.

. . .

Banshee and I arrived early at the perpetually open cemetery, where subtle lighting gently illuminated narrow shadows. The heavily landscaped meeting place, invisible from the main entrance, ensured privacy, especially on a Sunday night. I scouted the area with Banshee, outfitted in his full tactical gear, and set up east of the meeting site, where several large grave markers provided cover. I found a small collection of bushes to the north for Banshee, who lurked still and deadly in their shadows. He had his earbuds in and could hear my whispered commands to stay calm and silent. He rested his head on his paws and waited for something to happen.

Lana arrived fifteen minutes before the meet time and stood unarmed near the statue with her back to me. She had two separate recording devices to pick up her conversation. I provided our only security with a Glock I hoped not to use and with Banshee in full war gear.

Lana fidgeted, as five minutes past the hour ticked by. Finally, headlights turned in at the nearest lot, and Roberts marched to her with a backpack on one shoulder. I commanded Banshee to stay alert and remain still. Banshee tensed under his bush and remained nearly invisible.

"I figured it was you," said Roberts. "You've been a pain in the ass from the beginning."

"I suppose that's why you tried to have me killed at Hoover Dam."

"Just business, nothing personal."

"This whole thing has been just business for you, hasn't it?"

"It was a complicated job to pull off the perfect crime, and I performed it well."

"You mean almost perfect crime. Otherwise, we wouldn't be here."

"Before we do our deal, how about you tell me how you figured it out."

"Someone identified your voice on the 911 calls."

"Bullshit. Not even the FBI has identified a voice from those recordings."

"We used a different technology. After you were identified, I reviewed the records. The only anomaly was the mortgage payment you made to your dad that never arrived at his bank. So when I looked at the back of the check, I saw where the money had actually gone. A little digging saw that money disappear into crypto. You had the means and the opportunity. I assume the head injury was self inflicted, and you set Krug up to take the fall."

"His debt would have been the end of him eventually anyway. The death I gave him was easy compared to what he would have faced."

"I'm sure his family is thankful for your kindness. Did you bring the diamonds?"

Lana tensed, as he reached into his bag. He brandished only a candle and tossed it to her. "There're about twenty million in diamonds in the wax. I didn't have time to melt it. Do I have your word that this is the end of our interactions?"

"I'm an accessory to sixteen murders as soon as I accept these diamonds."

"Yeah," Roberts said, pulling a gun, "I might be at seventeen, momentarily. How many copies of the records do you have, and where are they?"

He advanced on her with the gun straight out in front of him. I whispered for Banshee to advance in silence. Slinking low to the ground, he glided toward Roberts.

"You can't shoot me here. The info will be released automatically," Lana said.

"I don't doubt it, you devious bitch. I'm going to take you somewhere private and you're going to tell me everything, or I'm going to peel your skin off, starting at your feet and working my way up. Move to the car."

Lana held her ground, and Roberts lunged toward her. "I said move, now!"

"Disarm, gun," I whispered.

After two strides, Banshee launched. Roberts sensed a shadow in his peripheral vision before Banshee's jaws clamped around his wrist, destroying muscle, tendons, and ligaments. The gun flopped harmlessly on the lawn, as Banshee yanked Roberts to the ground. The pain seared like a conflagration, as Banshee held his wrist. With his left hand, Roberts grabbed his knife and plunged it into Banshee's chest, but it bounced hard off the titanium plate in his vest.

"Banshee, retreat!" I advanced with my gun. Banshee let go and guarded, scanning for potential threats. I stood six feet from Roberts and kicked his gun further away. He cradled his injured wrist, but still held the knife. "It's over. Put the knife down. We recorded everything."

"No."

"There's no way out. I don't want to shoot you, but I will if I have to. Put the knife down and lawyer up. You may be able to trade the location of the jewels for your life."

"Spend my life in prison? As an ex-cop? No, thank you, and fuck the billionaire. Little miss detective over here will probably find the diamonds eventually, but no one will see those jewels for another sixty years. Zhang will be dead by then. People will still be talking about me in sixty years, and no one will remember the billionaire."

He stood up and I took two steps back. "There's nowhere to run," I said.

"I have no intention of running." He turned to Lana. "You were the only one to figure it out. Make sure all those assholes know I outsmarted them." With a fanatical smile, he drew the knife deeply across the left side of his neck. Arterial blood shot almost ten feet, but by the fifth heart beat, Roberts collapsed, and died by the tenth.

CHAPTER FIFTY-ONE

Sunday, 10:17 p.m.

Horrified, Lana rushed to him, but I held her back. "He cut the carotid and jugular. There's nothing we could do, even if we were in an OR." Lana leaned into my shoulder and cried as the last of the blood drained from Roberts.

"I didn't want it to end that way," Lana said, looking away from the body.

"It was his choice. He decided a long time ago that he wasn't going to jail. I think it's time we called Detective Roland."

Lana put the phone on speaker. "Detective Roland, this is Lana Hearns."

"How can I help you, Ms. Hearns?"

"We solved the robbery and recovered some diamonds. The perpetrator is deceased."

"Start at the beginning."

Roland listened without interruption, while Lana summarized.

"Stay there, don't touch anything, and don't talk to anyone. Detective Stillman and I will be out there in less than twenty minutes."

I looked at the blood-soaked body with the knife still clutched in his hand and at the bloody candle lying at his side. "C'mon, let's find somewhere to sit with a better view."

I steered her to a bench under a large shade tree and Banshee curled up at our feet. "Banshee was a hero, again," she said.

"He's the best. I'm gonna need to get him a new vest. This one has two knife marks on it. You're such a good boy." Banshee leaned into me.

"I've been on a lot of bad dates, but this one is the worst," Lana said.

"Unfortunately, I don't think this is my worst date ever. Do you really think the diamonds are in that candle?"

"I hope so. Miss Judy, who lives next door to him, has the same brand of candles all over her house. If there are diamonds in this one, I bet the rest are in her house somewhere."

"Call me crazy, but I don't think it was ever about the money."

"I agree. It was about the infamy, his dying wish to be remembered."

"You have a helluva story with that recording."

"Thanks for reminding me. Let me email a copy before the police confiscate the original."

"Do you think the cops are gonna be mad?"

"A little, but they'll be happy the case is closed and the diamonds recovered."

"What do you think he meant by the jewels wouldn't be found for sixty years? That was oddly specific."

"Agreed, but I'm too tired to think about it at the moment."

She laid her head on my shoulder and we rested silently until the first car pulled into the lot. "Over here, Detective Roland," I called. Her flashlight swung in our direction, and she marched over.

"Where is he?"

"Back there," I pointed.

"You sure he's dead?"

"He cut his carotid and jugular. He was dead the moment the knife went through them."

"And there're twenty million dollars of diamonds sitting there unguarded?"

I patted Banshee. "Definitely not unguarded."

"Lets wait for Stillman to go through this, again."

We waited in silence until Detective Stillman joined us. "Here're the rules. Our next conversation is off the record, but I need to know everything you did to get here tonight, no holding back. Nothing will be used against you. You have my word," Roland said.

I nodded at Lana, and she began her summary. After twenty minutes of frequent requests for details from both of them, they listened to the recording and confiscated her phone. They stepped away from us to talk.

"Do you think we're in trouble?" Lana asked.

"No, I think they're getting a slightly modified version of our story together."

Stillman and Roland reached an agreement, and Roland addressed us. "Technically, you broke the law with the tracking device, the financial hacking, and the breaking and entering of his house. Our understanding is that Ms. Hearns suspected that Roberts was the bomber after Little Mac's voice recognition. She went to his house to confront him, and he set up this meeting tonight to buy your silence. You brought Doc and Banshee for security, and the rest went down as you say. Does that version sound about right?"

We nodded.

"Here's what I need you to do. Get in your cars and go home. Don't talk to anybody. In a few hours when we've processed the scene, I'm going to call you downtown for the official version of your story. That testimony will be recorded and will be part of the official transcript. It would be convenient if that version matches what I just said. Any discussion of your breaking and entering and your tracking device is unnecessary. Understood?"

"Yes, ma'am," we said in unison.

"Good, get out of here and practice that story. Again, don't talk to anyone. The media will be here in the next half hour, and I don't want them anywhere near you."

"Thank you, Detective."

"Thank you, both of you, and Doc, stop by Roberts' car and make sure that transmitter is gone before I get over there."

"Yes, ma'am." Banshee ran ahead, as we walked to our car. I swiped the GPS tracker almost as smoothly as Rick had placed it, and slipped it into my pocket.

· · ·

Word spread quickly, and the crowd of media and onlookers swelled. Additional officers showed up, as Stillman took charge of processing the scene. Roland, equipped with a picture of the candle that possibly contained diamonds, led a group of officers to Judy Akins' home. She answered in her nightgown, and Ruby barked vigorously at the intrusion.

Roland calmly explained that the house might be part of a crime scene, and she and Ruby needed to relocate to the Mandalay Bay, that had graciously offered to host them. Judy gathered her things, and an officer drove her to the hotel.

Roland and her team searched the house and found over a hundred candles, and photographed and tagged each one as evidence. Back at police headquarters, X-rays of each candle revealed nine with objects contained in their wax. They placed one upside down over a fine metal mesh screen and heated it. After the wax dripped through the mesh, a pile of diamonds glittered defiantly in the sickly fluorescent light.

A second team secured and extensively searched Roberts' home, ripping out floorboards and drywall, but finding nothing. A piece of paper in the trash read, "answer me when I ring." The anomaly was noted in the report, but no correlation to the case was discovered.

CHAPTER FIFTY-TWO

Monday, November 13
6:58 a.m.

Under the anxiety inducing, flickering fluorescent lighting of an interview room at police headquarters, we clarified our story in a brighter beam of Roland's intense gaze. A small, curious group of cops had gathered outside the open door to listen. Stillman played Lana's recording with the volume maximized.

When it ended, Roland asked, "What do you think he meant by the jewels wouldn't be found for sixty years?"

"I have no idea," I stifled a yawn.

"Actually, I have a thought about that. As part of my story, can I be present when you search the area I suggest?"

Roland and Stillman locked eyes to communicate silently. "We have no problem with that. You've led us to the killer and to the diamonds, so the least we can do is allow you to be there, if you can lead us to the jewels."

"I think he hid the jewels in your evidence room."

"What makes you think that?" Roland asked.

"Listen to the tape. He didn't say we wouldn't find them for sixty years, he said we wouldn't find them for sixty more years. Roberts was precise in everything he did, and I don't think his word choice was incidental. After an internet search last night, I learned that evidence for all unsolved murders is stored for seventy-five years. Roberts had access to the evidence room, a perfect place to store them, because they're too distinctive to sell. He wanted his name to be heralded sixty years from now when those boxes were cleaned out and those jewels discovered. Check the fifteen-year-old cold cases first, with dusty boxes of evidence that would languish for sixty more years before they're opened again."

"Wait here, please." Roland and Stillman left the room together.

"When were you going to let me in on this?" I asked.

"I just did. I would have welcomed your help last night, but you were asleep and needed it badly. A good reporter never sleeps on a story." She winked adorably.

"If those jewels are down there, you're going to get a Pulitzer." I leaned over to kiss her.

After only a few minutes, Roland motioned for us to join her. "The Chief authorized the search. You two are welcome, but no photos, and don't touch anything." Two officers joined us, and a time worn officer named Murphy showed surprise at our excited group's enlivening his solitary, subterranean domain. He straightened in his chair behind a low, faded counter. "How can I help you?"

"We're conducting a search of the file room. No one enters without my permission. These two are going to keep you company," Stillman said. The two officers blocked the door.

The remaining four of us stepped into the gray, cavernous file room, and Roland consulted her list of thirteen fifteen-year-old unsolved murders, and she led us to the first box. With gloved hands, she opened the box and quickly sorted through the contents to match them to the evidence list on the box to find nothing missing and nothing extra. She placed the box back on the shelf, aligning it to fit into the dust-free rectangular space where it had waited for years.

Excitement melted to boredom, as we watched Roland methodically sort through old evidence. Some boxes were pathetically empty with others packed full of labeled bags. The search dragged into a second hour.

"One more, and we'll be over half way done," Roland pressed on. Next one is Mathew Adkins' that should be two rows over there."

She set the box on the floor and began the inventory. She abruptly stopped. "Stillman, ask the photographer to come down here." Stillman radioed for one, as we leaned to peer into the box. She pointed to a black canvas bag. "That definitely does not belong in here."

The photographer arrived and took pictures of the box, the shelf, the contents that had been removed, and the mysterious bag. Roland removed more items to expose the bag completely, and he snapped more photos. She removed it, set it on the concrete floor, and unzipped the bag. A thousand facets of multi colored jewels sparkled under the photographer's stark, bright white light.

Lana beamed.

Roland carefully slipped it into an evidence bag and checked the rest of the box. Finding nothing else that didn't belong, she returned the otherwise unremarkable box to its dusty place on the shelf. "Let's go upstairs to see what we recovered, and if anything is still missing, we'll check the rest of the boxes."

Roland led us to the evidence room to a round of cheers, as word of the find quickly spread. We watched silently from the back, as they inventoried watches, necklaces, bracelets, and rings, each as magnificent as the last, and laid them on a clean white paper on a table. Each item would be photographed and bagged separately.

Lana and I slipped out and headed home. Lana pulled out her phone.

"Hello, Feng. It's Lana. I assume you heard by now that the real robber is dead and your diamonds recovered."

"I am aware. Thank you."

"Please inform Mr. Zhang that his jewels have been recovered as well."

"He will be most pleased. Were you involved in their recovery?"

"Yes, right now I need to finish my story by the deadline, but I wanted to let you know that the ordeal is over."

"Thank you, Ms. Hearns. I look forward to reading your story."

.   .   .

Lana feverishly finalized her story. Finally, she pressed send and sat across from me with her legs tucked under her and with a glass of wine cradled in her hand.

Her phone buzzed nine minutes after her submission.

"Aren't you going to answer it?"

"No, I'm going to take a shower and get cleaned up. Then I'll look at all the messages and decide who gets first interviews." She set her empty goblet on the coffee table and strode to the shower without her vibrating phone.

She emerged from the bathroom a half hour later looking stunning with perfect hair and makeup and dressed in the blue silk blouse that highlighted her eyes. "You look beautiful," I said as I approached her.

"Thank you. How many calls?"

"Seventeen, including the networks, and you're trending on Twitter."

Lana called the three major networks to schedule her interview times, then handed the list back to me. "Congrats, you're now my agent. I've numbered them by priority. Can you please call them back in order and schedule times for interviews. They should be six minutes maximum, and I need at least ten minutes between each one. Thanks, sweetie."

"How much does an agent get paid?"

"You'll find out later tonight. Get to work."

Lana set up in her office, where she had installed professional lighting, and finished eleven interviews, refusing more, as she said she had absolutely nothing new to say.

"You haven't mentioned much about Roberts' confession and death."

"That information is reserved for the next round of interviews tonight. I plan to stretch this out a little."

The networks jumped at the opportunity to air more details on a crime that had mesmerized the nation and much of the world. Lana kept up the interviews until nine o'clock, then fell asleep on the sofa. I gently draped a blanket around her and slept more deeply than I had in months.

CHAPTER FIFTY-THREE

Friday, November 24
6:54 p.m.

I had reluctantly followed an insistent Lana to the ceremony that should honor her much more than me, where Rick, still playfully mad about his missing the final showdown with Roberts, gleefully anticipated his time on stage with us. The ceremony at the Mandalay Bay, in true Las Vegas tradition, was an epic show in their largest ballroom on a huge stage, where Lana, Rick, Banshee, and I were seated with the Mayor on one side and a state senator on the other. Members of the media mingled with celebrities and VIPs, including Feng, the Chief of Police, Roland and Stillman, and Charles Hedenfeld III, the event's host.

"Just over a month ago, tragedy struck our Mandalay family, when a robbery led to the murders of thirteen of our team members." After a moving eulogy honoring each of the fallen employees, he gave the microphone to the Chief to honor Sergeant Krug, once wrongfully vilified and now recognized as another tragic victim, buried with full honors for falling in the line of duty. Roland and Stillman accepted awards for their work closing the case.

"Can I please have Ms. Hearns, Dr. Docker, and Banshee come over here?" We rose to applause and stood awkwardly in a spotlight. Rick loomed fiercely behind us in a dark suit with a black shirt, looking like our bodyguard. Lana squeezed my hand, and I turned my attention back to the Mayor.

"The City of Las Vegas thanks you for your service and your risking your lives to aid the investigation and to find justice for the fallen members of our community. It is my honor to award you the Keys to the City of Las Vegas." Applause thundered, as they handed each of us a certificate and a key.

I turned to step back to my seat, and Mr. Hedenfeld stopped me. "Hold on. We're not done yet. I'm handing the two of you a key to Mandalay Bay." He shook our hands and whispered something to Rick, who laughed softly. "Everyone, please celebrate our newest lifetime platinum members, welcome to stay at our hotel any time, on the house." His raised hand quieted the crowd. "And to make sure that Banshee feels welcome, too, we're building a three-thousand-square-foot indoor dog park called Banshee's Playhouse to accommodate our canine guests."

I leaned down to tell Banshee to smile and bow, which he performed perfectly. The applause roared. Mr. Hedenfeld again silenced the crowd. "We have one more honoree tonight. As you know, we promised a million dollar reward for information that led to the bomber. One young man's special talent identified him instantly. Mac Kennedy, or Little Mac as he likes to be known, please come up."

Little Mac's smile lit up the room, as he shook the casino owner's hand and received a large replica check for one million dollars. The story of his talent of voice recognition had garnered public interest as well as the attention of the FBI. Agents from their technical division were working with him to understand how he could identify voices that their best computers couldn't. After his clearances finalized, he would be a paid consultant for the FBI.

"That was so fun. I'm gonna go ask that casino guy if I can get platinum status as well," Rick said, as we walked through the casino together.

"Rick, you may not have platinum status, but you're trending on Twitter under the hash tag, #whoisthebigguy." Lana held her phone to show him.

"Hot damn. Trending on Twitter ain't bad. I'm famous." Rick broke away and disappeared into the crowded casino.

"Excuse me, please, do you have a moment?" Feng asked.

"Of course. I assume you are here to take the jewels home," I said.

"That is one reason for my visit, but Mr. Zhang asked me to offer his thanks with a small token of his appreciation." He motioned to an assistant who handed him two beautifully carved wood boxes, handing one to Lana and one to me, gesturing for us to open them. Resting on red velvet was the most beautiful watch I had ever seen. Lana inhaled sharply, as she admired her matching watch.

"As you may know, Mr. Zhang collects fine watches and enjoys sharing them as gifts. He had these commissioned a year ago from Phillips Patek and has waited for the right opportunity to share them. They are unique models produced exclusively for Mr. Zhang. Inside the box, you will find a card. If you call that number, someone will come to you to fit the watch and explain its functions. They will also come to you anywhere in the world to fix it should you ever have a problem."

"Feng, please thank the Mr. Zhang for us. This is an extremely generous gift," Lana said.

"I will do so. Also, Mr. Zhang would like to offer to create a new vest for Banshee. We understand the current vest was nicked. He is offering to have one made of the latest carbon fiber, stronger and lighter than his current titanium, with integrated electronic functions. He would be honored, if you would aid in the design of the vest."

"The honor would be all mine. Please pass on my gratitude."

"Very well. As a racing aficionado, Mr. Zhang would like to have you as his guest at any F1 race. You have my number. Do not hesitate to call, and we will send a plane for you and have a suite ready on your arrival. Now if you will excuse me, I have a long flight home."

Feng slid silently into the crowd, now dispersing throughout the casino. I pointed to a group of reporters surrounding Rick. "I wonder what he's saying?" I asked.

"He's most likely talking about a superhero movie, where to play games online with him, about his favorite case from the ER, or about that time he almost got in a fight with a whole white supremacist bar."

"He is so charismatic. Everyone loves Rick."

Lana laughed at Rick, now performing backflips for the reporters.

I felt a hand on my elbow and turned to find a smiling Little Mac. "Hey man, you did great up there. Did you enjoy it?" I asked.

"Yeah. It was lots of fun with nice people. Hey, can you hold this check for me and let me take Banshee for a walk?" He leaned down for kisses from Banshee.

"We'll do better than that. We'll walk out with you."

Banshee and Little Mac joyfully jogged ahead of us, as they split the crowd on their way out the door.

THE END

ACKNOWLEDGEMENTS

Let's start with an easy one. If you are thinking of robbing Mandalay Bay, this is not a good blueprint. I am sure that they have a security center with guards and a vault filled with cash and occasionally with valuables from guests, but I have no idea of actual security arrangements at the hotel. For some reason, they wouldn't share a detailed security plan with me, but I am sure any robbery attempt based on this book would fail.

The F1 race details are accurate and provided a natural distraction for the plot. Although I did not get a chance for a hot lap at this event, I have been a passenger in hot laps in a Mercedes driven by a real life AJ. He is a professional racer, and if you ever get a chance to ride in his car, buckle tight and enjoy. AJ will throw the car around the track at the limits of the car's performance.

Many thanks to the guides at Hoover Dam, who did not report me when I asked them where the best place would be to attempt to murder someone inside the dam. Instead, they had a lively discussion of possible locations for me. The security force at Hoover Dam is real and well trained to handle any threat.

The character of Rick is based on a good friend I grew up with. If he had been a doctor, he would have chosen emergency medicine and was every bit as fun-loving as the character described in this book. He always had time to make a child laugh and smile and never met a problem he didn't want to solve.

Hats off to the unnamed nurse supervisor at Sunrise Hospital who refused to allow me access to the ER. I just wanted to see the inside, but I was considered a security risk. She did her job well. No matter how old I get, there is always one more charge nurse who wants to bust my balls.

This book would not be possible without my agent, Cindy Bullard at Birch Literary, or the fine team at Black Rose Writing, Reagan,

Minna, David, Justin, Chris and all the others who put the book together.

Finally, and most importantly, I need to thank my wife Tamara for her editing skills. I am full of ideas, and my words splatter onto the page in a jumbled mess. Tamara is a master at bringing order to my chaos and making the story communicate what she somehow knows I meant to write.

Doc and Banshee's next contract will be in Washington, D.C., where trouble will find them again.

I hope you enjoyed the book, and I always appreciate positive reviews on Amazon and hearing from readers through my website, GaryGerlacher.com.

ABOUT THE AUTHOR

Gary Gerlacher is a pediatric emergency physician who trained and worked in multiple Texas emergency rooms before opening his own pediatric urgent care clinics. His thirty years in medicine have focused on expanding access to high quality care for all children, and his stories give a unique view of the inner workings of the emergency room. He has three adult children and resides in Dallas with his two rescue dogs and his wife Tamara. Visit Garygerlacher.com to stay up to date on future books.

THE AJ DOCKER & BANSHEE THRILLER SERIES

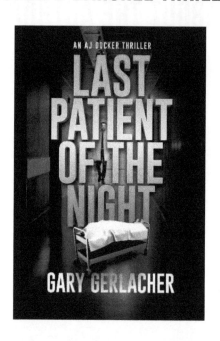

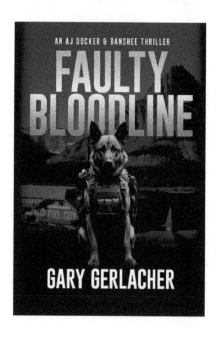

NOTE FROM GARY GERLACHER

Word-of-mouth is crucial for any author to succeed. If you enjoyed *Sin City Treachery*, please leave a review online—anywhere you are able. Even if it's just a sentence or two. It would make all the difference and would be very much appreciated.

Thanks!
Gary Gerlacher

We hope you enjoyed reading this title from:

www.blackrosewriting.com

Subscribe to our mailing list – *The Rosevine* – and receive **FREE** books, daily
deals, and stay current with news about upcoming
releases and our hottest authors.
Scan the QR code below to sign up.

Already a subscriber? Please accept a sincere thank you for being a fan of
Black Rose Writing authors.

View other Black Rose Writing titles at
www.blackrosewriting.com/books and use promo code
PRINT to receive a **20% discount** when purchasing.

Milton Keynes UK
Ingram Content Group UK Ltd.
UKHW012153090624
443713UK00001B/144